PRAISE FOR ALEXANDRA SOKOLOFF

Huntress Moon
A Thriller Award Nominee for Best E-Book Original Novel
A Suspense Magazine Pick for Best Thriller
An Amazon Top Ten Bestseller

"This interstate manhunt has plenty of thrills . . . keeps the drama taut and the pages flying."

—*Kirkus Reviews*

"The intensity of her main characters is equally matched by the strength of the multilayered plot . . . The next installment cannot release soon enough for me."

—*Suspense Magazine*

"Who you know: Agatha Christie, Gillian Flynn, Mary Higgins Clark. Who you should read: Alexandra Sokoloff."

—*Huffington Post Books*

The Price
"Some of the most original and freshly unnerving work in the genre."
—*The New York Times Book Review*

"A heartbreakingly eerie page turner."

—*Library Journal*

"*The* Price is a gripping read full of questions about good, evil, and human nature . . . the devastating conclusion leaves the reader with an uncomfortable question to consider: 'If everyone has a price, what's yours?'"

—*Rue Morgue magazine*

The Unseen

"A creepy haunted house, reports of a 40-year-old poltergeist investigation, and a young researcher trying to rebuild her life take the "publish or perish" initiative for college professors to a terrifying new level in this spine-tingling story that has every indication of becoming a horror classic. Based on the famous Rhine ESP experiments at the Duke University parapsychology department that collapsed in the 1960s, this is a chillingly dark look into the unknown."

—*Romantic Times Book Reviews*

"Sokoloff keeps her story enticingly ambiguous, never clarifying until the climax whether the unfolding weirdness might be the result of the investigators' psychic sensitivities or the mischievous handiwork of a human villain."

—*Publisher's Weekly*

"Alexandra Sokoloff takes the horror genre to new heights."

—*Charlotte Examiner*

"Alexandra Sokoloff's talent brings readers into the dark and encompassing world of the unknown so completely, that readers will find it difficult to go to bed until the last page has been turned. Her novels bring human frailty and the desperate desire to survive together in poignant stories of personal struggle and human triumph. But the truly fascinating element of Sokoloff's writing is her deep dig into the human psyche and the horrors that lie just beneath the surface of our carefully constructed facades."

—Fiction Examiner

Book of Shadows

"Compelling, frightening, and exceptionally well-written, *Book of Shadows* is destined to become another hit for acclaimed horror and suspense novelist Sokoloff. The incredibly tense plot and mysterious characters will keep readers up late at night, jumping at every sound, and turning the pages until they've devoured the book."

—Romantic Times Book Reviews

"Sokoloff successfully melds a classic murder-mystery whodunit with supernatural occult overtones."

—Library Journal

The Harrowing
Bram Stoker and Anthony Award Nominee for Best First Novel

"Absolutely gripping . . . it is easy to imagine this as a film. Once started, you won't want to stop reading."

—The London Times

"Sokoloff's debut novel is an eerie ghost story that captivates readers from page one. The author creates an element of suspense that builds until the chillingly believable conclusion."

—Romantic Times Book Reviews

bitter moon

Also by Alexandra Sokoloff

The Huntress/FBI Thrillers

Huntress Moon: Book I
Blood Moon: Book II
Cold Moon: Book III

The Haunted Thrillers

The Harrowing
The Price
The Unseen
Book of Shadows
The Space Between

Paranormal

D-Girl on Doomsday (from *Apocalypse: Year Zero*)
The Shifters (from The Keepers trilogy)
Keeper of the Shadows (from The Keepers: L.A.)

Nonfiction

Stealing Hollywood: Screenwriting Tricks for Authors, III
Writing Love: Screenwriting Tricks for Authors II
Screenwriting Tricks for Authors

Short Fiction

The Edge of Seventeen (in *Rage Against the Night*)
In Atlantis (in *Love is Murder*)

bitter moon

Book IV of the Huntress/FBI Thrillers

alexandra sokoloff

THOMAS & MERCER

Published by Thomas & Mercer, Seattle

www.apub.com

Amazon, the Amazon logo, and Thomas & Mercer are trademarks of Amazon.com, Inc., or its affiliates.

ISBN-13: 9781503940369
ISBN-10: 1503940365

Cover design by Ray Lundgren

Printed in the United States of America

For Craig Robertson

CARA

Chapter One

It is the moon that wakes her.

It is always the moon that tells her, somehow, that sends the rush of fight-or-flight chemicals into her blood, galvanizes her body with a warning of danger, a command to wake and act. The eerie light is bright through the window, shimmering in the room.

Now the metallic scratching on the door announces *Its* presence.

It is here again, the monster, coming for her. The thing that butchered her family. That left her scratched and bleeding and almost dead.

But she has that few moments' advantage because she knows. She knows the sound of *It*, *Its* smell, the hoarse and grating breath, the stench of sweat and malevolence. She knows what has come for her because she has been in a room with *It* before. She was small then, small and innocent and helpless. But she is bigger now, bigger and stronger and deadlier.

And she has something else. This time she is angry. This thing has stolen her family, has left her alone and scorned and shunned. This time she will fight, and fight to kill.

The creature slips stealthily into the tiny locked room, the counselor with the pitted skin and fat sausage fingers, and the fifteen-year-old bully he has brought for company or for camouflage or maybe for both.

The man is muttering, his breath reeking with alcohol. "Hold her down. Little whore . . . you know you want it. Strutting around like you own this place. Grab her arms. Hold her down—"

She launches upward, out of her bed. *It* is caught unawares, and she is a spitfire, punching and scratching and kicking. It happens in moments: the boy's nose is broken, his eye bleeding; the man's testicles crushed. And as the boy shrieks and the man lies moaning and clutching himself on the floor, she breathes through the fire in her chest and picks up the man's foot in both hands and holds the leg straight and brings her foot down as hard as she can on the knee to snap the joint—

The man screams once . . . and is silent. Passed out. She stands in the dark over the still bodies of the man and the boy, her whole body shaking, her heart slamming in her chest. The harsh breathing is still there, all around her, resonating in the room. Then *It* slowly recedes, foiled, but not vanquished.

She breathes in, breathes out, calming the frantic racing of her heart.

It will be back, she knows.

For now, she sits and waits for *Them* to come to take her to jail.

She is twelve years old.

TWO YEARS LATER

Chapter Two

She sits in the back of the ugly dark official transport van and watches out the window as the van speeds on the freeway, and the foothills roll away from the road. The sun is blinding after two years of confinement, the sky a brilliant blue. Everything seems vast.

The feeling of movement is alien. She has been transported only a few times during her captivity. She feels the drugs in her bloodstream, dulling her senses. Even so the speed of the van on the freeway is exhilarating, so fast it feels like flying.

She has been two years in *The Cage* in Ventura, and she has to fight down the impulse to open the door beside her and jump from the moving vehicle.

She does not know where *They* are taking her. Since she was five, she has never known where *They* will send her next, or what she will have to face when she gets there.

This morning was the release from *The Cage*, the low brick prison of the California Youth Authority, maximum-security juvenile detention. The van had gone south first, the 101 to the 5, then came the long drive through all the counties bordering Los Angeles, the suburban sprawl, the sameness of the housing developments. Past the seemingly endless snarl of L.A., freeway turned into highway, and now the hills on either side of the road are barren, beige curves.

The van is headed east, away from the ocean; she could tell that by the sun even if she couldn't read the signs. But she has become very good at road signs. The numbers tell her everything she needs to know. When you know the numbers, you always know where you are.

She can easily picture the map of the state in her head, the veins and arteries of the freeways and highways and interstates. During the two long years in *The Cage*, she had often journeyed these roads in her mind. They are etched in her soul. So she knows exactly where they are when the driver turns off the 15.

It is Riverside County, the same county where her aunt lives. The county that she was arrested, convicted and sentenced in two years ago.

Suddenly the land opens to desert, a wide sand-and-scrub corridor with foothills on either side of the highway. She stares out at pale dunes dotted with yellow black-eyed Susans and barrel cactus.

And she allows herself the slightest, faintest hope. The desert is better than the city. There are far fewer people. And in the desert, you can see things coming. You can run.

When the van turns off the highway, the off ramp is to the town of Las Piedras. She looks out the window at mountains with striking scattered rock formations which must have given the town its name.

They pass vineyards and horse ranches on the right, at the base of the foothills. The horses stir a memory of life before *The Night*, before the monster came and took her family, left her scarred and alone—

She slams shut a door in her mind to avoid looking back.

There is a sign for an Indian reservation; she knows there are many in this area. And then there is a warren of houses, and the van turns, rolls up a long, curved drive toward a low, wide suburban box with two wings, a brown lawn, scruffy palm trees, and a dry fountain with a dusty angel.

The group home. She has been in so many. They are all different. She has no idea what this one will be.

She sits in the back seat, waiting for the driver to come around and let her out. When he doesn't move, she remembers the door is not locked; she can open it for herself.

She gets out of the van holding her cheap backpack, containing one change of clothes: jeans and a turtleneck, and socks and a sleep shirt. All the possessions she has in the world.

Outside the overcooled vehicle, the sun blazes above. She feels the desert wind on her skin, smells the juniper and lavender and honey mesquite.

She could run now, before she checks in, before anyone steps forward to process her. Before anyone can find out who she is.

"Let's go," the driver says beside her. "I don't got all day."

She fights down the feeling and forces herself to walk with him up the path to the door. As she moves up to the porch she is looking at the doors, the windows, the gates, checking escape routes, even as the game begins.

The game of *Normal*.

She must play it—play it and win.

She will never go back to jail, ever.

She is fourteen.

Inside the entry hall she looks around quickly, memorizing the floor plan and exits. There is one wing for the bedrooms, one for the offices and kitchen, and the living room-slash-lounge and dining room are in the center. Across from the front door there is a large round clock on the wall, so big it seems to be screaming the time.

The group home director's office is immediately to the right.

She steps in and gets the first look at her new jailer. Ms. Sharonda. The director sits behind a wide desk with neat stacks of papers and a thick open file in front of her. She has a dark, regal face and suspicious eyes. Her mouth is a hard line, a warning: *Don't mess with me.* She is more than tough; there is an animal strength about her.

There will be no slipping past this one.

Ms. Sharonda nods to the chair on the other side of the desk, and she sits, holding herself still. It is very, very important to look *Normal.*

Ms. Sharonda continues reading the file in front of her.

She tries not to be distracted by the bracelets Ms. Sharonda is wearing: plain bronze circlets that clink softly when the director moves.

She has not seen pretty things in two long years.

Finally Ms. Sharonda looks up. "So. Cara. We're on a level system here," she says. "This home is a Level Five. Do you know what that means?"

Cara nods. She knows. She is an expert on group homes, and group home staff. She has lived in them since she was nine years old. The homes are classified by levels that range from 1 to 14. She has been in every level.

Levels 13 and 14 serve the most troubled children; they are basically small mental institutions. If this is a Level 5, there is no psychiatrist on site, but one will come every week. There will be five other wards of the court, and a staff that changes shifts every eight to ten hours. The staff's stated job is to watch you. Keep you from hurting yourself, the other residents, and other people. Most of the staff works for the paycheck. A few are crusaders. Others . . . others best not to think about.

Ms. Sharonda taps the file on her desk. "You got placed here because of good behavior in YA. If that changes, you're outta here."

Cara nods. Ms. Sharonda looks back at her sharply. Cara says nothing.

After a moment, Ms. Sharonda continues. "Your case worker will be by on Friday. You're old enough to be in ninth grade. That's high school. Think you can handle that?"

Cara has not been in school since seventh grade. There were only textbooks in *The Cage*. School could mean anything, any level. She is often put in remedial classes. Special Ed for special problems.

"I can handle it," she answers tonelessly.

Ms. Sharonda stares at her. She swivels her chair to the bookshelves behind her and removes a book, then turns back and hands it across the desk.

"Read something."

Cara stiffens. It is a test. In the system there are always tests. Her first instinct always is to hide any ability from strangers, until she knows what the test is for.

Ms. Sharonda is waiting, frowning.

Cara looks down at the book. It is some collection of poetry. After a moment she opens it at random, looks down at the page, and reads aloud.

"Oh sea . . .

let me wrap my darkest me
in your drape of flame and sapphire,
my arms raised to night . . ."

She glances up. Across the desk from her, Ms. Sharonda is silent in her chair, and the verse is short, so Cara continues to the end.

"Whatever it takes
to conduct this flight, the moon's music
tearing the silence
where I inevitably fall
and never mind the drowning."

She closes the book, and looks up.

"All right, then," Ms. Sharonda says gruffly. "Las Piedras High. You start tomorrow. There's a minibus that takes you over and brings you back."

She knows. She knows all of it.

She will go to school, then straight back to the group home. Ask permission for everything: to get food from the refrigerator, to watch TV, use the phone, go into the backyard, or take a shower. Bedroom doors must be left open at all times. The mirrors in the bathroom will be polished steel, not glass, to prevent wards from breaking the glass and slashing their wrists—

Ms. Sharonda has said something and Cara forces her attention back to her. The director is holding out a bundle in a rolled-up pillowcase. A survival kit. Inside there will be two pairs of socks, two pairs of underwear, two T-shirts, and a little bag with a bar of hotel soap, a mini toothpaste, a mini pencil, a shaving razor.

She takes it, tucks it under her arm.

"Breakfast at six. You need to be dressed and out in front at six thirty. There are extra clothes in a box in the closet in the hall."

She nods.

"You'll see the psychiatrist first."

Of course. The psychiatrist.

The director frowns. "Now, you've petitioned for a name change. We don't normally do that."

Suddenly her heart is beating out of control in her chest. The name change is key. If she can be someone else, anyone else . . . then maybe the monster that killed her family, that attacked her in the last group home, will not be able to find her this time.

For a moment she is back in the tiny dark room, the weight of the creature on top of her, pinning her to the bed, breathing its rank and stinking breath . . .

Ms. Sharonda is looking at her through narrowed eyes. She forces herself back to the present, forces herself to meet the director's eyes.

After a moment, Ms. Sharonda finishes. "But under the circumstances . . . the school thinks it would be in everyone's best interests. I've talked to administration and they've changed your name on the rolls.

It's not a permanent, legal change, you understand. But at this school, they're willing to try."

Cara nods hard, hoping to appear grateful. She is limp with relief. She walks out of the office as Eden Ballard.

It is a start.

The psychiatrist sits behind an ugly desk in a long room lined with books. It is the all-purpose meeting room, for appointments with social workers, sessions with therapists. Dr. Everhardt begins the way they all begin.

"How are you feeling today, Cara?"

He is already looking at her neck and it is all she can do not to lunge across the desk and scratch out his eyes.

"Eden," she says, without inflection.

"Of course," he says. "Eden. I'll just start by asking a few questions, all right?"

The questions are always the same:

In the past week, did you have trouble falling asleep or staying asleep? Did you feel depressed or sad? Were you afraid of things? Did you think or worry about bad things that you have seen or have happened to you? Did you have thoughts of harming yourself? Did you have thoughts of harming someone else?

Her answers are carefully calculated. Of course she doesn't think about harming herself. Of course she doesn't think about harming anyone else. For some of the lesser questions, like *Were you sad this week?*—it's safe to answer yes or "once or twice" or "on a few days." That's *Normal.* Every answer she gives is designed to make her appear *Normal,* just as every question is designed to trick her into seeming *Not Normal.*

And then come the crucial questions, the ones she must always answer with *No.*

"Are you seeing anything that shouldn't be there?"

You mean the shadows that are more than shadows?

"No."

"Are you hearing voices?"

Just the moon talking, and the air, and the lizards . . .

"No."

"Any flashbacks?"

Like the monster in my room?

"No."

"Nothing that scares you?"

"No," she says.

No matter how she answers these questions, *They* will give her medication anyway. All the group home kids are medicated. She wants the medication. She would like it to work.

She sees things, of course she sees things, and hears things too, ever since *The Night.*

According to *Them,* the things she sees aren't real. So they give her drugs to make them go away.

The problem is, they don't.

When she leaves the psychiatrist, she walks back to the bedroom wing, past the signs on the walls. Instead of pictures and posters, there are charts and lists of rules. She notes the doors. Every door. Front door, back door, side door.

In her waistband is the pen she picked up from the psychiatrist's desk. The rules on pens vary from group home to group home. The wards here may be allowed pens, they may not. But a pen is as functional a weapon as a knife, and less likely to result in jail time, since the meaning of a pen is ambiguous. There is nothing ambiguous about a concealed knife.

In the closet she finds the trunk of clothes that Ms. Sharonda mentioned: worn, drab items that will never call attention to themselves. But among them, there is a turtleneck sweater. She grabs for it, feeling a surge of relief. It is a bit small, but it will hide what it needs to hide. There is also a hoodie, always good for concealing your hair, to make yourself invisible. A good haul.

Now to the bedroom. There are three of them for the six residents, so each girl has a roommate. Hers is so medicated she barely looks up as Cara unpacks her backpack.

When she is sure no one is watching, Cara checks the doorknob. There is no inside lock. The outer door can be locked with a dead-bolt key. Hard to pick, but not impossible. Spending most of her life locked up has meant that she has spent most of her life learning to pick locks and break out of and into places. Jail is a school for such skills. She will make a pick from the clasp of the pen tonight.

Now her eyes case the windows. Windows that won't open. They are not safety glass, though. They will break. And there is a chair sturdy enough to shatter the glass, if need be. That realization is calming.

Otherwise, the room is like any other in a group home. Cheap suburban. A dresser for each girl, a closet, a desk they will have to share, but she can't see her roommate demanding much use of it.

All told, it is better than YA. There are windows. There are no shackles. Little things like that. And for the moment, it is safe enough. There are worse things out there than zoned-out kids.

Much worse.

At dinner the night staffers take over, Ms. Nicole and Ms. Sheila, and Cara meets the other residents, her roommate plus four more girls of varying degrees of crazy. They eat tamale pie, the other girls chattering to each other and pretending not to look at her.

Like the kids in YA, they are deeply scratched. A spectrum of psychiatric disorders: Asperger's, attention deficit, bipolar, depression, BPD, OCD, PTSD, schizophrenia.

Monique, the largest of the girls, watches Cara. She is heavy, burying her scratches. She doesn't breathe so much as wheeze. Her clothes look uncomfortable on her, but not as uncomfortable as her skin.

When Ms. Sheila leaves the room to get dessert, Monique's focus is instantly on Cara.

"Whatchu do to get sent up to YA?"

Under the challenge, under the aggression, there is awe. Girls don't often get sentenced to YA. Much less for two years. Much less at twelve years old. Cara had been the youngest in the jail. Some inmates had told her she was the youngest girl ever.

"Musta been some serious shit," Monique presses. "Girl getting sent up to YA. Musta been bad."

In her mind, Cara hears the cracking of bone, the pulping of flesh.

It was bad.

"It was YA," she says flatly, and doesn't speak further. There is nothing to be gained from the conversation.

Ms. Sheila returns to the room and Monique shuts up.

After dinner the girls line up for night meds. Ms. Nicole hands them out in small paper cups. Cara throws her pills back, swallows, and opens her mouth wide to show she's swallowed. Not a chance that she would not swallow. The moon is rising and she wants the haze that the meds give her. Without them, she sees. Too much.

The other girls head for the TV room. Cara asks Ms. Nicole if she can go to bed.

Ms. Nicole gives her permission and she washes up and changes into her sleep shirt and sweat pants in the bathroom, since bedroom doors can't ever be shut. And she will not let anyone see her scratches.

Then she lies on her bed with the door open and the rectangle of light in the door and the drone of the television in the common room outside.

She feels the chemicals spreading through her body. Already she can tell the dosage is much lower than what she had in YA. She has begun her bleeding and it seems to affect the medication.

Behind the curtain of drugs, she can hear the moon whispering outside the window. The light is hot on her skin. She can feel the singing of her blood in her veins, thrilling along just under the surface of her skin.

But there is no immediate threat. The shadows in the corners of the room are just that: ordinary shadows.

It is not home. There has not been such a thing as home since she was five. But it is better than being alone with what is out there in the night.

She lies still and watches the moon climbing into the sky beyond the windows.

And she remembers the full moon on *The Night*.

She is lying on her bed, holding Tiger, looking up through the veil of light. And the moon is whispering.

Then the moon starts to scream. She can hear it in the sky, screaming. And then everyone is screaming. Her mommy. Her sister. Her brothers. Everyone screaming and screaming.

And then so infinitely much worse . . . the silence.

The door explodes open and a shadow shuffles in. Bulky, manlike, but not a man. A beast, with a snout and jagged teeth and dripping jaws. Holding a glinting blade. And dripping with blood—

She jolts out of sleep with her heart thumping, fear running up and down her nerves, her jaw clenched tight to keep from screaming.

It is not here. She is alone. Just the sleeping roommate in the other bed.

She uses all the mental force she has to push away the image of the monster.

But she will never forget what *It* looks like.

It looks like evil.

She thinks about the pen she has tucked into a hole in her mattress.

"Do you have thoughts of harming yourself?"

Every day. Every night.

She thinks about opening her wrists. It would be easy to do. But she doesn't move, and after a while, she sleeps.

ROARKE

Chapter Three

Roarke startled awake in bed. His heart was pounding, his back drenched in sweat. He'd been dreaming, but the only thing he could remember was the glare of the moon.

He lurched up to sitting, as if there was something that he needed to do, something urgent, something vital that he'd forgotten about . . .

But of course there was no case, no work, no one waiting for him. It only felt as if there were.

He lay back in the dark predawn, listening to the dull and soothing sound of the ocean outside the cottage.

After a moment he reached for his phone to check the time. There was a message on the screen, an unfamiliar number, an area code he didn't recognize. The call must have been what had woken him.

He pressed the Play arrow. A recorded voice came on, curt and unfriendly.

"Special Agent Roarke. I've been trying to get you for a long time."

There was an underlying menace, almost a double entendre to the words that had Roarke automatically tensing.

The voice paused, and then: *"This is Detective Ortiz. Riverside County Sheriff's Department. Again."*

Ortiz. Riverside County, Roarke thought. *Something familiar there, but . . . "again"? What?*

The voice on the message dripped sarcasm. *"I guess you Feebs really don't care about catching Cara Lindstrom, do you? No matter how many people have to die. Unbelievable."*

Roarke felt the familiar adrenaline jolt at the mention of Cara's name.

That's over now, he reminded himself. *But what the hell is this?* The guy sounded wasted. *A crank caller? Drunk dialing?*

The caller spoke again. *"I'd appreciate a call back. If you ever get your head out of your ass."*

There was nothing more, just a phone number.

He played back the message and again was struck by the seething animosity in the detective's voice. He couldn't figure out where it was coming from; he'd never spoken with Ortiz before.

Cara Lindstrom, the mass murderer, had been Roarke's case. And his obsession. He'd caught her. Last month, through a combination of circumstances, she'd been able to get bail, and promptly jumped it. She was a fugitive now. God only knew where. And that was the parole board's problem, not his. He was on voluntary leave of absence from the San Francisco FBI. Hoping to clear his head of Cara Lindstrom for the sake of his own sanity.

He stood, pulled clothes on, and walked out into the living room of the beach house.

Outside the wide windows, beyond the stretch of sand, the ocean was a vast canvas of rolling black.

He stepped outside, onto the porch, and sat in one of the chairs, looking out into inky sky and cold starlight as the crescent moon slipped down into the shimmering water.

Before Cara, he had not known that every month's moon has a name. Sometimes different names for different tribal nations. This month was a Wolf Moon. But it was also called Bitter Moon. And that well enough described what was in Roarke's heart.

He had lost everything, it seemed. Rachel Elliott, the one chance at a decent relationship he'd had in years, possibly ever. The girl Jade, prostituted teen turned vigilante killer, whom he couldn't decide whether to protect or arrest.

He'd lost his job, his integrity, his moral compass, his life's mission. And worst of all, his faith that he was doing something worthwhile in the world . . . or that there was even any chance of doing something worthwhile in the world.

Since he took his leave three weeks ago, his team had called him almost every day. Epps, Singh—both separately and together. Snyder, too—his FBI mentor.

Roarke never called back.

He was done with the case that had made him cross that line into bleak and utter chaos.

He was done chasing Cara, for any reason. He had held her in his arms on a beach, under a pier just like the one he could see down the beach, and had felt bony death in his hands. His own death.

He heard Detective Ortiz's voice in his mind.

"I guess you Feebs really don't care about catching Cara Lindstrom, do you? No matter how many people have to die."

No, he didn't care about catching her. He hoped he'd never hear from or about her again, for both their sakes.

What he was going to do with the rest of his life was another question.

CARA

Chapter Four

The minibus departs the driveway of the group home exactly at 6:30 a.m., exactly as Ms. Sharonda dictated. The bus drives through a clear and windy predawn, through the rocky foothills, past the horse ranches and vineyards.

Cara has dressed in jeans and the black turtleneck. Even in January, it is already so warm she has cut off the sleeves, while keeping the high collar, which hides her throat so no one will stare. She sits still in her seat and looks out the window, watching the wind turn the oak and scrub into mini-tornados.

The bus stops to pick up kids from two other group homes before heading for the high school. Cara surveys everyone that boards, without seeming to look at them. And they watch her, too. The eyes, always the eyes on her. The newbie. The pumpkin. The fish. Fresh meat.

But there is no immediate, conscious threat.

She watches every turn the bus makes, memorizing the route. The town is nestled in the desert mountains. It is not big. The bus passes blocks and blocks of long white posts, beyond which are the Indian lands.

The minibus makes a turn into a residential neighborhood with public bus stops on every block, and Cara gets her first look at Las Piedras High.

The buildings are sand-colored brick, the same pink and tan as the scattered boulders on the hills, pale against the sage green scrub. A tall, plain chain link fence surrounds the athletic fields. On the main building, **HOME OF THE WOLFPACK** is painted in huge red cursive letters.

It is a medium-sized school, which is good. It is big enough that she can be relatively anonymous. She can do her work and keep to herself, not attract attention. And there is another good thing about the school. The hills. They are right there, dull green, dry and beautiful, with those strange and mesmerizing rock formations. She can breathe better, just being able to see them.

If only she has been put in real classes, something that can keep her mind occupied, keep the monsters at bay . . .

The minibus pulls up in the teacher's parking lot in front of the school and disgorges its passengers.

Cara steps off the bus into the strong, warm wind. The Santa Anas. She remembers them from before *The Night*. They were a constant, live thing, sweeping through the desert day and night, sometimes comforting, sometimes exciting, sometimes ominous.

She looks around her and sees nudges and knowing looks from the milling students on the front lawn. The minibus is a dead giveaway that they are group home wards. The other kids split up immediately and Cara moves away from them, too, walking as if she knows exactly where she is and exactly where she is going. Eyes straight ahead. No faltering. No weakness.

She walks up the path, steps through the steel front gate . . . and is startled by the image of a snarling wolf, a larger-than-life mural painted on the building beside her. It freezes her for a moment, then she forces herself to walk forward. Her hands are sweating and she hates herself for it.

Ahead is a plaza with scattered stone planters where students sit and stand in groups. There are rows of picnic tables under metal roofing, to keep the tables shaded in the intense heat that must come in the spring. Rows of lockers surround the quad at sidewalk level.

It is so strange to see kids walking around free. Sitting where they want, how they want, on the picnic tables and benches and brick planters. People slouching, play-fighting, sprawling on the grass. There are no lines. No COs. Instead of the prison uniform of blue jeans and gray sweatshirts, there are so many styles, so many colors. So much skin.

And there is a surprise. In *The Cage* she was the youngest, smallest. But she is not the smallest here. She has stretched in *The Cage*. She is not small, now.

She identifies the administration building and stops into the office for her schedule, as Ms. Sharonda instructed. Beyond the front counter there is an office with an open door. A tall man sitting behind a desk looks out at her with a sudden sharp interest, a look she knows too well. She stiffens and turns away, reaching across the counter for the schedule the secretary is handing her.

Outside again, she quickly assesses the layout of the quad, scans the hierarchy. The school yard is not much different from a jail yard: there is always a pecking order. The center quad has four square center planters with low bench-like walls all taken by the obvious jocks and cheerleaders, other less dominant cliques shunted off to the sides.

She passes along the periphery, keeping her face a mask as her eyes skim the crowd. *The Cage* has made her an expert in seeing without being seen.

Don't let them know what you're thinking. Don't look into the corners.

Despite her best vigilance, she draws attention almost immediately.

There is a cluster of letter-jacketed jocks ahead and she gives them a wide berth, but not wide enough. A mock-fight breaks out, the biggest one shoves someone to the side of him, and the momentum sends the big one stumbling backward into her path. She freezes in her tracks but he collides with her anyway, and twists around in surprise and instant, blustery rage.

"Out of my way."

She looks at him, keeping her posture neutral, while inside she tenses to fight. She knows she should step aside; he isn't worth the hassle, not on her first day. But the words come out of her mouth anyway. "*Your* way?"

There's an instant hush from the jocks and other students around them, people suddenly tuning in, greedy for blood.

The big jock's eyes flare. Cara can see the anger build in him, slow realization that he is being defied, that he will need to assert himself—against a girl.

She fingers the pen in her pocket, fixes on his neck, the smooth tube of the carotid, now bulging slightly with his anger. She pictures the pen driving into the soft flesh, the spurt of crimson it will be—

Someone bursts out laughing. "Burned you, Martell."

It's another of the lettermen who has spoken. Cara refocuses, takes him in quickly, standing behind the angry one. He is slimmer, easygoing, with longish blond hair and surfer looks. The stitching on his jacket reads *Devlin*. The stitching on the big one's reads *Martell*.

Devlin's eyes flicker over her and she tenses, then he smiles at her briefly and shoves his friend back. "Quit yer trippin', dude."

They start to spar, throwing fake punches, no threat involved. While the one called Martell is distracted, Cara moves on quickly. No one follows her. But she hears Devlin call after her, "Welcome to Las Piedras."

And then there is class.

English Lit. Ms. Brooke. A stern African-American woman who sits at her desk for ten minutes after the bell rings, working on something of her own without even looking at the class. *Good,* Cara thinks. She'll be able to read this period.

Gym. Ms. Brand, a stocky and militant jock. A clique of cheerleaders who have obviously all signed up for the same period because they can't do anything on their own. Brand starts the class off with three laps around the track. The running is agonizingly good; the first freedom Cara has had in ages. She has to force herself to hold back so that the teacher doesn't get any ideas about signing her up for team sports, which she loathes. But she feels her whole body working as it's meant to, strong, lithe, unstoppable.

Spanish. Señor Aceves. He speaks nothing but Spanish to the class and they are to speak nothing but Spanish in class, and this is good. Languages are power. Languages are freedom.

Chemistry. Mr. Pring. A boyishly enthusiastic man who greets everyone effusively as they wander in. The lab cabinets on the walls hold a treasure house of chemicals. She can't believe all of this is simply available. The potential for lethal destruction is staggering.

The blond jock from this morning, Devlin, sits in the front in a group of his friends. Cara sees him look up as she steps through the door, feels his eyes follow her as she takes a seat in the back. He is still looking at her when she finally glances his way. He smiles, easy, friendly.

She turns her eyes away and focuses on the chalkboard, the teacher. Like Spanish, chemistry is practical. She doesn't want to miss anything.

Lunch she eats alone, sitting in the almost forgotten pleasure of the sun, and no one bothers her.

The last class of the day is Social Studies. When Cara walks in, the teacher, Mr. Easel, is standing at the front, a clean-cut, square-jawed man in white shirtsleeves and blue trousers. An American flag droops behind him in the high corner of the room.

But Cara barely registers any of this. She has stopped still, staring toward the third row.

A girl with short, curly brown hair sits at the second desk. She is pale, freckled. There are deep, ugly scratches down her face, her neck, her bare arms. She is bleeding from the scratches.

The floor below her desk is pooled with violent red blood.

Cara is frozen in her tracks. The fear is a wave of nausea . . . her legs are jelly and she can't move, can't breathe, can barely stand . . .

Through the blackness and the screaming in her ears, she hears a voice. Someone calling her name. The new name.

And then there are hands on her, holding her up; someone speaking into her face. The teacher.

The brown-haired girl is staring at her, as is everyone else in the class. There are no scratches. There is no blood.

The tall man who scrutinized her from his office this morning is the vice-principal. The name plaque on his desk reads *Mr. Lethbridge.*

Cara sits in the chair in front of the desk in his office, keeping as still as possible. Her heart is pounding so loudly she is afraid the VP will hear it.

"So there was a bit of trouble in class?" he asks.

She fights to calm her heart. She must not let him know what she feels, what she knows.

"What happened?" he asks, oozing fake sympathy.

"Nothing."

Of all the things she has seen since *The Night,* she has never so clearly seen blood like that. Whatever has happened to the brown-haired girl is terrible, terrifying.

She can say none of that. She can't tell anyone. She can't let anyone know what she sees. They will put her away again.

"Car—Eden. We need to know what's wrong so we can help you."

The VP's gaze on her is like spiders on her skin. She wants to scream, to claw them off, to claw his eyes out to stop the spiders.

Instead she sits on the edges of her hands and tries to breathe.

"If there's a problem with your medication—"

"No," she says, too loudly. "No."

The vice-principal repeats himself. "What happened in class?"

"I was just . . . dizzy for a second. I didn't sleep last night."

"Nightmares?" the vice-principal says, fake-sympathetically.

This is a trap. Admit to a bad dream and she could end up back in Level 14. She shakes her head emphatically.

"Just a . . . a new place . . ."

The vice-principal nods. "Of course. It's hard. Would you like to talk about it?" he asks, so gently hinting.

Now she is on full guard. She can see the gleam in his eyes, the avid curiosity. He wants to hear about *The Night*. He wants to know what it's like to lie in a pool of your own blood while a monster eats your family. He wants to suck her pain out of her marrow like some vampire in an ugly suit.

There is nothing that she wants to give this man. Nothing.

She sits back in the chair, and waits.

The vice-principal waits with her, but when it becomes clear that she is not going to speak, he sighs.

"Cara . . . Eden, I want you to know that I'm here to help."

Black anger buzzes in her head. It always comes to this. People with their fakey kind faces and voices saying they can help, encouraging her to talk. Talking means tests and pills and institutions.

There will be no talking.

The vice-principal has flinched back, and she realizes she is on her feet, standing over the desk. She forces something that may pass for a smile. "Thank you."

She is released from the office, and walks as calmly as she can out the gates, toward the parking lot.

Run, her senses are screaming at her. *Get away from this place. Get away from whatever is here.*

After the minibus ride, back at the group home, she says nothing to anyone. She goes to her room and lies down, curls up in a ball.

Her mind goes to the brown-haired girl, the pool of blood.

She has seen such things since *The Night,* when the monster disguised as a man slipped into her house and ate her family.

It scratched her, ripped her throat open, and left her with the other bodies, left her for dead.

But she didn't die.

And since then, she has seen *It.*

It hides in people. *It* sometimes shows her *Its* face, just for a moment, as if *It* is laughing at her, taunting her, popping up to remind her that *It* never goes away.

She sees *It* in the crawly looks of men who are too old to be looking at her the way they do. She sees *It* in teachers and counselors who use their jobs and their power to hurt and torment. She can feel *Its* presence when the hairs stand up—on her arms, at the back of her neck, a frantic choking feeling that tells her *Run.*

And today, in class, the pool of blood around the girl was the same as *The Night.* The blood that her sister lay in. The blood that Cara lay in.

She knows only one thing. The monster that killed her family, that tried to kill her, is *here,* now. *It* has scratched the brown-haired girl. Not killed her, not yet, but wounded her deeply. There is no other explanation. *It* is there in the school, somewhere. Cara has been released from *The Cage* of YA only for this. One day out and *It* has found her already, or if *It* hasn't, *It* will.

Underneath the turtleneck, she can feel the throbbing of the scar on her neck where *It* slashed her that night.

She goes to the polished steel mirror and pulls the turtleneck down to look at her own scar. She sees the open wound, her own blood running from the deep slash in her neck.

Help me, she whispers to no one. *Help me.*

ROARKE

Chapter Five

When Roarke opened his eyes, it was morning, and he was back in bed. He got up, pulled on old khakis and a sweatshirt. The clothes were worn, soft on his skin. After the formal tailored suits he'd worn as an agent, it was a feeling almost like being naked.

He moved out into the living room of the beach house. Through the broad pane of window, the ocean stretched out beyond the sand, a pewter mirror in the dawning light.

The cottage was simple and functional, an original from 1940, with hardwood floors, a fireplace and built-in shelves in the living room. A bit shabby, but with far more character than one of the ubiquitous condos in town. It had looked out on all kinds of weather and had housed any number of people, and it remained serene and somehow untouched. Seeing the ocean and the strip of sand out the wide front windows was profoundly calming.

As he did every morning, he made himself coffee, poured it into a metal canister, and zipped up a hoodie to walk on the beach.

The air was soft and, in mid-January, already warming. There was peace in the glimmering ocean, the tang of salt and sand, the papery yellow flowers on the dunes, the wind, the lulling rumble of waves.

It made sense, in the midst of emotional turmoil, to seek refuge in such surroundings. But California has over three thousand miles of tidal shoreline. And any number of charming beach towns. So Roarke could give himself all sorts of reasons that he had chosen the central California shore town of Pismo Beach to retreat to and have his quiet meltdown. He could say it had nothing to do with the fact that it was one of the few places he knew that Cara Lindstrom had stayed for any length of time. Length being relative: in Cara's case, a whopping total of six days in one place. It was not in her nature to stay still.

But the truth was he looked for her every time he walked on the funky downtown streets, past the beach shops and surfboard shacks and bike rental booths. He looked for her browsing the outdoor racks of batik clothing and shell jewelry, in the lobbies of the much-faded, formerly elegant hotels with original thirties and forties architecture.

And on the beach. Especially on the beach, and most especially when he crossed under the pier, with its forest of posts, its cathedral-like echoes, and felt the ache of his memories of their night encounter on the sand. What had happened, and what he wished had happened.

When those memories threatened, there was another to halt them: the one of Cara standing in the wreck of the farmhouse, staring into his eyes with her breath clouding white in the frozen air . . . and blood dripping from her hands, just after she'd sliced a razor across Darrell Sawyer's throat.

And then there would be the shame . . . the shame of what he'd done as an agent, the overwhelming guilt of destroying evidence, abetting two known criminal fugitives, and perhaps worst of all: creating a third. Rachel Elliott had not been seen or heard from since that night that she'd taken Jade, the sixteen-year-old killer, out of that same farmhouse and presumably hidden her with a shadowy, revolutionary feminist underground that might or might not exist.

All of his thoughts on that subject were wild speculation on his part, and yet, he knew he might not be that far from right.

He moved up the stairs and onto the pier.

A large compass was painted on the planks at the wide entrance, a constant reminder that he had lost his own. Pelicans perched on the wooden railing, in ragged defiance of the **Do Not Feed Birds** sign beneath their webbed feet.

He gave them their space, and moved further down the railing to look over the vast and glimmering crescent bay. And as always, his eyes scanned the beach, before he could order himself to stop.

He knew that Cara was long gone from California, this time. She knew that all of California law enforcement would be watching for her. That *he* would be watching for her. The media had made her famous again, almost as famous as she had been as a little girl, the "Miracle Girl," the sole survivor of a psychotic mass murderer—

And then it clicked.

He knew who the midnight caller was. It was a detective who had handled the investigation into what Roarke suspected was Cara's first murder: the homicide of a group home counselor who had been killed in Cara's signature style, just a week after Cara had been released from juvenile prison.

Sixteen years ago.

Not the lead detective, but the junior on the case. Ortiz.

Why was he calling now?

Roarke's pulse was pounding as he fumbled for his phone and hit the callback button. He felt a surge of impatience bordering on anger when all he got was a voice mail message. He composed himself, spoke into the phone.

"This is Agent Roarke returning. You can reach me any time."

He disconnected. Then he played back the message, to see if he'd been imagining the implied threat. He hadn't. The menace was clear in the detective's tone.

Why? What the hell is that about?

And that needling insult: "*I guess you Feebs really don't care about catching Cara Lindstrom, do you? No matter how many people have to die.*"

Does Ortiz know where she is?

Do I want to know?

He went back to the cottage, and walked a circle around the living room, but he knew he was only postponing the inevitable. Finally, he went into the bedroom, pulled open the bottom drawer of the battered dresser, and took out the file.

Cara's history—police, psychiatric, and otherwise. Singh had requested it when the team had first tied Cara's prints to the murder of a trucker at a rest stop not far from Pismo. The file covered only the early years of her life, since at the age of eighteen she had disappeared from all public record.

At the top was the photo Roarke had found of her in one of those case files: a slim blond waif in her early teens, with enormous and watching eyes. Too intense to be called beautiful, too mesmerizing to look away from.

He put it aside.

There was a document inside the file that was completely unofficial, but Roarke suspected it belonged anyway: an informal written summary by a retired police chief about the Palm Desert murder of a counselor named Clive Pierson, sixteen years ago.

Pierson had been employed at a group home where Cara had been living. He'd testified that twelve-year-old Cara had beaten an older boy into unconsciousness. She was sent up to the California Youth

Authority, juvenile jail for the state's most violent offenders. Two years later, a week after she was released, Pierson was found dead in his mobile home, his throat slashed. No one had ever been arrested for the murder.

The retired police chief, Jeffries, was from a different district, and had not been part of that investigation. But he had voiced his suspicions to Roarke that Cara had killed the counselor.

Roarke put Jeffries's report aside, opened an envelope, and dumped out a series of crime scene photos.

The images were as bad as it comes. Blood-drenched sheets. Arcs of arterial spray on the walls.

From the time Roarke had heard about it, that murder had always been under his skin.

Did a fourteen-year-old girl do that?

He smoothed a hand through his hair, reached for his phone, checked for messages. No call back from Detective Ortiz.

He could call again, yeah, and start the inevitable phone tag that goes along with trying to contact a police detective. He could do that. But it was a lot harder to say no to a flesh-and-blood FBI agent, or whatever Roarke was at the moment, standing in front of you in the office.

On impulse he checked the distance from Pismo to Palm Desert on Google Maps. Nearly a five-hour drive.

In the end he couldn't say what made him go. He could never say why when it came to Cara.

He got in the car and drove.

CARA

Chapter Six

When she wakes in the morning it takes her a moment to focus on where she is. When she does she is surprised to find the walls of a bedroom rather than of a cell. There is no monster, no blood.

Just her, and her roommate asleep in the other bed, in the dark blue of predawn.

She lies still, evaluating the sensations inside her. There is a slight nausea, dizziness. And she can see glimmering around the edges of things.

She knows what it means. The medication isn't strong enough.

She sees it in a flash, so real—

The girl with the curly brown hair, sitting at her desk with a pool of blood at her feet . . .

She presses her hands to her head to force the image away. She breathes in. And again. She feels her heart start to beat.

If her medication isn't strong enough, is that why she's seeing these things? Would the blood go away if she just got a stronger prescription?

She debates telling Ms. Sharonda, or the shrink. But reporting these things can end you up in more trouble. She must appear *Normal*.

After a time, she rises, dresses, and eats with the others. And says nothing.

Today there is a traffic snarl at the high school, a long line of cars waiting to get into the parking lot drop, so the minibus releases the group home kids beside the sidewalk, some distance from the front entrance of the school.

They step off the bus into the wind, and as yesterday, the kids quickly disperse in different directions, distancing themselves from each other. Cara walks slowly, dropping behind them.

The wind is strong, huge, billowing gusts: the hot, dry Santa Anas, rattling the palm fronds above. She has to fight to make her way across the sidewalk against the force pushing her backward with every step.

As she struggles, she becomes aware of something besides the relentless wind. A presence. Her heart is suddenly pounding, a feeling of anxiety and dread.

She knows the feeling. An early warning.

Of what?

With just her eyes, not turning her head, she surveys the sidewalk, the people around her.

A van is parked at the curb. Not like the school minibus, but another, a white one with no writing on it, no logo from a business. No back windows either. There is a man's shape at the wheel, obscured by the brightness of the sun.

She drops her backpack to the ground and crouches, pretending to tie the laces of her Keds. And from that crouch, she looks backward toward the street.

When she looks back, she sees that the man inside is turned toward her, watching her.

And there it is: a whispering at the corners of her mind. In her mind, but also outside of it, dark and ominous . . .

Her heart is suddenly too tight in her chest.

She twists around and walks straight onto the lawn, where no car can follow.

She can feel the eyes on the back of her head, following her. An intention.

She passes quickly through the painted steel gate of the school, past the mural of the snarling wolf, rounds the corner into the quad . . . and nearly runs her over.

The bleeding girl.

The girl startles backward and the two of them stare at each other, facing each other.

Before she knows what she is doing, Cara is speaking. "Did you see *It*?" she asks, low, so that no one else can hear. Possibly not even the bleeding girl. Her face seems frozen. And then she turns without a word and walks away from Cara.

Cara watches, with a cold band around her chest.

As the girl walks though the scattered groups of students in the quad, she leaves a dripping trail of blood on the ground.

But no one looks. No one sees.

The girl disappears around a bank of lockers. Cara comes to life and runs after her, past clusters of students who turn to look, whispering.

She ignores them, tears around the corner of the lockers . . .

The bleeding girl is gone.

Cara stops in her tracks. And then beside the row of lockers, she sees the door of the girl's bathroom just closing on its hydraulic hinge.

Cara strides forward and slams through the door.

Inside the dim tiled space, the bleeding girl is there, standing at one of the sinks, just reaching for the faucet.

She twists around when the door bangs open behind her. She is pale and hollow-eyed, and Cara feels a stab of pain just looking at her.

"What is it? What's happening?" Cara demands.

The girl backs up from her, bewildered. "What?"

Cara lunges forward, grabs the girl's hands and turns them palms up. No gashes. No blood.

The girl pulls away. There is no strength in the move.

"Who is it?" Cara says harshly.

"I don't know . . . what you mean." It seems to be a great effort for her to talk, and Cara wants to shake her, to wake her up.

"Yes, you do. The man in the van."

The girl flinches, as if she's seen a ghost. Cara seizes the girl's arms and she cries out. "You're hurting me."

"*I'm* not hurting you—"

"Let me go—"

"I know you saw. Who is he? What did he do to you? *Tell me.*"

The girl breaks free. They look at each other in the silence of the cold, tiled room. The girl is trembling.

"Please . . ." Cara whispers.

The girl's face crumples. "Leave me alone. You have to leave me alone." The girl pushes past her and out.

It takes Cara a moment before she can walk out of the bathroom. She stops beside the lockers, her legs shaky, her head buzzing.

Am I crazy?

Maybe. But the bleeding girl's pain is real. Not just pain. *Fear.*

A group of girls passes by her, looking her over surreptitiously, and Cara realizes she is standing still in a thoroughfare, where other people can see her.

Normal. Must look Normal.

She starts to walk again, although at the moment she can't remember what her first class is. She forces her legs to move, hoping her brain will catch up.

In the center of the quad, the jocks are seated on a concrete wall, legs apart, feet planted on the brick, like young kings. The Wolfpack. She sees Martell look at her and make some comment she can't hear. The others laugh.

Don't look. Don't react. Don't feed them.

Without increasing her pace, she moves toward the periphery of the quad . . . so intent on avoiding Martell and his friends that she nearly collides with the vice-principal, standing at the door of the administration building, arms crossed on his chest, watching the students coming in for school.

"Whoa, hold on there, Eden."

She backs up. Her heart is racing again as she is overcome by the urge to flee.

But Lethbridge steps toward her, with a wide crocodile smile. "How are you doing this fine day?"

She mumbles a reply.

He keeps talking, in that fake sweet voice. "Are you finding all your classes? Any problems with your schedule?"

She forces herself to speak, to sound *Normal.* "I'm fine. Everything's good."

"I've been looking at your test scores. You're a very bright girl."

She doesn't trust what he means by that, so she remains silent.

"We should be thinking about building up your resume for college applications. There are many fine clubs and activities at Las Piedras. I'm thinking particularly of Palmers, which sponsors a number of scholarships for its members."

Cara can barely concentrate on what he is saying. All she can see is the shadow in the van. "I don't . . . know if I'm allowed to."

"I'm sure your caseworker would approve. And they'd be lucky to have you. You think about it, talk to her about it."

"I will," Cara says, to end the conversation. "I don't want to be late to class."

"Good girl," Lethbridge says. She can feel him watching as she walks away. She forces herself not to run.

At the sound of the bell, she remembers that her first class is English.

She sits in class, and tries to calm herself.

The bleeding girl knows something. She has encountered *It*, and *It* has scratched her, recently and profoundly, and she is wasting away.

But the girl is too badly damaged to help herself. Whatever is happening to her, she is denying it with every fiber of her being. Cara knows one thing: if people do not want to see, they will not see.

All through the school day her thoughts return to the white van, the man watching the school.

She has seen this kind of thing before. There are often men watching the group homes, parking their cars and vans down the street, looking to swoop in and scoop up the girls who have never heard kind or flattering words, who believe the promises of photo shoots and stardom, who are pathetically eager to believe that a smooth older man could have any interest in a teenage girl other than selling her on the street.

Is that what this is, now?

Cara thinks suddenly of Ms. Sharonda.

There is something so strong about the director. And she would know about the men in the cars and the vans. She sees things about people, too.

Can I tell her?

Does she dare?

Maybe. Maybe.

She doesn't know. But it is the first hope she has felt.

In Chemistry class, Pring claps his hands and exhorts everyone to "Partner up!" as if that is a normal and everyday occurrence. Cara stands up with the others, holding the work sheet Pring has passed out, but moves on her own to one of the lab tables placed at intervals around the periphery of the room.

When she turns from the cabinet, he is there. Devlin. Taller than she is, blond hair falling across his blue eyes. He smiles at her, puts his work sheet down on the lab table.

"Not my best subject but I'm ace at faking it."

She tenses, quickly assesses. His intent is not predatory; that, she is too expert at recognizing. But there is intent there. And she is not here to be scrutinized. She turns away from him without speaking, skims the instructions on the work sheet, opens the cabinet behind her to look for the requisite compounds. He doesn't budge.

"Are you pissed because of Martell?"

She gives him a stony look. The brown-haired girl is bleeding to death in full view of the school, and he thinks she cares about his sociopath road dog?

Devlin laughs, but it's a pleasant sound, not cutting. "He's harmless, I swear."

She assesses him quickly. This one is not malicious. But she has seen what is crawling behind his friend's eyes. *It* is not fully awakened yet. But *It* is waiting.

"You think?" she asks flatly. And slowly, the smile dies on Devlin's face.

"I've known him a long time." It sounds lame, and he knows it. He shakes his head. "I've never seen him—"

And then he stops, his eyes widening slightly, and he doesn't finish. Because he realizes he had been about to lie. He *has* seen. But if you don't talk about *It*, *It* doesn't exist.

She turns to the work sheet on the lab table in front of her, focuses on collecting the equipment: beakers, a Bunsen burner. Ignoring him.

He sees things, this one. That doesn't change what he is. A good boy. Good family, good grades, good sportsman. Good future.

Not for her.

At the end of the school day, she walks out to the minibus, scanning the street for the white van. She doesn't see it.

But it was there before. That wasn't a vision. It was real.

On the ride home, she rehearses what she will say to Ms. Sharonda. There was a van parked outside the school, with no windows and no writing. A man was watching her from the front seat. He whispered something at her, and she didn't hear what it was, but she was afraid.

The last part is not the exact truth, mostly because she doesn't know what the exact truth is. There was whispering, that's true. The whispering told her she is in danger. But she doesn't know where the whispering comes from, only that it is rarely wrong.

When there is whispering, she knows she must listen.

The minibus drops the six girls off beside the fountain with the angel. Cara walks with the others into the house, and turns down the hallway toward Ms. Sharonda's office.

At the end of the hall, a man walks out of the conference room, heading down the hall toward the front door. Pitted skin. A pudgy roll around his middle. Fat sausage-like fingers.

Suddenly Cara can't move. She is shaking. Her hands, her legs . . . even her teeth are chattering.

She has not seen him in two years. Not since the night he and the boy came into her room. Not since she had to fight for her life.

It has been so long, she can't remember his face. But she knows by the smell. *Its* smell.

He knows her. She knows he knows her. He looks straight at her and smiles, that horrible, stretched-mouth smile. She can feel the violation of his hands on her. She is choking on his stinking drunken breath as he holds her pinned to the bed and tries to shove his tongue down her throat, tries to force her legs apart. She feels the icy fear and white-hot rage . . .

As he walks past her, he whispers, "I'm watching you."

She sees jagged teeth.

When he is out the door, she forces herself to move, runs to the front window, stares out, looking for the white van.

The counselor is there, getting into a beat-up old dark blue Tercel. *Not* the van.

She backs away from the window and strides toward the lounge. Three of the girls are already parked on the sagging sofa, watching TV. She stands in the doorway, her heart beating so loudly she is sure the others must hear it.

"What was he doing here?" Cara asks. She can hear the tremor in her own voice, and digs her nails into her palms to stop it. "The man who just left?"

"Just some caseload," Monique says indifferently. Caseload—the system's weird, ungrammatical slang name for caseworkers.

"What did he want?"

"How the shit do I know?" Monique says, not even bothering to look at her this time.

Cara turns away numbly and goes down the hall to her room.

She lies on her bed with a book open on her chest as camouflage and tries to think through the waves of confusion and sick apprehension.

She knows it was the counselor. Pierson. She knows it. She knows *It*.

What was he doing here?

He said he was watching me.

So has he been watching the school? Is that the man in the van?

But he wasn't in a van.

But he wouldn't drive his own car for what he wanted to do.

And what does he have to do with the bleeding girl?

This is what is confusing. There is never just one. *It* turns up everywhere.

But that was *Pierson. He's come looking for me here. He knows where I am.*

And one thing is clear. She cannot tell Ms. Sharonda now. Not about the bleeding girl, not about the van, not about anything. Because a counselor is a counselor. They stick together. It cost her two years in *The Cage* to find that out.

He knows where I am.

She reaches into her pocket, fingering the ballpoint pen there. How easy it would be to end this.

But finally she knows what she must do.

That night, when Ms. Nicole calls the girls forward to take their meds, Cara takes the paper cup and swallows the pills obediently, shows her tongue and cheeks.

Then she locks herself in the bathroom.

Vomiting is easy. Sometimes there is a pain so deep in her gut that the only way to feel better is to puke it out. This time, all she needs to do is think of the pool of blood at the brown-haired girl's feet for her bile to rise.

She bends over the sink and gags the pills up into her hand.

She looks at the capsules. Depakote. Clozapine. A mood stabilizer and an antipsychotic.

They have been effective, in their way. They have been a curtain between her and the whispers, the visions, the screams.

But she cannot afford the haze that the drugs provide. She must be clear, no matter what horrors she sees. She must be able to see *It* coming.

She flushes the pills and goes to her room. Through the window, the moon is a perfect half in the blackness of sky.

She lies back on her bed . . . and waits for the moon to talk to her.

ROARKE

Chapter Seven

When people outside California think about California, they picture Hollywood, Disneyland, the beaches. They picture San Diego and San Francisco. The connoisseurs might imagine Sequoia, Yosemite, the Sierra Nevada mountains.

But in reality, vast stretches of California are desert. The Mojave. Death Valley. Joshua Tree. Anza-Borrego. And Palm Desert, where Roarke was headed, straight east on the 10.

It was a perfect Southern California day, windy and clear as only January can be in California, pushing eighty degrees on the inland roads. Global warming might be a disaster for the planet at large, but at the moment, it suited Roarke just fine. His Land Rover ate up the miles, and the driving was a relief. It felt like movement, like life. The foothills rolled down in thick folds from the snow-topped peaks of the San Bernardino Mountains; the valley stretched out before him with its sandy washes and patchwork squares of orange groves, intermittently feathered with the tops of palm trees.

He reached to turn on the radio. As he scanned through the stations, he came across one of the shock-jock commentators he hated. He was just about to punch past to another station when a name stopped him.

"Cara Lindstrom's arrest and escape has sparked a national debate about 'rape culture.' We're taking callers."

Despite himself, Roarke left the station where it was.

"Hello, Ron from Bakersfield," the host said.

The caller didn't need coaxing. His voice blasted through the speakers, a self-righteous outrage silenced only periodically by censor bleeps. *"Rape culture? Please. We're f***** Americans. We're the best at everything. If we actually practiced rape culture, there would be a trail of bleeding pussies from New York to Los Angeles and back again. If rape culture actually existed in America, there's no way we'd let ourselves pass with only sixteen percent of women experiencing it. That's bush league."*

Roarke's hands tightened on the steering wheel in disgust and anger. He'd been careful not to turn on the TV because he didn't want to know how much hate was being focused against Cara by the men's rights groups, the talk show hosts and shock jocks like the one on this station.

"You just watch. This Lindstrom c*** is going to get a taste of rape culture—"

Roarke punched the button to silence the rant.

Multiply this psycho by ten thousand, a hundred thousand . . .

The thought made him almost sick with fear for her.

If any one of them ever gets to her . . .

He prayed that Cara was so far away no one could ever find her. Including him.

It was just before noon when Roarke hit Palm Desert, an oasis in the Coachella Valley at the base of the stunning San Jacinto mountain range, with its sheer cliff faces and views of pristine dunes.

The town was now famous for the music festival, which had started with impromptu parties out in the dunes and canyons, musicians on acoustic instruments playing spaced-out psychedelic desert rock. The music scene had exploded and brought not just gentrification but real wealth to the formerly scruffy town. Sixteen years ago it wouldn't have been so posh. But now El Paseo, the town's main drag, was a sand-colored version of Rodeo Drive. Large and colorful pieces of public art decorated the median on a street lined with stores with names like Tiffany, Givenchy, Wolfgang Puck. The opulence seemed garish and obscene against the pristine purity of the desert, the staggering beauty of the mountains.

Roarke found the Palm Desert Sheriff's Station on Gerald Ford Drive, just past a stretch of golf course. The large parking lot was full of black and white trucks and SUVs.

He got out of his Land Rover and looked at the building, built in a vaguely adobe style: red flagstone with pillars, a front plaza with red-gold ceramic tile. Instead of lawns, there were planters with pebbles, and well-tended desert vegetation: bushes with red and orange flowers, squat palm trees. It was the cleanest police station he'd ever seen.

He reached into the back seat for the suit coat he'd hung on the side hook of the vehicle, and shrugged it on. He may have been on the beach for weeks, but it would take a while for the habit of FBI dress standards to die.

Inside the spotless lobby were pink sandstone walls, a few rows of plastic chairs. Several deputies and a couple of plainclothes milled inside the glass-enclosed reception cubicle. Roarke walked up to the counter and addressed the male deputy perched on the front stool.

"I'm looking for Detective Ortiz."

"You have an appointment?"

"Just hoping to catch him."

"And you are?"

Roarke was suddenly faced with the new problem of how to introduce himself. No longer technically an agent, at least in his own mind—but not quite a civilian, either.

"My name's Roarke—"

A sunburned man with dark hair, solidly built in his suit, turned from the counter where he was standing. "I'll take care of it, Benson," he told the deputy.

He stepped to open the door of the reception cubicle and walked out into the lobby, then stopped in front of Roarke, a boxer's stance. "I'm Ortiz."

That's a bit of luck, Roarke thought. "Matthew Roarke—"

The man's face turned darker. "I know who you are. You think you can just turn up here without an appointment? Who the fuck do you think you are, Mr. G-Man?"

The detective's hostility caught Roarke off guard. He willed his fists not to clench, willed his voice to stay even. "*You* called *me.*"

"Yeah, I called you. *Now* you want to talk. Now that Lindstrom's in the wind again, thanks to your fuckup."

Ortiz wasn't just angry. This was a barely contained rage. Roarke tried to keep himself together.

"You said you had information—"

"Had. I *had* information. I *called.* After that whole Bitch thing— the media shitstorm. But no, the FBI had it under control, didn't you?" His voice was bitter. "So Lindstrom makes fucking bail."

"Hold on. You called?" Roarke asked. This was coming out of nowhere.

"And no one ever called me back."

Roarke couldn't fathom it. That wasn't like Singh, at all. She was probably the most meticulous person he had ever met, let alone worked with. Then again, in the days before Cara's hearing, they had all had their hands full, the team. And he hadn't been thinking clearly himself, not by a long shot.

He forced himself to focus back on Ortiz. "I'm here now. Do you have information relevant to the whereabouts of Cara Lindstrom?"

Is that what he thought? Or hoped? Now that he'd said it aloud he actually hoped the exact opposite.

Ortiz's voice was grim. "I coulda told you plenty that woulda kept her behind bars."

The anger was beginning to grate on Roarke. "What would that be?"

"She killed a man in cold blood in this county."

Despite his own suspicions on that front, Roarke found himself rising to her defense. "My understanding is that she was never charged."

"She was never charged," Ortiz said, grinding the words.

Roarke pushed it. "Did you ever have anything on her, really? Las Piedras is forty-five miles away from Palm Desert over a mountain road. How do you place that fourteen-year-old girl at that crime scene?"

He'd thought it through a hundred times. Of course he had his own idea about how it had happened. He just wanted to know what the detective had.

Before Ortiz could answer, Roarke added, "And why do you think she would go to that kind of trouble? The planning, the danger. We're talking about a fourteen-year-old girl—"

"Because Pierson sent her up to YA. He had her put away for two years. Kids kill for less."

Roarke shook his head. "It never bothered you that there were two of them against one of her? A grown man and a fifteen-year-old boy with a history of assault?"

Ortiz looked ready to jump him. "*You* didn't see that crime scene. *I* did. It was a blood bath. Girl does that at fourteen, it's not hard to figure what comes next. And I guess we saw, didn't we? Christ only knows how many men she's killed since."

Roarke had to stifle his dislike. There was blistering resentment there, but also triumph. Ortiz had been vindicated, and he wanted everyone to know it.

The detective almost spat his next words. "But she makes bail because she's a woman. A *serial killer,* and she just walks."

Ortiz was wrong about that. What was interesting about Cara was that she *wasn't* a serial killer. There was no sexual motivation to her murders whatsoever. She was an extraordinarily prolific vigilante who was convinced that the men she killed were evil. But under the circumstances Roarke wasn't about to correct him.

"And you have no idea where she is, do you?" Ortiz challenged.

Roarke suddenly had the distinct impression that there was a motive here, that he was being played. "Do you?"

Ortiz looked angry, and also sly. "You don't even have a guess. With all your FBI resources at your disposal. Fucking useless." He shook his head. "I'll tell you what, though. She'll get hers. There are all kinds of people gunning for her."

He was sounding just like the radio callers.

But Roarke held back his own anger, because something wasn't adding up here. "Did you have an actual reason for contacting me?"

Ortiz's lips curled in something that was not quite a smile. "I got what I expected. Go the hell home, *Agent* Roarke."

Chapter Eight

R oarke stood by his Rover in the parking lot outside, at once agitated and mystified by the encounter. On one hand, he knew where Ortiz was coming from. Every lawman had one. For Ortiz, Cara was the one who got away. He'd known all along she was a killer, and now the world knew.

But there was more there than a desire for justice or closure. That level of rage against a fourteen-year-old? It didn't make sense.

Why would he want to contact me at all? Was it just drunk-dialing? Blowing off steam?

There was something underneath it. Roarke could feel it festering. He just didn't know what it was.

So I've driven all the way out here for nothing.

He looked out on the desert landscape, the towering wall of the mountain range.

What now? Back to Pismo?

He didn't relish the thought of another five-hour drive back the way he came. But beyond that, the prospect of returning to the beach, to his state of limbo, was almost panic-inducing.

But . . .

But . . . there was an alternate route home that would take him through Las Piedras.

The exact route that fourteen-year-old Cara would have to have taken to get to Palm Desert that night.

He felt the pull of the thought, like a nicotine craving, like an alcoholic's urge for *just one* drink. He knew the danger, the seductive undertow of the case.

But I'm here . . .

He gave in, opened the driver's door, and got back on the road.

The drive from Palm Desert to Las Piedras was an hour and twenty minutes by the Garmin, that began with twenty miles on the famously scenic Highway 74, up and over the San Jacinto and Santa Rosa mountain range.

Roarke turned onto the highway and began the ascent into the mountains, turning off frequently at the vista points to look back in awe over the huge sprawl of the Coachella Valley. Bare sand, house-sized boulders, cactus . . . and a stunning vastness. It wasn't a drive for the faint of heart: just two lanes with an occasional turnout for slower vehicles, and whiplash-inducing curves, every new turn opening up staggering desert panoramas and new contrasts in landscape and vegetation.

He found himself gripping the steering wheel with both hands to negotiate the increasing highway elevations on the winding road, the hairpin turns with their deadly drop-offs.

More and more he realized it was a crazy thing to think that Cara had driven it herself, at night, at fourteen.

He couldn't fathom how she would've been able to do it. The winding road through the mountains at night would be perilous in the extreme. He knew the adult Cara was an expert car thief, and she would have had to learn somewhere, some time. But at the time of the counselor's murder she had been in CYA, juvenile prison, for two years. In order to make this drive at the time Ortiz was alleging, she would have had to learn to drive at *twelve*.

If she had done it, how the hell *had* she done it?

On the other side of the mountain, the road descended gradually, with equally stunning canyon views. In between watching the road, he went over the time line in his head. He'd practically memorized it.

Twenty-five years ago the Lindstrom family was massacred by the serial killer known as the Reaper, after which five-year-old Cara lived with her father's sister, her aunt Joan, and Joan's new husband in the wine country town of Temecula.

Cara's mental scars from that night proved overwhelming. The husband left the family almost immediately, and Joan gave Cara up to the foster care system only a few months later, citing extreme behavioral problems and overwhelming mental issues.

Cara was in and out of foster homes, and then group homes, for the next seven years. During all that time she was on psychotropic medication. The trouble with that was, the diagnoses of her mental state were so conflicting that it wasn't possible to properly medicate her. No one really knew *what* they were medicating. But whatever else it was, there was certainly PTSD: severe, sustained psychological anguish stemming from the unspeakable tragedy of that long-ago night.

Then came the attack on the boy in the group home, Pierson's testimony against her and her incarceration in CYA, the old name for the California Division of Juvenile Justice. She was released in January of 2000, and sent to a group home in the Riverside County town of Las Piedras. She was at the high school there for just two weeks, after which she was transferred again.

And during which the former counselor from the group home was murdered in Palm Desert: almost an hour and a half drive from the high school.

Had Cara been planning that murder, plotting revenge, all the time she had been incarcerated? Or was there more to it than that?

Roarke had always wondered. Because with Cara, there was always more to the story.

The state road turned into Cahuilla Road, a twenty-mile two-lane highway through hills and valleys, skirting and sometimes crossing several separate Indian reservations: Santa Rosa, Cahuilla, Pechanga . . . each one so distinct topographically. Native American nations, sovereign territory, with their own laws and justice system.

Cara would have grown up with that, too. Roarke filed that thought away as he stared out at vast stretches of unpopulated wilderness.

So many places to hide. And this is just one state.

He felt a spark of hope. She really could be anywhere, by now. She had the resources . . . surely she had the sense to get lost and stay lost.

He thought suddenly of Ortiz, the detective's explosive anger. And a traitorous part of him whispered to Cara, *Go. Stay gone.*

Chapter Nine

He reached Las Piedras in the early afternoon.

It was one of the weird little towns in the hill-lined corridor between the coast and the desert: hippified Lake Elsinore, Murrietta with its hot springs, the Temecula wine country. Las Piedras had not experienced the land boom or the resulting traffic congestion that some of those other towns had. It was nestled beneath sage green hills dotted with the huge pale boulders that must have given the town its name. Isolated, quiet, not too different from what it must have been like sixteen years ago. Roarke had the feeling of traveling back into a simpler time.

He had told himself he would just drive by the high school, a cluster of two-story sand-colored brick buildings with a scattering of oaks and palm trees. But it only took one glance for him to pull to the curb and get out of the car.

He stood on the sidewalk, feeling the wind on his skin, while students milled on the front lawn under the dry, rustling palms.

And he stared up at the front of the school, at the words painted in red cursive letters:

HOME OF THE WOLFPACK

He didn't live his life by synchronicity, although he had a healthy respect for intuition in general. But Cara had attended the school for just two weeks.

In January.

A Wolf Moon.

Before he was aware what he was doing, he was walking across the school lawn toward the administration building.

He stepped through the metal gates, and was confronted by a snarling wolf effigy on the wall outside of the building. As if the thoughts in his mind had assumed form.

He turned away from it, glanced over the quad: a core defined by four discrete but interconnected two-story brick-and-glass buildings. Rows of lockers surrounded the quad at sidewalk level.

The plaza was a study in the student pecking order, the four square center planters with low walls all taken by jocks and cheerleaders, other less dominant cliques shunted off to the sides. All of them looking impossibly young to Roarke's eyes, children playing at an adult game.

Sixteen years ago there would have been no smartphones. No iPhones. Facebook hadn't even launched yet. It was a less connected time, and a more connected time.

A blond girl, slender and waifish, glanced at Roarke as she walked by. Not Cara, of course, or her ghost, either.

He didn't look after her. But he turned, opened the door of the administration building, and walked in.

He'd already decided to use his Bureau credentials to pave the way. The receptionist was suitably impressed, spoke hurriedly into an intercom, and then he was ushered behind the counter and into Principal Lethbridge's office.

Lethbridge was a surprisingly tall man, broad shouldered, just starting to develop a paunch. His hale and hearty persona was a thin veneer stretched over an inner core of menace. Kids would think twice before fucking with him.

He stood and reached a hand across the desk. "Agent Roarke, is it? We don't often get the FBI coming around."

Roarke shook hands briefly, got right to the point. "I'm looking for information on a former student of yours. Cara Lindstrom. She would have been enrolled as Eden Ballard."

The principal's face changed to a combination of wariness and something else that Roarke couldn't quite interpret. "I'm not sure I'll have much to tell you. You're talking about fifteen years ago—"

Roarke kept his voice pleasant. "Sixteen. Were you at the school at the time?"

"I was. Vice-principal."

"Are you saying that you don't remember Cara Lindstrom? Surely you were aware of her history. *All* of her history."

"The school was aware," Lethbridge said stiffly. "But she was only here for two weeks. "

"What happened after two weeks?"

"As I remember, she was transferred elsewhere in the county by Social Services."

"Not because of something that happened here at the school?"

"Nothing to do with the school. It was Social Services' decision."

Roarke's next question came out of the blue, even for him. "Did anything odd happen that month, while she was here?"

"Odd?" the principal repeated.

"Anything violent or traumatic . . ."

Roarke could see from the subtle, sudden tension in Lethbridge's body that there was something. Definitely something.

"That's a very strange question," the principal hedged.

"But?"

Lethbridge deliberated. Roarke waited him out. Finally, he answered, "A student committed suicide."

Roarke stared at him.

"It was unexpected, and obviously very disturbing to the whole school."

"A boy or a girl?"

"A girl."

"When was that, exactly?"

"I would have to look it up."

"Thanks, I'd appreciate that," Roarke said, as if Lethbridge had offered.

The principal seemed to struggle internally between anger and acquiescence, but ultimately leaned forward and hit the button on his intercom. "Karen, would you bring me a copy of *The Wolf,* from 2000?"

Roarke felt a jolt at the words, but realized the principal was talking about a yearbook.

Still, the name . . . worrisome.

The office door opened and a secretary came in with a slim bound volume and a much thicker one. "Didn't know if you meant the year-book or the paper," she said, holding both up inquiringly.

"Both," Roarke said immediately. "Please."

She glanced at him, then put both books on the desk in front of the principal, and stepped out again, closing the door behind her. Roarke saw that the thicker binder was bound newsprint: the school's papers for the year.

The principal opened the yearbook and flipped to a page near the front, looked down at it for a moment, then turned the book around to face Roarke.

Roarke looked down on a studio-posed photo of a girl with short, curly brown hair, a few prominent freckles.

There were words and dates below the photo:

Laura Huell

April 2, 1985 – January 22, 2000

Rest in Peace

Fourteen years old.

She was fresh-faced and pretty without being either beautiful or memorable, and her smile wasn't a full-wattage one, but it wasn't haunted or visibly troubled, either. Just a teenager. Before sex. Before trauma.

But something had happened to make her take her own life, and it had happened when Cara was in the school.

On the same day that the group home counselor had been murdered.

CARA

Chapter Ten

Just one night without the medication and already she can feel the buzzing in her veins. It startles her, the power of it. She has been medicated for the past nine years of her life; she can barely remember what it feels like not to be. But this is something unlike anything she has felt before.

She walks down the hallway of the home carefully, as if she is balancing on a tightrope, and sees Ms. Sharonda watching her from her desk as she gathers her school things from the coat rack.

"You all right, there, Eden?" she demands.

"I'm fine."

She's not fine. But she has purpose. She heads for the shuttle with the other girls.

On the way to school she stares out the window at the hills, and she plans.

This is what she knows. There is the bleeding girl, and there is the counselor, and there is the man in the van.

And there is the blackness, the danger, around all of them.

But she doesn't know if all three things are connected. That's what she has to find out.

At school, she begins.

The bleeding girl's name is Laura Huell. She shares only one class with Cara. She eats lunch alone at the picnic tables outside the visual arts studio.

When she sees Cara coming, she scurries away like a frightened mouse. It is impossible to ask her what she knows, about the counselor or the man in the van or anything else. She simply will not speak.

Cara is frustrated. Angry. But she understands. She's just a girl, herself. There's nothing she can do about what is out there. She can't help.

So she goes to class, and she does her homework, and she waits, and she watches.

In two days, she sees the white van three times. Once it is parked beside the curb outside the school, too far away for her to see a license plate. Twice she sees it driving on the street as the minibus takes the group home kids to and from school.

But is it *the* van? That is the point, obviously, of using an unmarked, windowless white van. They can be rented. There is no telling one white van from another. It is a useless clue, good only for scaring her and making her doubt herself.

She uses twenty-five cents from her weekly Social Services allowance of five dollars to make a phone call at the school's payphone, and check up on the counselor. She remembers the phone number of the group home in Palm Desert. The one where the monster last struck. She stands in the open box and deposits her quarter, dials, waits nervously. When a female voice answers, she tries to make her voice lower, older.

"May I speak with Mr. Pierson, please?"

"He doesn't work here anymore."

Cara's heart sinks. Then she steels herself, and makes her voice gruff. "This is Ms. Lewis in Las Piedras. He was up here at the home yesterday and left some keys. How do I get in touch with him?"

When she hangs up, she has a phone number and an address in Palm Desert: the Golden Shadows RV Park.

A small relief. He's not living here, in town. And now she knows how to check up on him.

The voices are slithering noises in the back of her head. They grow louder as the moon fattens, but what they say is still elusive.

Reading helps. Chemistry equations help. Focusing on her homework can be lifesaving; it turns down the volume on the constant whispering.

On the fourth school day, the minibus does not have to stop at the second group home, consequently they arrive at school early.

As Cara walks in through the front gates, she sees Laura walking down across the quad. There is a blankness to her face that Cara recognizes. She is far, far away. She moves on autopilot, like the walking dead. But there is no blood. Not now.

On impulse, Cara changes directions and follows her.

Laura enters a building and turns right into a corridor. This early in the morning, the hall is empty. Cara hangs back, watching from the intersection of corridors, as Laura walks down it, the tap-tap of her footsteps echoing softly on the walls. She stops in front of a door at the end of the hall, and stands there, still, before she reaches out for the knob.

Then she walks through the door.

Cara moves down the hall, closer to the door. There is a hand-lettered sign taped to it.

PALMERS MEETING

The door opens suddenly and the vice-principal is there. Lethbridge. Cara takes a step back.

He raises his eyebrows. "Hello there, Eden. Are you here for Palmers?"

Cara looks quickly into the room, behind him. A circle of boys and girls in chairs. A flag in front of the room, and writing on the chalkboard:

THREE PILLARS OF SERVICE:
GOD, FAMILY, COMMUNITY

And a name:

MEL FRANZEN, PALMERS CHAIR

A man in a suit stands in front of the circle, fleshy, with pale crew-cut hair; broad shouldered and big smiled.

Laura is there, in the circle of chairs.

And the blood is there, a crimson pool at her feet.

"Come on in, Eden. You're very welcome." Lethbridge holds the door open.

Behind him, the crew-cut man in the suit looks toward her. His eyes crawl on her skin. Suddenly Cara can barely breathe through the hammering of her heart.

"Wrong room," she says, backing away. "I'm late."

She turns away from the door and walks down the hall. She feels the vice-principal's eyes burning into her back and has to force herself not to run.

ROARKE

Chapter Eleven

R oarke had to push a little, but he walked out of the high school with
copies of the yearbook and the binder of school newspapers.

He sat in his car, and he looked down at the photo of Laura, the
dates of the obituary.

He checked the file of Cara's early years just to be sure, but he was
right. Laura Huell died on the same day as the counselor.

He didn't like it. Not at all.

He looked out the window at the school.

There are no coincidences with Cara. Something happened here.

Lethbridge was useless, clueless.

*There must be someone else I can talk to about this. Someone who was
there. Who would know?*

He reached for the file again and opened it, looking for a name.

◆   ◆   ◆

As it happened, Ms. Sharonda Lewis was still the director of the group home in Las Piedras where Cara had stayed for her two weeks in the town.

Many of California's one thousand group homes, or "congregate care," for teenagers in the Social Services system had been closed down since the end of the nineties because of criminal mismanagement, disorder, neglect, and abuse. The fact that this one was still open hinted at it being one of the better ones.

It was a stucco house in a residential neighborhood, a low, wide suburban box, with a long horseshoe driveway.

Roarke walked past a dry fountain with a worn, dusty angel statue. The sun was warm above. There was wind. There were palm trees.

Inside, the house was eerily quiet, devoid of its teenage residents; it was a school day. Sharonda Lewis met with him in her office. She was a strong, striking African-American woman. Roarke put her age at around forty-five, which would have made her not even thirty years old when Cara was in her care.

"I headed up the San Francisco FBI team that oversaw the Cara Lindstrom case. She was a resident here sixteen years ago. You may have heard something about her recently—"

"I heard," Ms. Lewis said. She was impassive, regal. A force.

"You remember her, then?"

"You're talking about sixteen years ago. And she was here for all of two weeks." Like the principal, the woman didn't seem about to give him anything.

"But she was something of a standout, wasn't she?" Roarke suggested.

Ms. Lewis stared at him hard, then for some reason, relented. "She was that."

"Why only two weeks?"

She shrugged. "She'd just been released from CYA. We had an open bed that week. It was a temporary placement. That's the way it works."

"Was there any trouble while she was here?" He watched her.

"I would say the opposite. She kept her head down."

"She was seeing a psychiatrist twice a week at the home, correct?"

She looked wary.

"It's in her file," he prompted.

"Yes, that's right."

"What was the diagnosis?"

Her face hardened. "You said you saw the file."

He tried the question a different way. "Did you believe the psychiatrist got the diagnosis right?"

"I'm not a psychiatrist."

"But there are things you saw and heard . . ." He looked at her, and waited.

She exhaled sharply. "These kids . . . they have combinations of so many traumas. Diagnoses conflict. Then add to that the normal adolescent hormonal spikes . . . I don't know how possible it is to *diagnose* all of that."

That was always the sense Roarke had gotten from Cara's files. Over the years she'd been labeled with early-onset schizophrenia, childhood bipolar disorder, borderline personality disorder, post-traumatic stress disorder, and every combination of the above.

"You didn't notice peculiar delusions?" he asked. *Did she ever talk to you about* It? was what he meant.

"I said, she kept her head down. She was high functioning."

"Were you aware that she left the home at night?"

She looked murderous. "Not on my watch she didn't."

Roarke believed her. But he also knew that group homes were most often understaffed, with underpaid and inexperienced workers. He knew that homes had wildly different house rules about curfew and leaving the homes. And he knew that Cara was infinitely, uncannily resourceful. Somehow she had gotten out, gotten herself out to Palm Desert. Somehow.

He tried again. "She was transferred just two weeks after she was assigned here. Are you sure there wasn't a particular reason she was moved?"

The director gave him a stony look. "She got a more permanent placement. Like I said. It's how it works."

"While she was here, did you counsel her? Did she confide in you?"

"About what?"

About It, he wanted to say. *About this idea she has that she can see evil.*

"About anything," he said aloud. "Did you have any sessions with her?"

"She had sessions with the psychiatrist."

"I meant—you didn't do any counseling yourself?"

"I'm the director here. I manage the house."

He looked at her, wondering why she was stonewalling him. "I'm sorry. It's just that—you seem like the kind of person . . ."

She stared back at him, giving him nothing.

"What I mean is, I've never in my life seen anyone who needed help as much as she did."

Her look was merciless. "Agent Roarke, are you familiar with California Youth Authority?"

"Somewhat."

"Whatever you've read, whatever you're imagining, it is worse. I assure you. It is not juvenile hall. It is not a youth home or a camp. It is prison. Before all the lawsuits they kept kids on lockdown twenty-three hours a day. Do you have any idea what it does to a child to be in solitary twenty-three hours a day?"

She shook her head, looking somewhere beyond him now. "When one of those lawsuits *forced* the facilities to perform their mandate of education, the system's bright idea was to put the wards in cages for school hours. We're talking a desk in a cage the size of a phone booth."

Roarke felt pain in his head, pain in his heart. It was horrific . . . and too easy to picture.

You want to know how a fourteen-year-old child becomes a killer? You just heard it. Do you really need to know anything more than that?

Ms. Lewis nodded. "They go into the system mental . . . they come out much worse."

"I've met Cara," he said, finally. "I know what it did to her."

The director sat up so fast her chair hit the desk, hard. "You are not hearing me. It's *all* of them. Kids who have spent *years* of their lives living in closets or basements. Some of them we have to train how to tie their shoes and wash themselves. We get kids so hyped up on rage it takes six, seven, eight counselors to restrain them. Last week a girl here tried to eat a light bulb. Last year I had a brother and sister who were forced by a relative to have sex with each other at the bottom of a dry swimming pool, while people lined up to buy tickets."

She stared at him, merciless. "You never in your life saw a kid who needed saving so bad? I see them every day. Every single day."

"I hear you," he said softly.

She finally leaned back in her chair, as if drained. "Cara wasn't feral. She wasn't violent or suicidal. She went to school. She took her meds. She did her work. She was in better shape than most. Wherever she learned it, the child knew how to conduct herself."

Or she was just smart enough to play it that way, Roarke thought, but he knew the director was right. What he saw was nothing compared to what Ms. Lewis had seen, because for her it was kids 24-7. And he also realized that even at fourteen Cara might well have known to show nothing to this sharp-eyed, sharp-witted force of a woman.

But he decided to let that be. Instead, he asked the question that kept tugging at him.

"Were you aware that a girl killed herself at the high school? That week that Cara was there?"

Ms. Lewis was suddenly a bit more still. "What does this have to do with the case you say you're on?"

He held her eyes. "I don't know. Do you?"

A strange look passed over the director's face. She didn't answer—quite. "That school was bad luck for girls."

Roarke felt a prickling of significance. "Bad luck how?"

"Two of them dead in a month."

The prickling became a four-alarm warning bell. "*Two?*"

"Ivy Barnes. You don't know this? The girl who was burned."

"Tell me," Roarke said, through a dry throat. There was a pause, and he could sense she was gathering herself. He found himself bracing for it.

For the first time the director's voice was soft. "Ivy Barnes. She was abducted by a man in an unmarked van while she was walking to school. He raped her and then set her on fire."

Roarke was very still. "I'm sorry, what?"

Ms. Lewis looked at him straight on. "You heard me."

The familiar blackness and sickness rose up in him, threatened to encompass him. He heard his own voice speaking, flat, completely disconnected from anything inside him.

"When was this?"

"It was June."

This didn't add up. "You said she died the same month as Laura Huell. June would have been five months after."

"It was seven months before. Ivy lived for seven months. She died the week after Laura Huell killed herself."

Roarke left the group home in a fog. He knew he had the line of his investigation, now. Whether he wanted it was a different story.

An inconceivably vicious attack on a girl from the school that Cara had attended. Another girl who killed herself the same month that the first girl died.

It's connected. It has to be.

He stopped in front of the fountain with its battered angel, and looked at the scrap of paper in his hand, at the address and the name that Ms. Lewis had scribbled for him, saying just, "This is who you want to talk to about that."

CARA

Chapter Twelve

Cara is still thinking of Laura in the Palmers meeting when she takes her seat for Chemistry.

The crew-cut man in the suit . . . and the blood on the floor.

Palmers.

The club Lethbridge had said she should join.

She becomes aware of eyes on her skin, the crawly feeling of being watched. She jerks her head up to see the jock, Devlin.

She relaxes . . . but not much. She has already made up her mind that she must speak to him, but he saves her the trouble. He gets up from his seat and comes over to the empty desk beside her. As he sits he shoots her what must seem to any *Normal* girl a killer smile and says, "I keep wondering, 'Is today going to be the day?'"

"What day?" she asks, wary.

"The day that you talk to me."

She sees the interest in his eyes, senses the opportunity there. She shrugs, as if she doesn't really care.

"Why don't you talk to me?" she says.

He spreads his hands. "Anything. What do you want to know?"

"What's Palmers?"

He wasn't expecting that. "Seriously?"

She looks back at him, impassive.

"Well, do you know what Wayfarers is?"

She shakes her head. She doesn't.

"A bunch of guys. Businessmen from the town. Like a business club. They get together once a week and talk about charity work. Put money into stuff like Little League and the football team, and scholarships. Palmers is the high school version of it. But you don't want anything to do with that."

"Why?"

"Uh uh. My turn."

His voice is light, teasing, but she freezes, instantly on alert. "What, then?" she asks stiffly.

"Did you really do time in CYA?"

She looks at him. It's answer enough.

"What for?" he asks.

"Aggravated assault," she says evenly.

His smile slips. "Are you serious?"

She just looks at him.

"You seem so . . ."

He is about to say *Normal,* she can see it. She stares him down.

Normal? Sane? Really?

"My turn," she says tensely. "Why don't I want anything to do with Palmers?"

He looks startled, but regroups. "Just—it's a lot of old guys sitting around jawing about community and church. Total buzzkill. The only reason to be in it is the scholarship money."

"Scholarships," she repeats thoughtfully. And then the bell rings and she is spared further conversation as Mr. Pring calls the class to order.

At lunch she sits alone at a picnic table, hunched over. Chattering students pass, boys shoving each other back and forth, girls gossiping about the weekend. The picnic table, like every other at the school, is covered with graffiti. Gang talk, dumb jokes, crudely sketched genitalia. *Elise is a cunt. Chloe S. sucks dick.*

Cara takes her pen and scratches her own word into the table: *Palmers.*

Laura was in the Palmers meeting. And she was bleeding.

But she was also bleeding in Social Studies, she reminds herself. *All this pain. Where is it coming from?*

And then, suddenly, like in a dream when you think about something and it appears, she is there.

Laura.

Walking alone, remote as a sleepwalker, as if on another plane from the rest of them. Walking right past Cara. Past the row of picnic tables.

There is a darkness gathered around her. Cara can feel the dread like a vile, thick smoke, choking her.

Laura makes a quick, furtive turn toward the handball courts, and is gone.

Cara sits still, suddenly in turmoil. She knows that cutting school can get her written up, get time added to probation. But Laura is going somewhere and it's lunchtime and Cara finally has a chance to know more, know *something* at least . . .

So she follows.

She leaves the rows of picnic tables, walks toward the handball courts, slips around the same concrete wall.

Ahead of her, Laura wends her way through the concrete maze of the tennis and handball courts, heading toward the athletic fields. Cara follows at a distance. The lunchtime chatter of students fades behind her, and a dry breeze picks up, swirling dust on the asphalt. At the edge of the football field, Laura slips under the bleachers, and makes her way along the chain link fence at the back of the school.

She doesn't falter; she knows exactly where she's going, and seems to have done it before.

Even staying far behind, Cara can see there is a gap in the fence between two metal posts, concealed by the frame of the bleachers. Not much of a gap, not one that an adult could squeeze through. But for a slim, pliable girl? Nothing easier.

Laura reaches the gap and squeezes out, then walks quickly to the sidewalk.

Cara waits inside the fence, behind the frame of the bleachers, to see what she will do next.

Laura walks down the sidewalk several dozen yards, and stops at the bus stop.

Cara hovers under the bleachers, thinking. She knows that the other girl isn't going to a dentist appointment or anything sanctioned, or she would simply have walked out the front gates. But this is complicated, now, because Laura will see her following. She doesn't know why it's so important for her not to be caught following, but she knows it is.

She scoops her hair up, pulls the hood of her jacket up over her head, and thinks herself invisible. She knows very well that thinking does not *make* her invisible; she is crazy, not stupid. But it always seems that when she *thinks* invisible she does not draw attention to herself; rather she seems to blend in with very minimal notice.

The city bus turns the corner at the end of the street and rumbles to a stop, trailing black smoke. The doors whoosh open. As Laura is boarding in front, Cara takes her chance. She times her walk . . . darting down the sidewalk just as Laura will be climbing the stairs inside and feeding her money into the coin machine.

Then Cara boards the bus and pauses on a bottom stair where she is hidden from the bus passengers. She looks through the railing at the aisle. Laura is walking down toward the end of the bus, her back to Cara.

Cara bolts up the stairs, drops her money into the coin machine, keeping her back to the passengers as she pays the fare, then slides into the first front seat and slumps as low as she can go.

Hunched against the window, she looks up at the mirror above the driver. She can see Laura in a back seat, staring out the window as if in a trance. It seems entirely possible that she is so in her own world that she has not seen Cara at all.

The bus heaves its doors closed, and wheezes its way through town. Cara watches out the window at the passing residential streets, no idea where they could be going. Then the bus makes a turn and motors up into the foothills.

Up ahead there is a grove of dull green trees—olives, Cara thinks—and the brighter, feathery green of peppers.

And then there is a high stone wall with a glimpse of some kind of old building behind it, Spanish style, with white walls and wood beams and adobe-tiled roof, shaded by huge oaks and willows. A church? Whatever it is, it seems very old.

There are open iron gates in the stone wall, and iron letters on the arch above the gates read: *The Mission.*

And Cara knows this is where Laura is going before the bus's stop bell rings.

Cara stays low in her seat, and as soon as the bus halts, she is up and out, keeping her back toward the aisle as she slips down the stairs.

She bounds out of the bus and walks quickly, right up against the side of the bus so that Laura will not be able to see her from the windows above.

She rounds the back of the bus and then darts to a cluster of trees she can hide behind.

She hovers beside the trees, watching.

The bus pulls off, leaving Laura alone on the sidewalk. She looks up at the gates for a moment, then walks slowly up to them and through, up the long drive toward the entrance, a shaded patio with heavy double wooden doors.

Cara moves to the pillars of the front gates. From here, she can see the building: there is a bell tower with a cupola, part of a church, connected to a long horizontal building with several arches along an outside corridor.

She thinks back, wondering. She has studied the missions in one of her classes before *The Cage*—sixth grade, maybe. But she can't remember there being a Mission Las Piedras.

Laura seems to move more slowly, her steps growing heavier the closer she gets to the front doors.

On the front patio she reaches to ring a buzzer on the wall. She speaks something aloud that Cara can't hear, then reaches for a door and pulls it open, and disappears into the building.

Cara moves forward, staring up at the building. It may not be a mission, but it looks just like one, with arched windows in white-washed walls and buttresses of old, dark wood. The drive up to the building is graveled, lined with olive and pepper trees and desert flowers beneath: cactus and Mexican sage. Hummingbirds dart between the purple flowers.

There is another high stone wall to her right, and somewhere behind it she can hear the high, sweet voices of young children.

She sees a glimpse of movement at one of the arched windows. A figure, hovering as if watching her.

She feels cold dread as she stares up, not knowing if this is real or another vision.

It looks like a skeleton. But it is moving.

ROARKE

Chapter Thirteen

I t was up in the foothills, in a grove of oak and pepper trees. A high stone wall surrounding a building with the adobe, timber, stone, brick, and tile construction of an early California mission: whitewashed walls, arched windows, wood beams like buttresses with painted designs.

Roarke left his car in the small private parking lot and walked toward the front entrance, a shaded patio with heavy double wooden doors.

To his right was a high stone wall with an immense arched wooden gate. Roarke was startled to see a very realistic-looking skull and crossbones embedded in the mortar above the gate. He stepped closer, looking up at it, and realized it was a real skull and crossbones, yellowed and splintering.

As he turned back to the main building, his eye caught a flicker of movement in an arched window and he swiveled to look. A shadow figure was watching him, dressed in what looked like robes. There, and then gone.

He moved up to the patio, rang the buzzer on the wall beside the heavy wooden front doors. One door clicked open, and he walked through it into a reception area with a floor of shining adobe tile. There was an instant, ancient presence about the place, a feeling like stepping back in time. It could have been a chapel, although he suspected there was a real one somewhere on the premises.

At the desk he asked the plainly dressed receptionist to see Dr. Dubrow, the name Ms. Lewis had scribbled for him.

"Do you have an appointment?" the receptionist asked pleasantly.

A woman's voice spoke from behind Roarke. "That would be me."

Roarke turned, and a woman stepped from a hallway.

She was in her late fifties, he thought, maybe on the other side of sixty. She had keen and luminous eyes, and an elegant face, the bone structure of a classic film star—although at the moment she looked as if she hadn't slept in a month.

And she was a nun. The cowl headpiece was the only official part of her garment, but she was dressed in a dark turtleneck and slacks, with a long robe-like black cardigan, and spectacles hanging on a chain around her neck instead of a rosary. Her air of authority was unmistakable.

Another nun, Roarke thought, bemused. *What is it with me and nuns?*

It had been just two months since a prickly sister in Portland had helped him at a crucial stage of his investigation into Cara Lindstrom. Roarke had not darkened the doors of a Catholic church since he was twelve. But extremely lapsed, half-Catholic upbringing aside, he couldn't help recalling Sister Frances's words:

"Agent Roarke, we're the same. We deal with good people and we deal with evil people. We hone our skills so we can separate the evil from the good, see what's coming before it has a chance to do damage. It's my work every bit as much as it is yours. We need to be able to name it to fight it."

He'd thought of those words often in the last two months. It had been a rare moment of clarity in the darkest and most conflicting case he'd ever encountered. Maybe another nun was just what he needed.

So he resigned himself and spoke aloud. "Sharonda Lewis said you'd be able to help me."

"Ah. Ms. Lewis. Then I suggest we do our best not to disappoint her." The nun reached out to shake his hand, a surprisingly strong grip. "And you are?"

Special Agent was on the tip of his tongue, but he moved past it. "My name is Roarke. I'm following up on a case for the San Francisco office of the FBI, and Ms. Lewis said you may have information."

"What case is that?"

Roarke wanted a clean interview, with no preconceptions. "I can't say. But I need to speak to you about Ivy Barnes."

The look on her face was completely uninterpretable. "I see. Well. Come into my parlor."

She turned and walked down a long hallway with the same gleaming adobe tile, and doors of old oak off to both sides. She stopped at the last door and ushered him in. Roarke stopped to take in the room. Whitewashed walls were barely visible between tall, dark bookshelves crammed full of thick texts. An intricately patterned wool carpet lay over the tiles; there was a huge cluttered antique desk with an armchair in front of it, a couch against the wall.

She closed the heavy wooden door behind them. "Please. Sit."

Roarke took the chair in front of the desk and the sister moved to a sideboard where a coffee pot and coffee makings were set on a tray. She picked up a can and a scoop, looked toward him.

"Do you like it extra strong, industrial, or lethal?"

Roarke paused. *Is she serious?*

"You pick," he said.

"Your funeral." She put down the scoop and poured from the can. Roarke watched her. "I'm sorry, is it Sister? Doctor?"

"I've always been partial to Your Grace."

The line was delivered without a trace of a smile. *Definitely a live one,* Roarke thought.

She poured water into the coffeemaker. "It's Mother, actually, but no need to stand on ceremony. The children call me Mother Doctor. They see this"—she half-turned to him, gestured to her name plate: *M. Dubrow, MD*—"and they draw their own conclusions."

Mother Doctor. That's one for the books.

And yet Roarke found himself warming to the crusty nun, feeling both intrigued and more relaxed than he'd felt in months.

"And what is this place, exactly? A clinic?"

"Our patients are children who have been severely abused. Some of them need medical care. All of them need spiritual care. Or psychological care, if you prefer."

"Which do you prefer?"

"That would depend on what grant form I'm filling out." She left the coffee to brew and sat behind her desk. Roarke had the sense she was steeling herself.

"So you want to know about Ivy Barnes. Sixteen years ago she was fourteen, a freshman at Las Piedras High. She was walking to school in the early morning when she was abducted by a man in a white van. He took her out to the desert, raped her for two days, and then set her on fire and left her to die."

Roarke was completely still, his throat so dry he couldn't even swallow.

"She didn't die. Somehow she walked, or crawled, out of the desert and stumbled onto a highway, where a passing motorist found her and called the paramedics. Somehow they were able to save her. Her flesh was melted onto her bones. Even months later, she looked like a living skeleton."

Time seemed to stop and a silence fell, in which Roarke felt the abyss open underneath him.

I don't know if I can handle any more of this darkness.

A voice was speaking from far away, and he realized it was his own. "That may be the worst story I've ever heard."

Mother Doctor's face didn't change. "There's always worse," she said, and stood to pour the coffee. She handed a large mug across to Roarke without asking him if he wanted cream or sugar, and took a deep swallow of her own.

Roarke lifted his mug. The brew was thick and scalding. They drank in silence, then Mother Doctor spoke again.

"She lived for seven months. No one expected it. She was blind. No vocal cords. No fingers. She was very strong."

Roarke couldn't begin to imagine.

"She was in a burn unit in San Diego for six months before she was transferred here. It was clear there was no point in putting her through the pain of further surgery, and a surgeon colleague of mine was on the case who thought I might be better able to treat her. You see, she had no parents to speak of. She was a ward of the court, taken away from her addict mother. There had never been any conclusive father."

Roarke felt a different stab of unease. "She was a foster child?"

"She lived in a group home."

A group home kid. Like Cara. Now Roarke was afraid he would be sick. "A group home—"

The nun looked at him. "Not Ms. Lewis's."

He wasn't sure why that was such a relief, but it was. Still, a group home child viciously attacked . . . by a man who was obviously trolling the high school . . .

He felt a cold rush of fear for young Cara.

It's done, he reminded himself. *Whatever happened, it's done. Sixteen years in the past.*

"How did Ivy die?" he asked.

Mother Doctor shook her head. "The real question is, how did she live? It shouldn't have been possible at all. But—she died in her bed, here. She went to sleep one night and didn't wake up."

"What about the rapist?"

"What about him?"

"Who was it?"

Her mouth twisted in something that was not a smile. "Who knows?"

Roarke stared at her. His voice sounded hollow in the room. "He was never caught?"

"No arrests, no suspects. The case is open. It was never solved." She stood abruptly, with a swish of cardigan that sounded like robes. "Come back tomorrow."

Roarke stood with her, disoriented. "Why?"

"Because we're done for now. And I think you will want to come back tomorrow."

Her voice brooked no argument. Roarke moved for the door. And then a hunch made him turn back to her.

"Just one more thing. Did a girl named Laura Huell ever visit Ivy here?"

There was a long silence and he thought she would not respond. Then her voice came softly.

"Yes. Yes, she did."

He opened his mouth to speak and she shook her head, holding up a hand.

"Come back tomorrow, Roarke."

CARA

Chapter Fourteen

Years of practice has made her adept at sneaking in and out of places. There is a high stone wall to the side of the building, with an immense arched wooden gate, and a skull and crossbones embedded in the mortar above the gate.

She flinches at the sight of the skull, the hollow eye sockets, the long chipped bones. She forces herself to look away, steps forward to the gate and tries the handle. Locked. But the wall is rough, lumpy. She walks along the side of it toward a thick oak tree growing close to the wall and slips between the trunk and the wall, bracing her back flat against the wall, and uses her feet against the tree and her hands against the wall to walk herself slowly up the coarse surface.

At the top of the wall, she throws a leg over and straddles the top, looking over to survey what's behind.

There is a rectangular plaza crisscrossed by paths, surrounded by plots of gardens, with lots of big, shady oak and olive trees. She can't see anyone outside, and the whole secluded space is quiet, no sound but the rush of water from some fountain. She can already feel the cool air from the garden on her face. The place feels old, and peaceful.

She drops from the top of the wall to the soft ground below, landing on her feet in a crouch, balancing with her hands and arms.

She stands upright and moves, staying along the periphery of the plaza, darting between trees and shrubs, to keep as concealed as she can be. Children's voices drift from another part of the plaza, but the bushes serve as a wall.

The side of the building has a covered outdoor corridor, with Spanish-style arches. She heads for those, in the direction of the window where she saw the skeleton figure.

There is a back door of heavy wood, and this one is unlocked. She listens at the crack of the door for any sound inside and hears nothing, though the walls and door are so thick that it would be hard to imagine any sound escaping.

She steels herself, and pulls the door open a few inches to peer inside.

Ahead of her is a long, dim, empty corridor. It takes her eyes a moment to adjust to the dark, but she can see the walls are the same whitewashed plaster as the outside of the building. The floor tiles are gleaming adobe and seem centuries old. There is a line of doors along the inside wall, all closed.

One of the doors opens, and Laura Huell steps out. She is pale as glass, with that unfocused look in her eyes.

She stands there, swaying, and the blood runs down her arms, dripping down her fingers into red pools on the floor.

And Cara knows that whatever she needs to know is inside that room.

Laura walks away from her, down the corridor, that same listless tread. Cara waits, watching through the crack in the outside door until the hallway is empty, then slips inside and approaches the door with dread.

At the door, she looks down at the floor tiles, but of course, the blood is gone.

She puts her hand to the knob, turns it. It is not locked. She does not know if she is surprised or not.

She steps through the heavy wooden door.

A girl turns from the arched window, and with the light behind her, for a moment she is nothing but shadow.

She comes into focus gradually, which is a kindness, although there is no way to prepare for what Cara is seeing. The girl seems to be a skeleton with no flesh, just melted skin. Cara can see straight through to her bones.

A torrent of feelings rushes through her. Grief and rage and terror . . . mingled with another, more surprising emotion.

Relief.

A relief so profound she feels lightheaded. For the first time since *The Night* she knows she does not have to pretend. She does not have to lie. She does not have to hide. Because she is with someone who knows everything that she sees. This girl has been face to face with *It*. She has felt the brutal touch of the monster and lived. She knows everything about *It*.

They are the same.

The skeleton girl knows she is there. She is alert, looking toward her with sightless eye sockets.

Cara takes a step forward. "I'm Cara," she says softly.

Through the open door behind her, she hears voices and steps. Not in the hall, not yet, but approaching.

She turns, slips back out the doorway.

At the end of the hallway are two nuns, an older one and a younger one. The older one stops, seeing her. "Why, child. What on earth—"

Cara turns away and runs, bolting toward the door.

She bursts out the back door, runs back through the garden, darting through the hedges, past the fountains, her feet muffled by grass. She does not have to climb the wall again; the first door she comes to in the wall opens from the inside. She shoves through it, pulls it shut behind her.

Outside the shade of the garden, the afternoon sun is roasting, but there is a coldness so deep inside her she can barely move her limbs.

She drops onto a stone bench beside the wall, breathless, willing herself not to be sick. The air seems to be pulsing around her. Images come in blinding flashes.

Her sister in the moonlight, in a puddle of blood. The monster turning with dripping jaws. Mommy screaming, screaming, screaming. Her brothers screaming. Everyone screaming . . .

And then the screams are coming from her, from deep inside her, screaming in her mother's voice, her father's, her sister's, her brothers' . . .

She presses her hands to her ears to shut out the sound and shuts her eyes against the images.

But she knows what she has seen inside the Mission is not because of medication, or lack of it.

Now, finally she is clear.

This is what she has felt at the school. This is what Laura has seen, too.

It was the watcher in the van who did this to the skeleton girl. This is what he wants. What *It* wants.

And one word reverberates in her head.

Run.

ROARKE

Chapter Fifteen

Roarke walked out through the graceful, timeless front of the Mission, moving blankly toward the parking lot.

He was suddenly short of breath, on the verge of being sick. He sat abruptly on a stone bench to the side of the gate.

A teenage girl, burned alive. Her rapist, never caught.

Two girls from the same high school, dying violently within two weeks of each other.

Violently because, however Ivy had breathed her last breath, however long past the attack that death was, it was the result of the most unspeakable violence. And Cara had been there when it happened. Right there.

He had not the slightest doubt that the deaths were connected, and that Cara would have become involved in some way. Because if there was one thing he knew in his gut, it was that Cara would not have been still for this kind of horror.

And there was a new, nagging unease. A deadly predator had been trolling the school at the same time that Cara had been attending.

He could not quell the feeling of urgency.

Ivy had been a ward of the court, a group home kid, just as Cara was at the time. If there was a predator stalking the school, had Cara, or Eden, become a target? It was too easy to picture.

He remembered something Cara had said to him, three months that seemed like three decades ago: "It *plays with me*. It *lets me see* It."

Whatever had happened, he couldn't stop it, sixteen years in the future. And yet the urgency was there.

He had to know.

CARA

Chapter Sixteen

In the end, she has no choice.

She knows fully what *It* is capable of. *It* is the same. The monster who killed her family. *It* is there, watching the school, disguised as some man.

Who, though?

The counselor. The vice-principal. Whoever *It* is playing at being now.

It has been at the skeleton girl, has savaged her, all but destroyed her. *It* is searching for others.

But she has nowhere to go. Nothing but the clothes on her back, and a few dollars in her pocket.

So she takes the bus back to school. There must be a plan.

As she sits huddled in her seat, watching out the window, her aunt Joan flickers in her mind, followed by the numbing memories. Her strongest recollection of her aunt is of her standing at the door, over and over, different time periods, different dresses, watching Cara being taken away from the house yet again . . .

No.

If she runs away, her aunt's is the first place they will check. They will show up instantly, seize her—if her aunt doesn't turn her in first.

But where can she go?

She rides in a daze, exits the bus a block from the school.

Her legs are trembling as she steps onto the sidewalk. The roller-coaster inside her makes it difficult to walk in a straight line. The glittering bits of silica in the concrete reflect the sun in shards of light, and she must concentrate to keep upright.

A thought is flickering at the edge of her mind. Something she must not let get away from her. A connection.

Laura has been going to visit the other. The skeleton girl. Why? What is there between them?

She knows that it is key.

She is so intent on the question that she may have missed the smell at first, but she becomes more and more aware of it. A rotting, dying stench. A smell like burning, like cooked meat. Then she feels the eyes. Crawling on her back. Trying to get into her clothes.

She turns her head, barely, and sees the white van. Driving in a slow creep behind her.

The images come all in a rush.

The following, the quick grab . . . the chains welded into the wall of the van. The duct tape and gasoline. The brutal invasion of her body and the unspeakable pain of burning, her skin, her hair, her eyes on fire . . .

The stinking malevolence of the man.

He. *It.* The monster. The man with the same monster inside.

There are two things then. A hatred even greater than she knew she was capable of. A desire to kill, hurt, destroy.

And then fear so encompassing she feels her legs lurch beneath her.

Then she runs for her life.

ROARKE

Chapter Seventeen

Isolated as it felt, the Mission was just a few minutes' drive from the high school. Roarke headed straight back there.

He was aware that he was high on rage when he walked back into the principal's office.

Lethbridge's smile was showing the strain. "Agent Roarke. What can we do for you?" The word *now* was silent, but obvious in the air.

Roarke stared down at him. "I asked about unusual incidents involving the students here. Violent or traumatic incidents." He set his iPad on the desk in front of Lethbridge. On the screen was a news article he'd downloaded about Ivy's abduction. "Wouldn't you say this qualifies?"

The principal looked down at the smiling school photo of Ivy . . . next to the horror of the headline.

Roarke had read over the articles he could find in an initial online search in the car. The details were even more sickening than from Mother Doctor's terse report. Then came the reports of press conferences, the tense vows of the Riverside County Sheriff's Department to hunt the rapist down. Then the follow-up articles on Ivy's care, dwindling quickly as no new leads were uncovered.

Roarke watched Lethbridge's face, but could read nothing in the impassivity. The principal looked up from the tablet screen. "I understood that you were asking about the two weeks that Cara Lindstrom attended this school. This . . . tragedy . . . happened the year before that."

"Seven months before."

"I meant the *school* year before. We academics have a slightly different calendar than the rest of the world." He smiled. Roarke didn't.

"Ivy Barnes died the same month that Cara Lindstrom attended the school," he said.

The principal's smile disappeared. "I don't remember it being the same month."

"It was," Roarke said tightly.

Lethbridge frowned. "Are you saying Cara Lindstrom had something to do with Ivy Barnes' death?"

That stopped Roarke for a moment. Was that what he thought?

Just what do *you think she had to do with Ivy's death?*

Behind the desk, the principal was watching him warily. Roarke gathered himself. "After the attack on Ivy Barnes, did you do anything to protect the students at Las Piedras?"

"Do anything to protect them?" the principal repeated stonily.

Roarke stared at him, incredulous. Was the man unaware that the overwhelming majority of rapists were repeat offenders? That ninety-eight percent of rape victims knew their attacker?

"Ivy was abducted while walking to school. Did you put extra security on? Provide transportation to students without cars or whose parents couldn't drive them?"

"The school left that to the police."

"No self-defense classes?" Roarke demanded. "No counseling for students who might have been traumatized by the attack on their classmate? Students like Laura Huell, for example?"

"Agent Roarke—or is it *Mr.* Roarke?" Lethbridge gave Roarke a thin smile that didn't conceal his anger. "What is your point, exactly? This is a sixteen-year-old case. I can't possibly imagine what you think you can do for these girls now."

Roarke stared at him. "I want the yearbook from the year Ivy was attacked. And the school newspapers. And if there have been any other similar attacks on students that you haven't mentioned, I want to hear about it. I hope I don't have to ask again."

But as he walked out of the office with the books, Lethbridge's words remained in his mind, taunting him. *"I can't possibly imagine what you think you can do for these girls now."*

His steps slowed, and he looked over the quad, the animated groups of students. The jocks, the cheerleaders, the rebels, the Normals.

So young. They're all so young.

He felt an irrational fear, the sense of someone walking over his grave.

They're safe, he told himself.

But are they?

Someone had brutalized Ivy, set her on fire, left her to die.

No suspects, no arrests.

What if he's still out there?

CARA

Chapter Eighteen

S he runs. She has never been so fast. Terror makes her as swift as the wind.

She can feel the van speeding up behind her as she pounds down the sidewalk. The school seems miles away and she is running in the sluggish slow motion of a dream.

She hears *Its* hoarse, hissing breath behind her, and in her ears is the screaming. Her mother. Her sister. Her brothers . . .

She reaches the visitor-side bleachers and hurls herself at the chain link fence, clambering up. The metal heaves and clinks under her.

Behind her she hears the gunning of the van's motor. She scrapes over the top of the fence, feels sharp pain as the wires slice into her stomach before she drops hard to the grass below. She staggers, and whips around . . . just in time to see the van hurtling around the corner of the block, disappearing from sight before she can spot the license plate.

Her heart is hammering in her chest and her breath comes in hot gasps. Her vision is edged with black.

The running, the breathlessness, the surge of adrenaline, has created chaos in her bloodstream. The grassy field in front of her is too green and seems to be shimmering.

She puts her hands on her knees, bending over, and gulps in air, a long inhale . . . another longer, slower release to try to still herself.

Then she stumbles forward, making her way along the fence, under the bleachers.

Have to get out. Have to get away. How? How?

She reaches the concrete maze of the tennis and handball courts and for a moment lets her guard down, thinking she is safe.

She is never safe.

She smells the smoky pungence of marijuana, and as soon as she hears the voice, she knows how much trouble she's in.

"Lookit here."

She hears the slithering of *It*. And turns to face Martell.

He is not alone. There are other jocks, in their letter jackets with the snarling wolf emblem. Five of them, glassy-eyed with pot, clothes reeking with the green smoke.

Her adrenaline is pumping, and her anger flares. *It. It. It* is everywhere.

In that moment, she could kill him, she knows. But she doesn't. She stands motionless, feeling the asphalt under her feet, settling on her legs. *Wait,* a voice tells her.

Martell moves closer. It is hard to be still with this predator so close to her, leaning toward her, breathing on her neck.

"I know who you are," he whispers.

Her insides go cold. She knew she would be found out. Of course it would be him.

"Miracle Girl, that's what they say."

The jocks shift on their feet, surrounding her. She hears someone else whisper it. *"Miracle Girl."* She can feel *It*, the mindless rage, slipping in and around them, and hears the low growling from the pack. Sometimes *It* doesn't take just one form. *It* is also plural.

"Freak," Martell rasps, and she feels his poison spittle on her skin. "How'd you do it, freak?

She has no idea what he means. She keeps herself very still, but her blood is racing, her limbs itching.

Martell circles her. The other boys watch. She knows she will fight, but they are so much bigger and there are so many of them.

"The Reaper gets your whole fuckin' family, and he doesn't kill you? Why not? What did you do to save your own skin? Did you fuck him? Did you? Did you offer that little pussy up and beg for your life? Whore. Freak—"

She leans in to him, surprising him, and whispers, "I know what you are." Her hand shoots out toward his crotch; she grabs the soft sack, and twists. He howls in surprise and rage. Then he is on her, grappling her, hurling her to the ground.

For a split second, she sees him. Devlin. Standing toward the back of the pack, looking torn, and defensive, and angry, all at once.

Then they surround her, the snarling wolves, tearing at her, slathering jaws snapping. The asphalt is hot beneath her. Someone is kicking her from behind. She tastes blood in her mouth. Claws rip at her clothes, forcing her legs apart. But she pins her arms to her sides, lets the blows rain down on her. Because she has heard it. The sound of running feet.

She senses rather than sees the teachers rounding the corner, heading toward the fray . . .

She feels hands pawing between her legs, and bites down hard on her lips. But she doesn't move. After seconds that stretch like years, she feels the fists cease, the hands withdrawing, the bodies being pulled away from her as savage adult voices berate her attackers.

She is being helped to her feet, and she stands shakily to face her rescuers. She knows from their expressions what the teachers see. One small, lone girl against five bigger boys.

And she knows she has won.

ROARKE

Chapter Nineteen

Out of long habit, Roarke kept a travel bag in the trunk of his car: a few changes of clothes and shoes, a down parka, a Dopp kit. More than enough for overnight.

He'd passed several golf hotels on the drive in to Las Piedras, so he headed back that way, intending to use the hotel finder app on his phone to price them. But the decision was made for him when he passed the manicured entrance of a resort hotel and caught a glimpse of its marquee, the words **GO WOLFPACK!**

He made the turn into the long drive of Shadow Mountain resort, following the sign.

The hotel was renovated midcentury modern, with a sprawling river-rock fireplace, sunken lounge areas, a spacious bar and restaurant looking out on the golf course. Roarke could see two outdoor pools, two Jacuzzis, moody lighting.

A plaque at the front desk read *Chris Devlin, Manager.*

"How long will you be staying with us, Mr. Roarke?" the young receptionist asked him cheerfully.

"Just tonight," Roarke said, and hoped it was the truth.

His room was a ground-floor business suite with sliding glass doors out onto a patio with a view of the golf course. The lowering sun was brilliant through the glass. Roarke had a feeling of being off the grid, untraceable. As if he'd slipped into a parallel universe, a different time. Cara's time.

He tossed his bag on the bed, stripped and showered in the bathroom, sluicing off the grime of the road. Then he wrapped a towel around his hips, sat in the low armchair and paged through the yearbook: the young, posed faces, the sports teams and clubs. The students were mostly white, with some scattered Mexican and Native American faces. There were no photos of Cara, of course. No mention of her, or "Eden Ballard." She hadn't been at the school long enough to leave a footprint.

He dressed, ordered dinner from room service, and then started on the school newspapers. He read every line of the papers for the two weeks that Cara was at the school, but again, there was no mention of her. The newspaper the week after had an obituary for Laura Huell, written in adolescently dramatic prose that skirted around the word *suicide* without ever actually using it. From the article he learned that Laura had been an only child, that her family had attended Calvary Baptist Church. Her father had been a real estate agent and a member of the local Wayfarers Club. Her mother had been a housewife and taught Sunday school at the church. Laura had played the piano at the church and at some Wayfarers events.

Vague details about a girl who'd now been dead longer than she'd been alive.

He opened the yearbook to the photo of Laura, put it on the bed. Then he found his own photo of teenage Cara in the file that he'd brought with him, and set it next to Laura's photo on the In Memoriam page.

Laura Huell had killed herself.

She had visited Ivy.

The obvious inference was that Laura had been attacked by the same man. Roarke knew the statistics: a conservative estimate was that thirteen percent of rape victims commit suicide. Far more of them have suicidal thoughts. Perhaps Laura had been attacked, had survived, possibly escaped without the mutilation that Ivy had suffered, only to end her own life because of the trauma.

The warm desert wind billowed the curtains at the open sliding glass door.

Roarke moved to the door, stepped out onto his patio. He looked across the golf course at the dark curves of mountains, lit by the rising half-moon. The palm fronds whispered in the dry wind. There was an itch on his skin.

His thoughts were racing.

Ivy was a group home kid. And Laura had killed herself on the same night that the group home counselor had been murdered in his own home.

Is there a connection there?

And why had the principal of Las Piedras High failed to mention the attack on Ivy when Roarke had asked him about unusual, violent, or traumatic events?

It was all one vast unknown.

He'd found what might be an ally in the nun. *Mother Doctor,* he thought, with the same bemusement he'd felt in her office.

She was calling the shots, for sure. And he knew something would be revealed. There was nothing to do now but wait until morning.

He looked out on the moonlight over the golf course, and finally the full horror of all he'd learned that day surrounded him. To be fourteen years old, alone in a world where predators not only existed but were actively hunting for the most vulnerable children . . .

No one was there for Cara then.

"I'm here, now," he said to the night.

CARA

Chapter Twenty

In the school office, the nurse tends Cara, applying some stinging rust-red tincture to her bloody scrapes.

Cara looks across the office to the mirror above the sink. Her face is bruised, her lip bleeding, her hands cut.

The door opens and the vice-principal looks in, his face blotched with anger. The nurse turns to him. "She should go to the hospital," she says.

"I'll handle it," Lethbridge says curtly. He gives Cara a furtive look, as if afraid to look at the damage full out.

And then the door slams open behind him, and Ms. Sharonda is there behind him, her body stiff with rage.

"What the *hell* is going on?" She looks from the vice-principal to Cara, huddled in a chair against the wall. "Eden?"

Cara makes her voice low, doesn't look at the VP. "They found out who I am. They were hurting me . . ."

Ms. Sharonda turns on Lethbridge. "What are you doing about this?"

"We'll be looking into what happened—"

She doesn't let him finish. "I heard what happened. Five of them against a fourteen-year-old girl—"

The vice-principal speaks through his teeth. "A fourteen-year-old girl with a record of assault. With a juvenile conviction—"

"*Five.* Against *one.* Don't you dare think this is going to slide because of their country club daddies—"

"The boys say she attacked first—"

Ms. Sharonda turns on Cara. "Is that true? Did you start that fight?"

Cara sits up, looking from her to the vice-principal. Then she lifts the bottom of her black shirt.

Lethbridge jerks back slightly and Ms. Sharonda expels her breath, as they take in the wide streaks of blood, the deep scratches in her skin.

Cara knows it looks worse than it is. On the way to the office she dug her own nails into her flesh, widening the cuts from the fence until she felt the sticky flow, smeared it across her stomach.

Ms. Sharonda turns and stares the vice-principal in the face. "Those boys are expelled, are we clear?"

Cara sees her chance and takes it. She makes her voice low and broken, pathetic. "I want to go to my aunt's. Please can I go to my aunt's?"

The adults turn to her.

It is the perfect opportunity. Her aunt can't turn the school down.

She hears the relief in the vice-principal's voice. "That's a good idea. A few days off. I can arrange that."

Ms. Sharonda marches Cara out of the office, staring daggers at everyone unwise enough to cross her path. Cara is quiet and subdued by her side, holding the ice pack the nurse gave her against her face.

As they step out into the quad, her heart is beating with wild exhilaration in her chest.

She is free. She is free.

ROARKE

Chapter Twenty-One

He is back in school, in the sunny quad where he used to hang out with the rest of the guys at San Luis Obispo High. His embroidered football jacket is tight across his back, a little too warm in the sun, and he can see the sweat on Aparicio's upper lip, too—but there is no freakin' way any of them are going to take off the jackets. Not on Game Day . . . not when the cheerleaders are prancing around, their hair shiny and soft and their lips wet with whatever junk they put on them that tastes like candy when they kiss. The sun is hot on his thighs, giving him that almost-hard feeling.

And then he sees her, the girl standing at the periphery of the quad, as apart from the rest of them as she can be. Blond and slim, fragile and strong, too intense to be beautiful, too mesmerizing to look away from.

He has never seen her before and yet . . .

I know you . . .

Roarke opened his eyes. He was in the armchair in the hotel room.

She stood at the sliding glass door, a pale slip of a girl in the darkness outside, her dress rippling in the wind . . .

He sat up . . . the image of the girl faded away.

The glass door was open; it was the gauzy under-curtain that he'd seen, billowing in the wind.

The yearbook was on his lap. He'd fallen asleep reading it. It felt like the middle of the night, but by his phone it was only just after nine in the evening.

On the table beside him were the notes that he had been making on Laura Huell earlier. Details from the obituary and the school paper, filled in with copious Googling—though details of anything about the school from sixteen years ago were hard to come by.

He'd found nothing that would suggest a connection between Laura and the murdered counselor, beyond the fact that they had died the same night.

But there was something from his dreaming . . . something about the kids at the school.

Something important . . .

He sat still in the chair. And then it hit him. He'd seen one of the names in the yearbook before.

He opened the yearbook and turned to the D's, found a photo of a blond boy, one of the varsity jocks. Letterman's jacket, surfer type, easy, dazzling smile. The kind that peaks in high school.

The name under the photo was Chris Devlin. The same name as on the plaque downstairs. The hotel manager.

At the front desk, a different but equally pleasant young reception- ist told him, "Mr. Devlin won't be in until the morning. May I leave him a message?"

After a hesitation Roarke answered, "I'm Special Agent Roarke, San Francisco FBI. I'd like to talk to him when he gets a chance."

He turned away from the desk, started automatically for the eleva- tor—then he changed course and walked across the lobby, past the leap- ing fire in the river-rock hearth, and stepped outside onto the deserted patio.

Torches burned in between the empty tables and chairs, and the night air was cool and dry.

He looked out at the stars, the soft manicured hills of the golf course, dotted with tiny arcs of light.

He was just debating a walk when an animal scream split the darkness.

He tensed, staring out toward the sound.

Wolf . . . he thought. And then shook his head.

Coyote, or a mountain lion, that's all. You're jumping at curtains. Seeing signs.

Yet the scream had set him on edge, so that when he heard the step behind him, he twisted fast, automatically reaching for the gun that he no longer wore.

Behind him was a blond, athletic man in his early thirties.

"Didn't mean to startle you." The blond man indicated the moonlit landscape. "Glad you're enjoying our view." He stuck out his hand in introduction, although of course Roarke already recognized him. "Chris Devlin. I'm the manager here."

Devlin's perfect surfer looks had coarsened since high school, but Roarke imagined he could still set his female employees' hearts fluttering. "The desk told me you weren't here."

Devlin gave him a distracted smile. "I'm not, officially. But they said you were with the FBI."

"I was with the Bureau." Roarke reached for his wallet, handed over one of the business cards that he'd never gotten around to removing. "Now I'm working privately." He hesitated. "Consulting."

"Is there a problem?" Devlin looked curious and mildly concerned.

"Not at all. I wanted to talk to you. I understand you went to Las Piedras High."

"That's right . . ." Then a strange look crossed Devlin's face. "Wait a minute. This is about Eden, isn't it? I mean, Cara . . ."

Roarke was startled. *That's one hell of a guess.* At the same time, he had the feeling of having struck pay dirt. Eden Ballard was the first alias Cara had taken.

He let none of that show on his face. "Cara?" he repeated neutrally.

"Cara Lindstrom," Devlin said.

"What makes you say that?"

"You're FBI, asking about Las Piedras High. She's been all over the news. I've been reading . . . everything. It's all so fucking hard to believe." In his distraction, he apologized automatically, "Excuse the language," as if it was somehow something Roarke wouldn't have heard before. And then he looked at Roarke as if he'd just realized: "You're looking for her *here?*"

Because the truth was too hard to explain, even to himself, Roarke improvised. "I'm just retracing some steps, talking to people who knew her. Obviously you did."

Devlin shook his head, his eyes clouding. "I knew Eden. Not for long."

"But you do remember her."

"She's not someone you forget."

There was an ambiguous tone in his voice. Something underneath it that Roarke recognized too well. Longing.

"Can you tell me about her?" he asked, neutrally.

"Tell you what?"

Everything, Roarke wanted to say, but didn't, of course. *This is why you should drop this,* he told himself. *Now.* Instead, he spoke aloud, "Whatever comes to mind," he suggested. "What interaction did you have with her? Did you have classes together?"

"She was in my Chem class," Devlin answered, reverting automatically to high school parlance.

"Did you know who she was at the time? Her history?"

"No. I mean, not then. She just showed up in class one day. I knew she was from one of the group homes. She was young to be in Chem, when I think about it. I don't think she was sixteen yet."

"Fourteen," Roarke said.

Devlin looked startled. "You'd never think that. She was . . ." He stopped, and for a minute it seemed he wouldn't complete the sentence. "Tough."

"Were there any incidents while she was at the school, anything odd?"

"With her?" Devlin asked, after a fraction of a second's beat that Roarke might have been imagining. "Like, her freaking out? Hurting someone?"

Roarke didn't want to lead him. Yet. He made a neutral gesture with his hands: *Go on.*

"No, nothing like that," Devlin said.

"Why would you ask that, particularly?" Roarke said. "'Freaking out. Hurting someone.'"

"Well, because of what she did later. All those . . . I mean, you're not asking if she actually killed someone back then, right? In high school?"

Roarke evaded that issue. "Just any incidents that stood out," he said.

"No," Devlin said, and Roarke had the fleeting feeling he was lying. "She seemed pretty focused on school, really."

There was a silence. Roarke waited, but Devlin didn't offer anything further.

"Do you remember a girl at your school named Laura Huell? She killed herself in January of that year."

Devlin's eyes widened. "I remember. Of course. Awful."

It was an adult thing to say, sympathy in hindsight. Not the reaction of a kid who had been there.

"Did you know her well?"

"Not really. We weren't from the same . . ."

He didn't say it, but he didn't have to. *Clique. Crowd.*

"Can you tell me anything you remember?"

Devlin frowned. "The family was pretty churchy. Her dad was in Wayfarers with my dad. That's really all I knew about her."

"Is the family still in town?"

"Her mother, I think. Over on K Street."

"How did Laura kill herself?" It hadn't been in the papers.

"I think she cut her wrists. That's what we heard around school." Then Devlin's face changed. He seemed genuinely startled. "Are you saying *that* had something to do with Cara?"

It has something to do with something, Roarke thought. Aloud he said, "I was just curious. Is there anything else you can tell me about Eden?"

"Like what?"

"Anything at all."

"She wasn't like the other kids. Not even close." Devlin's eyes went distant. "She wasn't like anyone I'd ever met. There was something so—alive about her."

Like an animal, Roarke agreed in his mind. *She is entirely physically present.*

"Did she really kill all those people?" Devlin asked.

It was not asked in the way Roarke usually heard it, with gleaming-eyed, prurient interest. And yet he had no idea what to say.

More people than I think we'll ever know. More to come, unless by some miracle she decides to stop.

He knew it would never happen. Not until she was dead.

He forced himself back to the moment, stuck out his hand. "It was good to meet you. Thanks for taking the time."

Devlin returned the grip. "Sorry I couldn't help."

That's okay, Roarke thought. *I don't know how to help, either.*

As he stood in the mirrored elevator, returning to his room, he thought about the manager, tried to picture him as a teenager.

There had been an attraction there, on Devlin's side. That was obvious. *Love* would be a strong word to use for a sixteen-year-old, but he'd been smitten. It was absurd to feel jealousy. But what about young Cara? Did she have teenage longings, for boys her age, for anything resembling normal?

She was a mystery. She would always be a mystery. And here he was, chasing the mystery again.

He looked at his own face in the elevator mirror.

What are you doing here?

Walk away.

The doors slid open.

And he knew it was already too late.

Chapter Twenty-Two

Mother Doctor saw him promptly at ten, and he stepped into the darkened office feeling a strange mix of relief and nervous anticipation.

The nun stood from her chair, and came around the desk. "Walk with me," she said.

She took him out the door again, and at the end of the hall, they moved out through a wood plank door that looked like it had been there for two hundred years.

In the sunshine, Roarke looked around at an open courtyard crisscrossed by gravel paths, a rectangular plaza with discrete, well-tended garden plots surrounding it, stone benches, a mosaic-tiled fountain, even an altar with a pensive statue of the Virgin Mary.

As soon as the door shut behind them, the nun was reaching into her pockets, drawing out a pack of cigarettes and a lighter. Roarke was unsurprised to see they were old school: Camel nonfilters. She lit up, drew in and exhaled with more satisfaction than he imagined nuns were supposed to indulge in.

They walked past a bronze mission bell set in a stone-and-mortar arch, and onto a gravel path. Roarke was struck by a sense of timelessness. It was like being transported back to the days of conquistadors and padres.

"What is this place?" he asked. "I know it's not an official mission." The twenty-one missions of Alta California were drilled into the heads of every California school child. Roarke had toured some of them and even now could probably recite the names of a good half of them.

"It was a sub-mission. The Spaniards called them *asistencias.*"

Asistencia. Help.

She exhaled smoke and looked him over. "So. Roarke. You're the agent who headed up the hunt for Cara Lindstrom."

Roarke blinked. "Yes, I . . . how—"

She sniffed. "Do I look unfamiliar with Google? You arrested Lindstrom."

He paused before answering. That wasn't exactly the way it had gone down.

For a moment he was back in the dark forest, with the weight of a madman on top of him, and Cara standing above them in the moonlight, raising her blade . . .

He banished the vision.

"We assisted local law enforcement in apprehending her," he said, finally. "I take it people here have been talking about Lindstrom."

She snorted. "This is a smallish town. Not much happens on the surface. A whiff of scandal . . . well, we're all over it."

"Not much happens on the surface," he repeated.

She regarded him from above her spectacles. "As opposed to in the hearts of men."

He was finding it hard to tell if she was being sincere, or ironic, or completely messing with him. He had a sneaking suspicion she enjoyed keeping people guessing. *We all have our hobbies.*

She was speaking again. "Yes, people have been very interested in the Cara Lindstrom story. Our very own mass murderess. Even if she did live here for only two weeks. But how do you think Cara Lindstrom is linked to Ivy?"

"I don't know." And then he realized. "But you do, don't you? Do you know Cara Lindstrom?"

"I have met her."

He stared at her.

"Sixteen years ago. When she was attending school at Las Piedras High. She came here to visit."

Roarke knew he shouldn't be surprised. "To visit Ivy?"

The nun nodded, and glanced toward the high stone wall. "The Mission is less than two miles from Las Piedras High. There's a city bus that will take you right from the high school to our front gate. But not many students came to visit Ivy. It was . . . I think . . . too much to take in. When Ivy walked out of that desert, she was like a living skeleton. The fire had eaten her down to the bone. I don't think that kind of pain is even comprehensible to the rest of us."

The image was disturbing on so many levels, Roarke had to force himself to breathe. All the obvious reasons, and one more. The walking skeleton. *Santa Muerte.* The unconsecrated saint known to her petitioners as Lady Death, whose name the media had begun to link with Cara.

Was this the beginning, then?

Mother Doctor was watching him, but if she was aware of his inner turmoil, she didn't say. "One must consider that if such a thing could happen to someone you know, that it could happen to you. There is a superstitious sense of safety in staying away."

Roarke had heard this kind of thinking before, in regard to Cara. As if tragedy was a communicable disease.

"Did she say why she was visiting?"

"I spoke to her, but it wasn't what you would call a conversation. I caught her leaving Ivy's room. She hadn't signed in at the desk. Went over the wall, I'm guessing. We frown on that here."

"What did she say?"

"The first time, she just ran."

"The *first* time," Roarke repeated.

"We'll get to that."

She dropped her cigarette to the gravel path and crushed it with her shoe, then removed a candy tin from one of the deep pockets of her cardigan. She opened it, stooped to pick up the butt, put it inside the tin, and slipped the tin back in her pocket.

"Now. You asked about Laura Huell, if she also visited, and I said she did. What I didn't say is that it was not only once. She came several times over perhaps a two-month period."

Roarke was electrified, and also mystified. He had been thinking Laura might have visited Ivy after having being attacked herself. He had no idea how to account for multiple visits.

"Did she say why?"

"She said she was a friend. And I wish to God I had asked more." She took off her glasses, rubbed her eyes. "She was devout. That I could see. Her parents were church people. Which doesn't necessarily make anyone devout, as well I know. But that girl was. So I assumed she was here out of what one might call Christian charity."

Roarke was about to speak, but she held up a hand, anticipating him.

"Did I see anything about her that would have tipped someone off to her suicide? I saw she was troubled. But anyone who came to visit Ivy would be troubled. Obviously the girl, Laura, wasn't in such distress that she raised any kind of alarm bells." She looked off into the distance. "But maybe I was distracted. Maybe it never occurred to me to ask. I think about that."

Roarke was sure she did.

She reached into her pocket for her pack of cigarettes, drew them out. But her hand was shaking so badly she fumbled the lighter. Roarke took it and lit the cigarette for her. Her eyes crinkled at him.

"Why, Roarke. You'll turn my head."

He nodded to the cigarette. "You know, those things—"

The nun held up a warning hand. "If you're about to bring up vapes, pray do not. I have few enough pleasures in this life." She drew a deep drag.

Fair enough.

"About Laura Huell," Roarke said. "I've been wondering—"

"If she was also raped," she finished bluntly.

Roarke found himself surprised again. "Yes, exactly. I've searched news articles about her death, but I haven't seen any report of it." He'd been up quite late the night before, looking. "But statistically, rapists . . . they don't do this just once. They're serial offenders. They do it until they get caught, if they ever do. Even if they're caught, they do time only rarely, and after they're released, they start up right where they left off—"

"I'm familiar with the statistics."

He stopped. Of course she was.

She nodded. "You're asking if there were other rapes of this kind. You would think something so heinous would be noticed, wouldn't you? But even Ivy's attack was only local news at the time. Ivy was a foster child. Not the kind to make the papers." She touched her fingers absently to her lips, brushing tobacco away.

Roarke knew what she meant. With the media, always, some victims mattered more than others.

"I did keep an eye out for news. I still do. There have been rapes, of course. Thousands. However, many more that are unreported. That scourge never leaves us. But that specific kind of attack? The burning? No. There was nothing like that here or anywhere else that I've ever heard or read." She nodded at him. "You would be the one with access to information like that."

And against his better judgment, he was having the urge to access those databases.

She sat on a stone bench, smoking and studying him. "You're off asking all these questions on your own, aren't you? It's not really part of your Cara Lindstrom case."

He found himself wanting to confess. *Yes, I'm totally off the reservation and I have no idea what I'm doing.* Instead he said, "It's a loose end. I don't like loose ends."

"But what are you after?"

It was a good question. He didn't know how to answer it. Instead he asked, "Did Ivy talk to you? Did she say where she had been taken, during the attack?"

Mother Doctor gave him a strange look, which he interpreted as her not understanding the point of the question.

"He left her for dead," he said slowly. "There could be others that he did kill, and buried."

"Out there in in the desert."

Roarke thought of Riverside County, the endless stretches of desert sand. So many unincorporated areas. So many miles of nothingness.

He remembered something a Southern California sheriff had once said to him: *"If you stuck a cross everywhere a body was buried out here, the desert would look like Forest Lawn."*

"It's a possibility," he said aloud.

The nun's eyes were clouded. "Remember, I never met Ivy until six months later. She couldn't speak. Her vocal cords were burned. The police questioned her, of course, in whatever ways they had of doing that. But her attacker used a hood to cover her eyes during the abduction and throughout her ordeal; she never saw his face or where he had taken her, only that it was significantly off-road. She could tell that by the jarring of the van over rough terrain. The police never found the spot of the attack. And you didn't answer *my* question."

Of course she hadn't forgotten.

"I don't know what I'm after," he told her. He turned where he stood, looked back at the Mission. "Something happened here, in this town, sixteen years ago, that had to do with these girls. Ivy—horrifically attacked. Laura, who killed herself." *And Cara, who became a killer that same month,* he added to himself. "It all goes together somehow."

"But why is it significant to you that Cara Lindstrom was here?"

Roarke paused. How could he explain Cara to someone else? When he didn't know himself?

"She knows things," he said. "She seems to see things in people." She was a vigilante, but her accuracy had so far been astonishing, almost preternatural. "She thinks she sees evil."

The nun raised her eyebrows. "And do you believe that?"

Roarke didn't know what he believed. But what he heard himself saying was, "Every person I've found that she's killed . . . I'd say the world is better off without them."

"So you believe in evil."

She sat with her head tipped back to observe him. *Great. Just what I need. A nun who's also a shrink.*

Although maybe it was exactly what he *did* need. But how to answer her? What did he want? Answers? An end? He knew there was no such thing.

Aloud he said, "What happened to Ivy—that's evil. Sometimes there's no other word."

"It is evil. It is an atrocity." She leveled her gaze on him. "And so?"

"I want to understand it."

"What evil is."

"I guess. Yes." His voice sounded raw. He wanted to be anywhere other than here, having this conversation.

"What did you do yesterday, after we talked?"

The query was so abrupt, he didn't know what to make of it. "I'm sorry?"

"I'd like to know what you did after our talk yesterday."

Roarke felt defensive, as if it were a trick question. But he answered anyway. "I went to the high school to talk to Principal Lethbridge."

"Why?"

"I wanted to know why he didn't mention the attack on Ivy when I questioned him about unusual events at the high school."

She nodded. "Interesting. And what did you learn?"

Roarke's hackles were rising. *What is this, some kind of job interview?* It actually felt like one. But at the same time he found he wanted to talk it through, make some sense of what was going on.

"He's hiding something. He definitely doesn't want me stirring up the past. There's some guilt there. I don't know how deep, but . . . I don't trust him."

"And what do you intend to do today, when you leave here?"

Jesus Christ. What does she want from me?

Across the grassy courtyard, a back door opened in the building, and three nuns walked out in the middle of a group of children. Boys, girls, ages five to maybe ten. There was something about them, immediately, that was different from ordinary children. One little boy fluttered a hand beside his face, the classic stimming gesture of autism. One nun held a little girl by the hand. Her head was down, her eyes fixed on the ground, and she seemed to move only because the nun was leading her.

Mother Doctor followed his gaze, then looked at him.

The words were coming out of his mouth before he knew he was going to say them.

"I'll probably go out to Palm Desert and ask a few people in the department there what the hell they've been doing for sixteen years that they thought was more important . . ." He had to pause, swallow back something that wasn't exactly anger. "Than putting whoever did that to Ivy away for seven lifetimes."

"All right, then." Mother Doctor leaned suddenly forward and stabbed out her cigarette on the ground, repeated the ritual of taking out the candy tin, placing the butt inside, and slipping the tin back into her pocket. Then she stood.

"Let's go inside."

Back in the dim comfort of her office, she sat at her desk and pulled open a drawer again. Roarke was fully expecting more cigarettes to come out. He was guessing a pack a day, easily. It would account for that husky, classic film star voice of hers.

But instead of the Camels, what she pulled out of the drawer was a satin surplice, folded over to create a silky package.

She placed the packet gently on the top of her desk, in the center.

"You asked if Cara came more than once. She did. I can't say how, but I'd known that she would. I had looked into her."

"Looked into her," Roarke repeated. Coming from the nun, in this setting, it sounded almost mystical.

Mother Doctor frowned. "I called the school. It took some show of force, but I was able to find out . . ." For a moment it was if she didn't know how to finish the sentence. "Who she was. All of it."

"The second time she came, I was able to speak to her a bit. And I believe she came once more, a few days later. I found these things in Ivy's room. They weren't there before, and Ivy did not go out, herself. I can only surmise that Cara left them for her."

She unwrapped the cloth on her desk, one end at a time, to reveal the contents.

A glittering lump of gold stone. A plant frond that looked like palm. And a heavy silver ring.

Roarke looked up from the objects to Mother Doctor. Before he could speak, she lifted a finger.

"And yes, of course. I gave them to the police."

He reached for the ring, picked it up. On the flat square surface was a tiny compass, embossed in gold. It seemed familiar, somehow.

A college ring? A lodge ring? There was no identifying inscription.

"That one I was able to figure out for myself," Mother Doctor said. "The compass. It's a Wayfarers ring."

Roarke was aware of Wayfarers, in a general way. Service clubs like Wayfarers, Rotary, Lions, Kiwanis, had been a pillar of small-town America, a more informal, more Protestant descendant of Masonic lodges. Vaguely churchy, very male dominated—even after they were forced to accept female members after a lawsuit in the late eighties.

And then he remembered. Laura had played the piano for the local Wayfarers Club.

He stared at Mother Doctor. "The police had *this*?"

"Yes."

"What did they do with it?"

"They took those things, had them for a week, and then returned all the items to me. Nothing to do with anything, apparently. I could see they thought I was foolish. It didn't help that one of the detectives was a Baptist."

He glanced at her, not knowing if she was serious. "It was the Sheriff's Department that you gave these to."

"That's right. They were the department heading up the investigation."

Ortiz's department, Roarke thought. *Why don't I like that?*

"But in the end, I see their point. How was it evidence? A girl brings another girl presents." She lifted her shoulders.

"It's a man's ring, though, isn't it?" It was too big to be a girl's.

"I would say so, yes."

"And after you found these in Ivy's room, how many days later did she die?"

She met his gaze from across the desk. "It was the next day."

Roarke felt a hollowness in his chest. He asked the next question with no small dread. "Did Cara . . . was Cara there the night Ivy died?"

The nun shook her head. "I don't know. I didn't see her. I never saw her again."

There was silence between them.

Then she reached for the surplice, folded the objects back into them, and extended her hand across the desk, offering the packet to Roarke.

He looked at the package stupidly.

She nodded at him. "I've been holding on to this for sixteen years. It's obvious now why. It's for you."

His mouth was dry. "I can't. I'm not on the job anymore."

"Ah, Roarke. You're not 'on the job.' You're on a mission."

He wanted to argue. No words were coming.

She shook her head. "I understand the conflict here. 'Look too long into the abyss—'"

Roarke finished the quote automatically. "'And the abyss looks back into you.'" The profiler's creed, or warning. The nun had just summed up his whole state of mind for the last three months in one quotation.

She inclined her head in acknowledgement. "But Roarke. They were fourteen. Three fourteen-year-old girls with no one to stand for them. In the end, I didn't help them. Or couldn't help them. Maybe you can set something—"

She started back and fell silent, and Roarke realized he was on his feet, that he'd shoved back his chair, and was staring down at her, shaking.

She finished gently. "Set something right."

He contained himself however he could, and took the package. It felt heavy in his hand.

"This should also be of use to you."

She handed across a file folder, plain manila, and not new. Roarke opened it to look down on a photocopied document. He could tell without even reading it what it was: a police witness statement. The name on the top line was Ivy Barnes.

He looked down at the form for some time, then up at the nun. "How did you get this?"

She gave him an inscrutable look. "I have ways."

"How did they even . . . you said that her vocal cords were burned . . ."

"And her fingers, too, to stumps. And her eyes. And still, she learned Braille and typed it out herself. She wanted it known, what happened to her."

He felt a wave of resentment that it had to be him. And he knew it had to be him.

"All right," he said angrily. "All right." He gathered up the surplice and the file, and stood.

"You'll keep me apprised?"

"Of course," he said tiredly, to the door.

"Nobody said it was easy," she said behind him.

He turned to look at her. "What?"

"Life."

Chapter Twenty-Three

R oarke stood at the sliding glass door. Outside the sun shimmered through the water from the rain birds arcing over the golf course green.

The packet in the satin surplice was on the bed.

Roarke turned and paced the hotel room, postponing the moment that he would have to sit down with it. The urge not to touch the packet again was extreme.

Why? After all, it was in the past, wasn't it? No one's life was at stake any more. No harm he could do to anyone.

Except to you, a part of his mind whispered.

But finally he sat, opened the silky cloth, and looked down at the objects: the gold stone, the palm frond, the ring.

Relics, he couldn't help thinking. Not just fragments from the past, but in the way of the religious meaning: the personal effects of a saint.

Were they clues to Ivy's attacker? Clues for whom, then? To whom? If Cara had left them for the other girl, what was she was trying to say?

He reached for the ring, felt its weight in the palm of his hand. It was a bit big on his finger, made for a larger man. Had the killer worn it? But apparently the sheriff's department had dismissed it as a clue.

The palm frond was dry as dust, and it was impossible not to think of Palm Sunday, the ritual anointment of ashes, from Masses he'd attended in childhood, before he stopped going to church for good.

He picked up the stone. The metallic glittering caught the sunlight. Pyrite, he was fairly certain. Fool's Gold.

Were that and the palm frond clues to a place?

He could have them analyzed, wait to see what came back. Forensic geology, it was called. Forensic botany. If the palm frond and the pyrite could be traced to a specific area, it might be a clue to the place Ivy was taken and attacked. Even someone's property.

Wouldn't the detectives have done that?

Sixteen years ago, not necessarily. Even now, not necessarily. But there was also the fact that in sixteen years, the plant life of an area would have changed considerably. The results couldn't be trusted. And would a fourteen-year-old girl be leaving a forensic clue like that, anyway?

He had no idea what Cara would have been thinking.

It took even more time to work up the nerve to read the document Mother Doctor had given him, Ivy's police testimony. He'd read the details in the news reports, but to hear it in Ivy's own words would be another story altogether. The palms of his hands were damp even before he took up the faded file, opened it to remove the pages.

WITNESS STATEMENT

Statement of <u>Ivy Marie Barnes</u>

Age <u>14</u> Occupation <u>High school student</u>

This statement consisting of <u>3</u> page(s) and signed by me is true to the best of my knowledge and belief and I make it knowing that, if it is tendered in evidence, I will be liable to prosecution if I have willfully stated in it anything which I know to be false or do not believe to be true.

On the morning of June 2nd, I was walking to school. It was early because I was going to a Palmers meeting before class, so it was still dark. There was a white van parked up the street on the side I was walking on. When I passed the van it felt like someone was inside it, but all I could see was dark.

I walked faster. Then someone grabbed me from behind.

Many stops and starts later, Roarke put the pages down and walked around the room. He pulled open the sliding door to let air into the room. And then he went to the mini bar and pulled out a small bottle of whisky.

There was a manila envelope inside the folder that he knew contained photos.

You don't need to look, he told himself.

Of all the things in the world that he feared, burning was the worst. The idea of being set on fire was an incomprehensible horror. The idea of being burned that badly and living . . .

It's what Cara saw, he told himself implacably. *It's what Ivy* lived.

He put the whisky bottle down, stepped back to the desk, opened the envelope, and looked down on hell.

Some time later, he left the room with the file and an envelope, took the elevator down to the lobby.

He had to weave his way through a group of golfers, some kind of convention, already taking advantage of happy hour. Their drunken chatter seemed too loud, grating in his ears.

The young receptionist standing at the counter looked up from her computer with a smiling greeting. "May I help—"

Then she stopped, staring at Roarke. "Sir, are you all right?"

She looked so alarmed that Roarke made an effort to sound normal. "Just a rough day. Do you have FedEx pickup? I need to send something overnight."

"Of course. I'll get you a mailer."

Roarke sealed the mailer with the lump of pyrite and the piece of palm frond inside, addressed it to the San Francisco Bureau, and deposited the package in the FedEx box.

In the hotel's business center, he printed out the photos he'd taken of the relics.

As the printer whirred, phrases and images from the report flashed in his head. Ivy's attacker had used a hood to cover her eyes during the attack; she never saw his face. He had kept her chained in the van for the entire two days, never taking her out until he dragged her outside to burn her.

And there was something else in those pages. Something right at the border of his consciousness, that he knew would come to the surface if he just let it.

On the way out of the business center he almost ran straight into Devlin in the corridor. The hotel manager gave him a smile that was meant to be amiable, but seemed strained. "Hello there. I didn't know you were still with us."

It was a lie, and not a very good one.

That's interesting, Roarke thought. *Why?*

He felt a touch of suspicion that Devlin was outside the business center just as he had been scanning Ivy's police statement.

Now that really is paranoid.

But in the same moment he remembered that Devlin had said his father had belonged to the Wayfarers Club, and knew he needed to stay alert.

This guy was never caught. He may still be out there. He may be right here in this town. So from now on, you assume nothing.

Devlin was still trying to make pointed conversation. "Still looking into Eden? I mean, Cara?"

There was a note in his voice that Roarke recognized. A desperate yearning. That addictive pull.

And at that moment, Roarke realized that he wasn't looking for her anymore. Not the adult Cara. He had no expectation that this search would teach him anything that could bring him to her. It was about the girls, now.

Three fourteen-year-old girls with no one to stand for them.

"Just some loose ends," he said to Devlin pleasantly. "Have a good day."

And he walked down the hall, leaving Devlin behind him.

In his hotel room he typed off a text to Lam and Stotlemyre, the Evidence Response techs he'd always worked with at the Bureau. He knew they'd make the time to get the pyrite and the palm frond tested, no questions asked. He felt a ripple of guilt. And then he reached for the two yearbooks and laid them both open on the desk, to Ivy's and Laura's photos.

Looking down on their faces, the guilt vanished.

Like hell you didn't make the connection, Roarke thought at the principal. *There's something you're hiding here.*

Then he looked more closely at Laura's picture, at the clubs listed below: Glee Club, Honors, Palmers.

Palm frond. Palmers.

He grabbed for Ivy's witness report. The name had registered when he'd first read it, then the other details of the attack had wiped it away.

"I was going to a Palmers meeting before school . . ."

Roarke felt a stirring of memory.

It was some kind of club, wasn't it? It hadn't been a club at his own high school in San Luis Obispo, but there had been one at some rival school.

And Ivy was in Palmers. Just as Laura Huell had been.

He turned to the photos of the relics spread out on the bed, picked up the ring from the opened surplice, and examined the embossed figure of the compass. He grabbed his iPad and Googled. A moment later he was staring down at the same image of the compass, on the national website of the Wayfarers Club.

Palmers was the junior branch of the club.

Chapter Twenty-Four

I t was a long, mostly sleepless wait until morning, when he could reasonably start knocking on doors.

Laura Huell's old house was on K Street, just as Devlin had said, a boxy '50s style stucco. The landscaping looked minimally kept up and the trees and shrubs were old, on their way toward dying.

The woman who came to the door had the same unkempt look as the house. She was probably not sixty yet, but looked older.

"Mrs. Huell?" Roarke asked.

Her face tightened. "Who are you?"

He could see she was about to shut the door, so in a split second he decided to play his highest card.

"I'm Special Agent Roarke, FBI."

That stopped her from closing the door, barely. But he knew he didn't have long.

He could see past her into the house. Everything inside seemed to have a film on it: the floor was dingy, the walls greasy with fingerprints; a layer of dust furred the carpet in the shabby living room. Clutter was piled on tables and in corners, cardboard boxes and bulging plastic sacks stacked against the walls. Not full-on hoarding yet, but it was escalating.

"FBI, huh," she said warily, but didn't ask him for ID. Instead, she waited expectantly.

"I'm here to talk to you about your daughter."

Her face turned stony. "She's dead. Years ago." She started to shut the door again.

"Then I'd like to talk to your husband—"

There was a sudden narrow, sneering look on her face. "You'd have to find him then, wouldn't you? He took off. A long, long time ago." And then she asked the question. "Let's see your badge."

It wasn't a badge, but he didn't have it, and even if he did, he didn't guess he'd get much out of her. Sometimes you just had to admit it and move on.

"Sorry to trouble you," he said, and turned away. Behind him, the door slammed on its hinges.

The local Wayfarers Club was just blocks from the school, and another few blocks from Laura Huell's old house.

Roarke had read up on the Wayfarers before leaving the hotel. The organization was made up largely of white and middle- to upper-middle-class businessmen and independent professionals. The clubs were high on traditional Christian values, more popular in suburbs and small towns than in larger cities, and the members tended to be members for life. And the Wayfarers were closely involved in their town's schools, donating to athletic programs and scholarship funds.

He'd found confirmation of the last in the Las Piedras High yearbooks: the club had a full page ad in the back pages, and the Wayfarer name was scattered throughout the books as sponsors of the football team, and several scholarships. Meaning lots of money invested in the school.

But as he turned onto the block, he could tell even from a distance that the building attached to the address wasn't big enough to contain a club. He stopped the car at the curb, looking out at a motorcycle repair and accessories shop. He checked the address he'd gotten from the yearbook.

The address was right, but the shop was wrong.

He got out of the Rover and headed for the building.

The doorbell jangled as Roarke stepped inside. A man looked up from the counter—tattooed and pierced, with a Hells Angels look to him, but the leather jacket was high end and his beard was grizzled. The owner, Roarke figured.

"Help you?" the man asked, friendly enough.

"I was looking for the Wayfarers Club. Must have written down the wrong address."

The man nodded. "Used to be here. Over on Highland, now."

Roarke glanced around the shop, the few display bikes, the travel gear and biker clothing. No way was the square footage enough for a clubhouse of any size.

"Is this a new building?"

"I wouldn't say new. Wayfarers moved after the old building burned down."

Roarke felt a buzz of significance. "The building burned down? When was that?"

"A while, now. Fifteen, sixteen years ago."

"Sixteen years ago?" Roarke asked, and heard the incredulous edge in his own voice. "Do you know what month?"

The man in the leather jacket laughed. "Not a chance. Why do you ask?"

Inside, Roarke was electrified. *Fire. Ivy was burned. If a Wayfarer member was to blame, burning down the club would be poetic justice.*

And Cara had dispatched one of her targets by fire not even three weeks ago . . .

He kept his voice even. "Do you remember if anyone was killed in this fire?"

This time the man didn't laugh. He glanced around the shop and looked more guarded. "That I would remember. Not that I ever heard."

"Thanks. Appreciate it."

Roarke left the shop, went back out to the car and did some Googling on his iPad.

The club had burned down the night after Cara left Las Piedras for good.

The night before Ivy died.

The present Wayfarers Club, on Highland Avenue, was not a new building. There was a run-down feel about it, not the look of a flourishing organization. It had stuccoed arches and security bars on the windows, and could have been anything from a small medical clinic to a Jehovah's Witness Kingdom Hall, except for the large concrete and metal sculpture of a compass sitting in the middle of the small, sloped front lawn.

There was only one car in the small parking lot, an oversized new Lexus with a bumper sticker of an ichthus, the Christian fish symbol. Roarke parked beside it, walked up concrete steps to the entry, and tried the door. Locked. He reached for the doorbell anyway. The chime rang through the building.

He stepped back and waited, while the dry wind rustled the fronds of the palm trees in the front planters.

He was just turning away when the door opened behind him.

A man stood in the shadows of the doorway. He was bulky without being fat, tanned like a golfer, dressed in dress slacks and shirtsleeves, his dirty-blond hair in a military-style crew cut. Roarke put his age at a fit sixty.

His eyes flicked over Roarke, a glance of subtly aggressive assessment. But his tone was genial. "No meeting today, friend."

"I wasn't looking for a meeting."

"Then how can I help you?"

Something made Roarke decide to softball his approach, make his interest seem personal. "I've been trying to track down one of your members. Dave Huell."

The big man looked pleasant. "Sorry. We don't have a Huell in the ranks."

"I think he may have left town a while ago."

"How long ago?"

Roarke stayed vague. "It may have been as much as ten years."

The man chuckled. "Ten *years*? Some days I don't remember my own name."

"His daughter committed suicide sixteen years ago. In a town this size, I would think people would remember that."

The man's face rearranged itself. "Of course. I know the little girl you mean."

Roarke kept his face impassive, but made a mental note. *Laura had been fourteen. Not exactly a little girl.*

"So you remember Huell?"

The man was looking at him more sharply, now, and apparently had sussed out that he was law enforcement. "Are you with the police? Sheriff?"

That perplexing question.

"I consult for the FBI. Huell is a potential witness in a case." *That should be neutral enough.*

The man looked blank, and then chuckled. "That must be a very cold case. Haven't heard anything about Dave for ages." Then he opened the door wider, stepped aside for Roarke. "Why don't you come inside, and I'll try to help you out."

Roarke stepped into a cool, dim corridor, with a row of doors that seemed to lead to offices, and a set of double doors that he guessed led to a larger assembly hall. The place felt hollow; the daylight outside was muted, seeming far away.

The man indicated an open door into an office, and as the men stepped inside, he turned and stuck out his hand.

"I'm Mel Franzen. Chapter President." Franzen's grip was as aggressive as his attitude.

"Matt Roarke," Roarke returned. "How long have you been president?"

Franzen chuckled as he sat down behind his desk. "Hard to believe, but going on ten years."

"And you knew Huell?"

"He was a brother, yes. Must've been a good two hundred of us back then."

Roarke recalled his very brief interview with the very bitter Mrs. Huell. "He left town some time after his daughter died, is that right?" He knew it couldn't have been before, because according to the obituary Huell had been at the funeral.

"Pretty soon after, as I'm recalling."

"Any idea why?"

Franzen gave him a sly look. "I don't like to say."

Roarke waited for the inevitable.

The Wayfarer's voice dropped slightly. "There were rumors. He traveled on business. Out of town a fair lot. You know how it can be. A younger woman, out of state . . ."

There was a gleam of lasciviousness in his eyes. Roarke stifled his distaste, nodded. And noted that for someone with a self-described poor memory, Franzen was suddenly being able to recall quite a few details.

"When his daughter died, he took off. I think the girl had been the only thing holding the marriage together." Franzen shrugged. "It's not a pleasant story. If he'd come to any of the brothers for counseling, advice, we would have set him straight. Head of the family, father, husband . . . those are obligations. But shame is a powerful motivator. When a man knows the advice he'd get and doesn't want it, well . . ."

"Can you tell me about Laura?"

"The daughter? 'Fraid I can't."

Roarke frowned. "But you must have been familiar with her. She played the piano for your club."

Franzen lifted his hands. "If you say so. We work with quite a few of the students from Las Piedras schools. The chapter sponsors a scholarship. We contribute to sports and the academic decathlon." He shrugged. "Every year, we're working with dozens of students."

"Not many who die, I hope," Roarke said pleasantly.

"Thank the Lord for that," Franzen said, ignoring the implication that he should remember Laura.

Roarke took a different tack. "Did Huell leave a forwarding address?"

"Hold on here, I'll check for you." Franzen made a show of going into the computer, clicking through some files. Roarke had the feeling it was just that, a show. Franzen finally looked up.

"No, nothing on Huell since 2000." He pushed back from the desk. "Sorry I can't tell you more. You know, his wife still lives over on K Street—"

"Yes, I've been by. They haven't been in contact." Roarke paused, then changed tacks. "There's another student I'm inquiring about. Ivy Barnes."

Franzen's eyes narrowed. "You said you were looking for Dave Huell."

"Do you know Ivy Barnes?"

"I don't believe I do."

"She was a member of Palmers, like Laura Huell."

"As I said, we have dozens of students every year—"

"She was abducted and raped that same year. Her attacker tried to burn her alive."

Franzen's face rearranged itself into a study in outrage, pity, and sorrow. "Well. Who wouldn't remember that? A terrible thing. There are godless people in this world, Mr. Roarke."

And bad ones, too, Roarke thought. *I'm more worried about the bad ones.* But he kept silent, and waited for Franzen to continue.

The Wayfarer frowned into the silence. "You've lost me. What does this have to do with the other girl?"

"You don't find it disturbing, two girls from the same school dying violently so close together?

"As I recall, the police found nothing. Never made an arrest."

Odd answer to the question, Roarke thought. *And that's exactly my problem. They never made an arrest.* But he didn't say that. Instead, he glanced around him. "This club used to be over on Mill Street, is that right? But it burned down."

"That's right."

"What was that, arson?"

Franzen laughed, but there was an edge to it that Roarke read as controlled anger. "You got that right. Never caught the bastard, either."

"Was anyone killed in the fire? Or injured?"

"No, thank God. But that was a sweet piece of property. Damned shame."

"Odd timing though, wasn't it?"

There was a flash of something on the man's face. "I don't follow. Are you investigating the fire, too?"

"I'm curious about it. It just seems like a lot of bad luck for this club."

"Bad luck?" Franzen repeated. His eyes had gone blank again.

"A member loses a daughter, his wife loses him, you lose your clubhouse in a fire. I'd say that's a lot of strange for one month."

Franzen laughed shortly. "I'd say that's the blindness of hindsight. You're focusing on a few events. Unfortunate events, to be sure, but I don't see any connection. Tragedies happen. It's life."

He was right about that. Roarke put his hands on his thighs, and stood. "I appreciate your talking to me."

Franzen smiled. "Here to serve."

Roarke stepped to the door, then turned back. "Is Principal Lethbridge a member of this club?"

"Yes. Yes, he is. A very valued member."

Roarke nodded. "Thank you for your time."

"Nice talking to you, Mr. Roarke."

Roarke flinched inside at the repetition of *mister*. But fair enough. As he left the hall and walked out to the parking lot, he muttered, "Get used to it."

He sat in the car without moving for some time.

He had a crawly feeling from the encounter, and had to admit that he disliked Mel Franzen, for no reason he could say.

He saw Franzen watching him from the window, and raised a hand to him as he started the car.

A girl kills herself. Her father disappears. A Wayfarers Club burns down. And no one wants to talk about it.

There's a whole lot wrong with this picture.

Chapter Twenty-Five

B ack in his room at the hotel, Roarke steeled himself, and speed-dialed a familiar number.

Antara Singh was the researcher on his four-agent team, what *had been* his team, a brilliant analyst and tech expert. Roarke found himself waiting nervously as the phone rang; he had been avoiding all calls from the team since he'd taken leave. When Singh answered, remorse made him abrupt.

"Singh. I need some help."

There was only the briefest pause on her end. "Of course."

His agent's voice was serene, but the gladness underneath was almost painful. He could tell how hard she was working to contain her relief at the call. And he knew, with a stab of guilt, she would do anything he asked, in the hope of getting him back to San Francisco, back to the office, back to work.

"Where are you?" she asked.

He paused. "Las Piedras."

There was a loaded silence. Singh would recognize the significance of the town to Cara's history. But whatever she was thinking, she said nothing, merely asking, "What can I do?"

"I'm doing some investigation into a cold case. I'm going to need the coroner's reports on two deaths that occurred sixteen years ago."

In California autopsies were automatic in the case of suicide; the same went for the death of a minor. Coroner's reports were public record, but Roarke would have to make a request in writing to the coroner's office and there was no telling when the inevitably under-staffed and overworked office would get it to him. Singh was a wizard at cutting through red tape. And there was no denying he would need her help—the word *asistencia* flashed in his mind—for what he wanted to do. It was better just to admit it from the outset.

"Yes, go ahead," she replied.

"These would have been conducted by the Riverside County Coroner, in Indio. The first report is for a fourteen-year-old high school freshman named Laura Huell, an apparent suicide. I need to know if there was any evidence of sexual assault, or any signs at all of scarring or bruising that could indicate previous sexual assault, and if there was ever an earlier report of rape. And if so, if a rape kit was ever collected."

He meant the box of swabs, slides, combs, and envelopes that con-tained the evidence collected during a post-sexual assault medical exam, and the corresponding documentation forms.

"Yes. And the second?"

"The second is another fourteen-year-old girl named Ivy Barnes. There should be an entire case file here, on a sexual assault, mutilation, and attempted murder. I need everything you can get. I also need to know if there was a CODIS database search done for matches to Ivy Barnes' rapist."

"Both girls fourteen years old, sixteen years ago," Singh said cautiously.

Roarke said nothing. He heard the silence thicken on the phone line. Of course Singh was doing the math. Of course she would see the connection to Cara.

"Then I need you to search for rapes with similar MOs to the attack on Ivy Barnes." He paused and then said, "I'm sending some news articles through, and her witness statement to the police. You'll find the details of that attack in the witness statement."

He clicked over to his email to forward her photographs of the police report and the articles he'd downloaded. He told himself she would get a better rundown from the reports, but the truth was he didn't want to have to speak the details aloud.

He listened to the quality of her silence and knew that she was skimming the articles and the statement. He could see her in his mind, her face tense with concentration, her glossy black hair curtaining her face as she bent over the screen, gold armbands glinting on her wrists.

"Singh?"

"I am here," she answered. "Am I looking specifically for incidences of burning, then?"

Roarke reluctantly called on his profiling training. "Any actual burning, any threat of burning, any use of gasoline. But also focus on the age of the victims, and the mode of abduction: snatching the girl from the street, especially as she is walking to or from school. The use of a van. And covering her face with a hood, or blindfold, something that the assailant brought or improvised. Check for any hits you can find in ViCAP."

It was fishing, and he'd be lucky if she found anything. Law enforcement officers more often than not *didn't* submit forms to the ViCAP database. Still, it had to be tried.

"What range of years would you like me to include in this search?" Singh asked.

Roarke paused again and then said it. "All the way to the present."

On the other end of the connection, Singh exhaled tightly. "I see."

"Proceed on the assumption that the rapist is still alive and operating. In California and/or possibly the Southwest. I'm also going to need full police records and background checks on a Robert Lethbridge and a Mel Franzen, both currently residing in Las Piedras."

"I will get back to you, Chief."

He felt a pang at the old nickname. He knew that he was taking time away from her official work. He also knew she would walk through fire for him. He could only hope he was taking her someplace worth going.

"Thank you, Singh."

She said only, "Of course." And then she was gone.

He hung up the phone, and stood, feeling the room too close around him.

He looked at the photos of the relics he'd taped up on the wall above the desk, and was drawn again to pick up the Wayfarers ring. There were hundreds, thousands, tens of thousands of men who owned them. But both Lethbridge and Franzen were Wayfarers who were directly involved with the school that both dead girls had attended. They were the obvious place to start the investigation—

But then he stopped, thinking about it.

Are they?

There was an even more obvious suspect, wasn't there? What about the man that he was sure Cara had killed that week?

He put the ring aside and looked at the photo of the palm frond.

Palm Desert.

It was the flimsiest of connections, more a hunch than a clue.

But let's not forget, that while all this was happening, Cara went out to Palm Desert and killed the counselor. Not Franzen. Not Lethbridge. The group home counselor, Pierson.

And Ivy was a group home kid, too.

So what if Pierson was a Wayfarer? It wasn't uncommon, in these midsized and smaller towns.

He needed information that he had to wait for. Singh was on it. But . . .

His own words to Mother Doctor came back to him:

I'll probably go out to Palm Desert and ask a few people in the department there what the hell they've been doing for sixteen years that they thought was more important than putting whoever did this away for seven lifetimes.

Why not take another drive? He had some bones to pick with Ortiz, anyway.

He stood, and reached for his car keys. And then he went to the closet, opened the built-in safe, to take out something else.

His Glock.

CARA

Chapter Twenty-Six

The corridor of highway between Las Piedras and Temecula is bounded by mountains. There are jagged rock formations, flat housing developments, an uncanny number of palm trees, and several golf courses.

Cara stares out the car window at boulders and barrel cactus. Ms. Sharonda is driving her. Cara suspects that Ms. Sharonda believes she would make a run for it if she put her on a bus.

Ms. Sharonda is no fool.

But Cara's desperate gambit has worked. Yesterday the vice-principal called her aunt and arranged for Cara to stay for a few days. A few days is a start. She is away from the school, away from the monster in the van, and that is the first step. She does not know how long she will be safe, but she has bought herself some time.

And her aunt will not be as vigilant as Ms. Sharonda. Once she is at her aunt's house, Cara can run if she has to. She may very well have to.

A bit at a time, she allows herself to think of what she is fleeing. She must go slowly, because there is so much that she is afraid she will be sick if she lets it all in at once.

The counselor, Pierson, suddenly showing up at the group home. Telling her he's watching her.

Laura, bleeding from the wounds of some terrible secret.

The darkness of the van and what happened to the skeleton girl—

In the driver's seat, Ms. Sharonda suddenly speaks. "You have something you want to tell me?"

Cara is jolted back to the present.

Tell her?

The thought makes her flush hot and cold.

Can she tell her? Does she dare? Would that do anything but get her in a Level 14 home, doped out of her mind?

Her thoughts feel so loud she can hardly contain them . . . but nothing comes out of her mouth.

Ms. Sharonda shakes her head, tight-lipped. "Well, you got away with it. You got yourself right out of that school." She glances away from the road, looks at Cara directly. "I don't want to see you back. You're out now—you stay out. Are we clear?"

After a moment, Cara nods. That's the plan. She's going to stay as far away as she can get.

The car leaves the flatness of the desert valley to ascend into the hills toward Temecula. Sunny grape fields sprawl over the hills, dotted with the olive trees and date palms that also thrive in the Mediterranean climate.

It all feels vaguely familiar. She has very few memories of the time before *The Night*. Before *The Night*, there were visits from a pretty, lively person who laughed hard and cried hard. After *The Night*, when Cara went to live with Joan, there was no laughing. There was a man, too, who wasn't nice. There was fighting, and crying. The man left. Cara left soon after, to the first of an endless parade of failed foster placements and group homes, and the dreams at night, always the monsters in her dreams . . .

She shuts that line of thought out.

The house, too, is familiar, a comfortable two-story tract home in a hillside community with quiet curving streets and cul-de-sacs. She has stayed there briefly over the years. Not often, and only briefly. She knows Aunt Joan got the house from insurance money Cara's father left her. Cara knows there is money for her, too, that will come to her when she is eighteen years old. But that is an abstract fantasy, completely inaccessible. Eighteen years old seems like centuries away. She has never believed she will live that long.

Ms. Sharonda pulls the car into the driveway and stops.

Aunt Joan comes outside and speaks to Ms. Sharonda for a long time, while Cara sits on the metal bench on the porch. Her cousins watch from the window. They are young: Erin a shy nine, and Patrick a bratty ten-year-old, sullenly staring at her.

Finally, her aunt turns away from the car. Ms. Sharonda looks up at the porch, toward Cara. "We'll be talking," she says, an assurance and a warning.

Aunt Joan forces a smile and walks up on the porch toward Cara. Cara can feel her aunt flinch even as she hugs her, and she pulls back again quickly.

Then Aunt Joan calls her by the other name, which Cara supposes is all right. The whole school will know by now. After the fight, there will be no going back.

"Well, Cara, it's good to see you. Let's get you set up in the guest room."

Joan takes her into the house, up the stairs, to a room that Cara remembers staying in before. Her aunt chatters nervously. "I was just going to start dinner. I'm sure you have homework to do . . . I remember the piles of homework we used to get in high school. I can drive you to the mall if you like, after, or maybe you'd like to take a walk . . . I'm not sure what you like to do."

As if she actually has a choice.

Cara says only, "A walk sounds nice."

That seems to please her aunt. "We've got some pretty great views in the neighborhood. Even just in the backyard."

Joan abruptly stops talking and touches Cara's face, looking at her. She winces at the bruises the fight has left. But then she looks deeper. "You look so much like . . ." There are tears in her eyes and she clears her throat. "You've grown up into such a beautiful young woman. Your father . . ." Her voice catches again. "Your father would be so proud."

All Cara can see is blood. Her aunt seems to be crying tears of blood. She looks away.

Joan brushes at her eyes. "What those boys did . . . it's not right. It's not fair." Her aunt's face becomes distant. "I want you to know I'm sorry I didn't visit more. It was just . . . I just . . ."

Cara knows. There will be no help from her. There never has been.

Patrick openly hates her. He follows her into the hall as she goes downstairs, and whispers "Freak" at her when his mother isn't looking. Cara stops that with a look, but his fury simmers underneath his skin.

"Nobody wants you here, freak."

She smiles and says something under her breath, too low for him to hear. It incenses him, the not knowing.

"What did you say, freak?"

She looks at him steadily, until he shifts uncomfortably.

"Stop it."

She continues to smile, not looking away, as Patrick starts to panic.

"Stop it. Stop it. *Mom!*" he yells, skittering away from her.

Cara turns and goes out through the back door, into the yard. The back of the yard slopes up to a hill overlooking the neighborhood, and she climbs up to the highest point, and sits on the ground, looking out.

Beyond the neighborhood, a quiet subdivision of curving streets and cul-de-sacs, the desert stretches out to infinity.

She breathes in, suddenly so tired she could lie back and fall asleep right here on the grass.

It has been three days since she stopped her medication. The shadows are becoming longer by day and at night the moon whispers to her as it grows. But on the hill, looking out, it is peaceful. The wind murmurs softly, but it is not the dark slithering of *It*.

The desert seems clean and peaceful and safe. She could hide in the desert. She could bury herself in the sand and sleep for a million years . . .

She feels a presence behind her.

She twists around . . . to see Erin standing some distance behind her. She is just a wisp of a girl. Her dark eyes and dark hair, almost black, make her olive-toned skin seem pale.

Erin looks up in the sky. "The moon is up."

Cara is startled to hear her say it. She looks up and realizes Erin is right. Just over the hilltops, she can see the faint white disk.

"Yes."

"But it's day."

"The moon doesn't go away because it's day. It's always there. Sometimes you can see it and sometimes you can't, but it's always there."

Erin looks at Cara and Cara can feel the need in her. She seems cowed by something, scared of her own shadow, something that has nothing to do with Cara's presence in the house. There is a bruised sense about her, without actual bruises. She is so small, and suddenly Cara is afraid for her.

Her aunt's voice comes from the back door of the house, calling. "Erin!"

Even from a distance, Cara can hear the frantic undercurrent beneath her words. Aunt Joan moves quickly up the hill, holding out a hand to the younger girl.

"Don't bother your cousin, sweetheart. Come on inside to play."

Erin looks at Cara. Cara nods at her to go.

As they walk away from her she has to breathe through a rush of anger.

Her aunt does not want her near Erin.

Cara knows she thinks it will happen again. That whatever killed Cara's family, Joan's family, is still out there, that it might come back at any time.

But she also understands that her aunt is afraid of *her*, has always been afraid of her.

She knows she is not *Normal*. But is she really so different?

It seems only that she sees how things are. There is someone in or around the high school who is evil, who wants nothing but to cause pain, torture and death. The skeleton girl is locked away, trapped in a living hell, and the thing that did that to her is walking free.

And people do nothing. Her aunt, Ms. Sharonda . . . they know these things happen, are happening, and they do nothing . . .

She fights another sickening wave of anger.

She knows she cannot go back to the school. She *cannot*. But her aunt is right to be afraid.

She escaped *It* once, as a child, and *It* has been after her ever since. *It* will come for her. As the counselor, as the man in the van . . . or someone completely else. *It* found her at the school and *It* will find her here—

She is breathless with the terror of the thought. She presses her hands into the grass, gasps in, forces herself to inhale.

You're here. You aren't dead. Sit. Be still. Think.

She breathes in . . . and out again, concentrating only on her breath.

The moon continues its slow climb into the sky. And gradually she is able to focus on it.

Out in the daylight. What does it mean?

She sits and watches the neighborhood, the mothers arriving home with kids in their cars.

The cars.

They seem to glow in the afternoon light.

She watches, and waits, and the moon begins to whisper.

After a time she stands and walks down the hill. She walks the curving streets of the quiet neighborhood and looks at the cars from a closer vantage point, with special attention to the Hondas and Toyotas and Acuras. She notices the newer cars are mainly parked in driveways and in garages . . . and that more of the older ones are parked on the street. One of the older ones has another thing about it that is particularly interesting to her.

She takes another slow loop around the block, then goes back to the house.

"Did you enjoy your walk, Cara?" her aunt asks, from the kitchen doorway.

"It was good," she answers.

She has seen what she needs.

Inside she helps Aunt Joan lay out a dinner table just like in shows on TV: place mats, cloth napkins, a centerpiece of flowers. She watches her aunt to make sure she gets the correct placement of flatware, and when she sits, she takes the napkin from the ring and puts it in her lap in the same way that her aunt and cousins do.

Normal.

The smells of spaghetti sauce and broccoli are sharp, too strong without the haze of medication, and she feels her stomach roil with nausea. But she swallows back the sick and eats gingerly.

Across the table, Patrick glares at her, Erin sneaks glances at her in between toying with her food. And Aunt Joan tries to make conversation.

She starts, "How is school, Cara?" and then immediately realizes the absurdity of the question. She looks away from Cara's bruises. "I mean, your classes . . ."

Cara understands the desperate need to hear something *Normal*, and plays along.

"It's a good school. I like Spanish. And Chemistry."

"Mr. Lethbridge says you're an excellent student."

Lethbridge. Another reason she must get away. She doesn't know what it is with the vice-principal, but there is danger there. She feels sick that he is watching her, has been talking about her.

"I'm trying," she says.

Patrick sneers at her and she stares back at him until he looks away.

After dinner she offers to clear the table while Patrick heads for the family room and parks himself in front of the television.

She carries dishes into the kitchen as her aunt flits in and out. Her chance comes when the phone rings, and her aunt goes upstairs to talk.

She begins a quick, furtive search. In a bottom drawer, there is a box lined with blue velvet, with a set of tarnished silver. The carving knife tempts her, but it is too big to conceal easily. But there is a whole set of steak knives shoved in with the more expensive pieces. One of these is deadly sharp and small enough to hide any number of places.

The laugh track of the sitcom her cousins are watching in the other room turns to the raucous music of a commercial, always so much louder than the show. Cara quickly pockets the knife and slides the heavy drawer shut.

As she stands, she has a flash of memory: her aunt's husband, the not-nice one, tinkering with his car inside the garage.

She looks toward the back door that leads into the garage.

Then she opens the lid of the trashcan, pulls out the bag and ties the edges, eases open the back garage door. She steps into the dim garage, standing in the rectangle of light from the kitchen, and holds the trash bag in one hand as she scans the shelving unit.

There is a cabinet with tools, a treasure trove. She puts the trash bag down and helps herself to a screwdriver and flashlight, various thicknesses of wire . . . and then hits pure gold: a packet of clip leads.

She tucks the clips into a pocket, the screwdriver and flashlight into the waist of her jeans, and arranges her shirt over the bulge.

There are footsteps in the kitchen behind, someone coming. She twists around to pick up the bag of trash. As her aunt steps into the garage, all she sees is Cara depositing the bag in the can.

Aunt Joan looks at her. "Well, thank you, Cara, that's very thoughtful."

"You're welcome," she says.

She goes to the guest room that is hers for the night, and slips the knife under her pillow. Step one, completed. Step two will come that night.

ROARKE

Chapter Twenty-Seven

It was late afternoon, and the shadows were long over the hills and valleys of the desert corridor crossing through the reservations at the base of San Jacinto Peak.

Roarke felt the knots inside him unraveling as he headed up through the mountains, with their stunning vistas at every turn.

Again, he found himself gripping the Rover's steering wheel with both hands to negotiate the hairpin curves. And again, though he was almost certain Cara had killed the counselor, he was at a loss to understand how she had managed it. He'd checked, and there was no bus line on the route, now or in the past.

Had she hitchhiked?

And what had compelled her to do it?

He'd always thought, much like Ortiz seemed to think, that it was simply personal: revenge on the counselor for getting her sent up to YA. But did it somehow, somehow, connect to the other two girls?

He tried to put himself in teenage-Cara's mindset.

As events unfolded at Las Piedras High, she must have thought, at least fleetingly, that the Reaper—*It*—was back to get her. How could she not? To have escaped that monster—only to end up in a school being stalked by a sadistic and deadly predator . . .

He felt the same rush of fear for Cara, a sense of urgency . . . the same feeling that had propelled him back on the road.

On one level, that was completely irrational. He knew that whatever had happened sixteen years ago, whatever encounter she may have had with this monster, she had survived it.

But did she really?

Was it whatever happened to her at that school that turned her into what she is?

His thoughts were interrupted by the sudden appearance of the red fuel light on the dashboard. He hadn't seen a single gas station since turning off of 371, and the road he was on crossed straight through tribal lands.

Do Indian reservations have public gas stations? he wondered. *If they don't, how would they feel about a white, obvious lawman who has no jurisdiction on their lands wandering in to borrow a gallon of gas?*

Something stirred in the back of his mind as he thought it. A new thought, something important . . .

But at that moment he rounded a corner and a general store came into view, with a couple of old gas tanks in front.

He pulled in to the drive in front of the fueling island.

Wind rippled the prayer flags hanging above an outdoor patio with picnic tables under oak trees. An unnervingly realistic dinosaur sculpture snarled down from the roof, something between a raptor and a T. rex, glaring balefully at all who dared approach.

Roarke got out of the Rover, removed a gas nozzle from a pump.

As he stood in the wind, waiting for the tank to fill, he saw that the moon was already up, a pale disk in the blue of the sky. He stopped in his tracks, looking up at it.

Wolf Moon. Bitter Moon.

And it was far too close to full for his liking.

It was easy to get mystical, this far out in the wilderness. But the fact was, for each of three months now, the full moon had meant havoc and bloodshed and the brink of death.

The nozzle clicked off as the gas finished pumping.

As Roarke turned back toward the car, he saw an old Native American man sitting on the rough burl bench beside the door of the store, watching him.

Roarke stopped, looking back at him, struck by the ravaged beauty of his face.

What have you seen? he wondered. *Would I even understand if you told me?*

The old man stared back. And then turned his face away, toward the daylight moon.

Back in his Rover, Roarke wound his way down the snakelike road on the other side of the mountain toward Palm Desert.

When he hit the town, he cruised by the Wayfarers Club of Palm Desert, but it was locked up, no cars in the parking lot. He'd called the club and left a message on a voice mail system requesting a return call. He'd have to wait for a callback.

He pulled into the parking lot of the sheriff's station just before five, but didn't go in. He wanted a private conversation with Ortiz. He parked where he had a clear view of the front doors, and waited.

The wind whispered through the feathery mesquite in the planters, and the sun lowered, blood-orange over the desert.

Finally, Roarke saw Ortiz leaving the building, walking out to the side parking lot.

Roarke got out of his car and followed at a distance. He caught up with Ortiz as he was opening the door of his SUV.

The detective's face twisted as he saw Roarke. "You. Again."

Roarke stood his ground and spread his hands. "You're the one who got me out here. Now I'm just finding so much fascinating stuff that I can't stay away."

"What are you talking about?"

"I'm here to get some information on an old case. Laura Huell."

Ortiz's eyes flared. Roarke braced himself for the rage. Then apparently Ortiz thought better of it. "I had nothing to do with that case."

"So you're familiar with it." Roarke took Ortiz's silence as agreement. "Just a few easy questions. Was there any evidence that Laura Huell was sexually assaulted?"

There was a loaded pause before the detective answered. "I have no idea. How would I know?"

"Your department investigated the suicide, didn't it?"

"Someone in the department did. I didn't."

"But the whole department investigated the attack on Ivy Barnes, didn't it?"

Ortiz stared at him, thrown. "What?"

"There was a rape case ongoing at the same time that Lindstrom was at the school. A girl named Ivy Barnes. A man out there raped, blinded, burned, and did his damnedest to kill a fourteen-year-old girl—"

The detective cut him off. "I know the case."

"Was there a Wayfarer connection?"

"Look, I'm not here for your damn—"

Roarke rode over him. "Was there ever a connection to the Wayfarers Club investigated in regard to either case?"

Ortiz took a threatening step forward. "This is bullshit. What the hell are you doing, fucking around in all this?"

Roarke stood his ground. "I want to see the file on Ivy Barnes."

"No. You have no jurisdiction here." The detective clearly relished the denial.

"But you're not the person to ask, anyway, are you?" Roarke said, softly.

Ortiz was silent, seething.

"So why not say that? Why are you so set against me looking into this?"

"Go fuck yourself, *puto*." Ortiz got into the driver's seat and pulled the door shut hard.

"I've already got it." Roarke slammed the copy of Ivy's witness statement against the windshield for Ortiz to see.

Ortiz stared at the statement through the glass, then lowered the driver's window and said the same thing Roarke had said to the nun. "How did you get this?"

"Have you read it? Because I don't think that anyone could read that and not want to move heaven and earth to find the monster that did it. So I'm wondering why, between the two cases, you chose to pursue Cara Lindstrom instead?"

Ortiz's voice was tight. "I work *homicide*. That counselor was murdered—"

"And Ivy was still alive? Only because she was strong enough to fight for her life." Roarke leaned toward the window, fixed on the detective's face. "You knew Pierson attacked Lindstrom, didn't you? He and the boy. You knew it was self-defense. But still, you were out for her. With no evidence. Nothing to back you up. Why?"

Wind rustled through the fronds of the mesquite trees, and the dusk seemed to close around them. And then it dawned, a feeling so cold and so certain that Roarke felt the chill through his body.

"She saw something in you, didn't she? She saw *It.*"

The look Ortiz gave him this time wasn't nasty. It was a killing rage. Somehow he mustered himself. "We're done here." He twisted the key in the ignition.

"What was it? Domestic abuse? Stalking?" Roarke's voice dropped with his own realization. "Or was it rape?"

Ortiz gunned the engine, forcing Roarke to step back as the vehicle careened out of the lot.

Roarke stood in the parking lot feeling the drunken buzz of adrenaline. It had been stupid Neanderthal posturing, the kind he didn't usually indulge in—because it scared him, how good it felt. But it was not entirely without purpose. He *had* seen the detective's face. And he had thrown the gauntlet down. Ortiz knew now that he was investigating, and what he was investigating. The trap was laid, the bait set. He would see what he could catch.

The last exchange was reverberating in his mind.

She saw something in you.

He'd said it on impulse.

But could it be?

Did Cara see something in Ortiz? Did that trigger this hatred in him?

It was an almost preternatural thing to think. It presupposed that Roarke believed Cara could see—whatever you wanted to call *It*. Evil. Wrongdoing. Past crimes or malevolent intent. And that she was seeing it as far back as fourteen years old.

But Ortiz seemed to have pursued her with an uncommon wrath; a zealotry that went far beyond professional duty.

Was that why?

He turned and looked at the sheriff's station. Then he walked toward the front entrance.

What he needed was a name.

Chapter Twenty-Eight

O rtiz had not been the lead detective on the investigation into the counselor's murder. The senior detective's name was Miller, and he was retired, but when Roarke called the number the deputy at the desk had given him, Miller answered the phone, and agreed to meet Roarke at a nearby Mexican restaurant.

Roarke parked in the half-empty lot of a pink adobe-style building with neon palm trees on the roof.

Inside he stopped in the doorway and looked over the restaurant, unnerved.

He was surrounded by skeleton figures: *Dia de los Muertos* dolls, Catrinas in their finery, skeletons painted on velvet . . . bullfighters, card players, musicians, brides. Behind the bar, on the walls, hanging from the ceiling, reflected in the gilt mirrors also hung around the room.

Santa Muerte. Lady Death. Here, too.

Roarke gathered himself and focused. There was an older man sitting by himself in a back booth, and Roarke knew him instantly as former law enforcement. He had a bristly gray beard, bushy eyebrows, wire-framed glasses. His once-muscular frame had gone soft, but he seemed comfortable in his bulk.

Miller stood as Roarke approached, and they shook hands across the table.

"Appreciate you meeting me," Roarke said.

They sat, but before either one of them could speak, a waiter appeared beside the table. "Something to drink, *señor?*"

Miller indicated the margarita in front of him. "They know how to make 'em."

Roarke nodded to the waiter. "Salt, rocks."

When the waiter was gone, Miller picked up his own drink. "So you want to know about Gil Ortiz."

Right to the point. Roarke was fine with that. "I got a strange phone call from him a few days ago. I've talked to him twice and I still don't understand what he's after."

"A phone call about Cara Lindstrom?"

Roarke looked at Miller, surprised. The older man nodded. "I got one of those, too, a few weeks back. My fault she's out there, apparently."

Roarke didn't know if he was feeling relief or apprehension. "He said it was mine."

Miller snorted. "Yeah. Gil was an angry guy. I haven't had any face-to-face contact with him recently, but I'm betting you have?" He eyed Roarke.

"He's angry," Roarke agreed. "Can you tell me about him?"

"I didn't work with him long. Too much of a loose cannon." Miller lifted his glass, took a minute before drinking.

Roarke realized the other man was debating something, and waited, giving him space. Finally, Miller admitted, "I never liked the way he treated witnesses. Or suspects, for that matter. He was a bully. We don't need that kind of person in uniform. Or plainclothes, either."

Roarke's drink arrived. He took a swallow, tasted the bite of tequila, and nodded appreciation before returning to the subject, trying to be as neutral as possible. "He seems pretty convinced that Cara Lindstrom killed that counselor, Pierson."

Miller sounded rueful, a bit defensive. "Well, with twenty-twenty hindsight, that theory might not've been as wacked as it seemed at the time. But at the time—the girl was fourteen and she had alibi witnesses."

"Who?"

"Her aunt and cousin said she was home all night. Plus, how would she have gotten herself there?" Miller shook his head. "Fact is, Pierson was a user. There was crack on the premises. People get killed for that shit. And not by fourteen-year-old girls."

Roarke realized now why Miller had never pursued Cara for the murder. It made sense. But . . .

"Her cousin . . . you mean her cousin Erin?"

"That sounds right. Younger girl. They slept in the same room that night."

Roarke nodded, but he knew that even at nine, Erin would have protected Cara.

The light from the red candle on the table glowed on Miller's face as he looked into his glass. "Maybe I should've pursued it. But Gil was off the rails. He'd split up with his wife, it was nasty. Couldn't get him to stop trash-talking her. He went around all the time like he was going to explode. And this case . . . there was just something off about the way he focused in on the Lindstrom girl. Made it hard to take him seriously. After all she went through . . ." He grimaced. "Tell you the truth—I didn't want anything to do with it."

Roarke understood, too well. He had felt the same thing himself. "Was he ever accused, or disciplined for domestic violence? Any kind of abuse?"

"Not that I ever knew, but can't say it would surprise me."

"Can I ask you—did you work on the Ivy Barnes case?"

Miller flinched. "We all did for a while. Whole department was knocking on doors through half the county, trying to find some lead on the sorry piece of human waste that did it. Worst thing I've ever seen." He stared off somewhere far away.

Roarke pressed it. "Was that case ever connected to the suicide of a girl named Laura Huell? Also a student at Las Piedras High?"

Miller frowned. "Laura Huell? I never heard anything like that. Far as I knew the thing with the Barnes girl was a one-off, someone passing through. There was never any evidence. I hope the guy is burning in hell." He drained his drink and signaled for another.

I hope so, too, Roarke thought. *But hoping isn't enough.*

Roarke sat in his car in the parking lot, looking out at the shadowed mountain range towering over the desert.

Before he'd left Miller, he'd asked if Ortiz was a Wayfarer, and Miller hadn't known. But it was pretty clear from the conversation with the detective that Ortiz was a bad guy.

How much of a bad guy he actually was, Roarke didn't know.

And Franzen might be a bad guy, too.

But those were feelings.

The fact was: when Cara drove out here to Palm Desert that night, she killed Pierson. And Golden Shadows RV Park, where the counselor had been murdered, was a ten-minute drive from the restaurant.

The RV park was nestled at the base of the mountain range, just outside the national park.

Roarke stopped the Land Rover on the sand shoulder of the road, got out of the car, and took his Maglite from the trunk.

It was easy enough for him get onto the grounds; he simply walked in through the gates. There was a manager's trailer at the entrance, but nobody came out of it when Roarke passed by. There was nothing remotely like high security going on, and he guessed there would have been even less sixteen years ago.

It was dark now, but the moon was high and dazzling in the sky. He didn't bother turning on the flashlight; the moon lit his way.

He walked further into the park, through the curved pattern of trailer lots, through well-kept double-wides. The resonant quiet, the feel of the dry wind, was intoxicating. He caught the smell of honey mesquite and desert lavender. The night pulsed with desert life. As he walked, he worked the scenario through in his head.

Pierson had been killed the same night that Laura Huell killed herself.

How could that be a coincidence?

The counselor might have attacked Laura, and like so many girls and women before her, she'd taken her own life. Then, knowing that he had attacked Ivy and now Laura, Cara went straight after him.

It was what the adult Cara would have done.

He found the right lot number: the spot, though probably not the same trailer, where the counselor was murdered. It was a standard double-wide, with a rocker on the tiny front porch and a small cactus garden at the side.

There were no lights on in the home, so Roarke could take his time looking up at the windows, the doors, envisioning Cara breaking in. A slim wraith, all in black, breaching the door, creeping into the trailer . . .

Somehow she had been out here that night. Somehow she had made that drive through Indian territory and the perilous roads, through forest and darkness, to kill this man.

Without realizing, he spoke aloud. "Because he was Ivy's attacker? Or just because he was bad?"

He'd seen the photos. It was too easy to picture the bloodbath it had been: the slash of the knife, the arcs of crimson arterial spray. A fourteen-year-old girl, up against a grown man, almost certainly a child predator. It could so easily have ended another way.

Anger rose in him, that she had been so desperate, so alone, that she would feel this was her only option.

The loneliness she must have felt . . . it was suddenly unbearable.

But it was possible, just possible, that it had all ended here, that night.

Miller's words in the bar came back to him. "*There was never any evidence. I hope the guy is burning in hell.*"

No one had ever been arrested. Maybe it was because the rapist was dead.

Maybe Cara had killed him to avenge the other two girls, and it was over now, a reign of terror and devastation stopped in its tracks by Lady Death.

Roarke's sense of relief at the thought was so overpowering that he halted on the sand, and sent up a fervent wish to whatever force in the universe could hear him.

Let that be it. Please let it be over.

CARA

Chapter Twenty-Nine

S he lies in bed, listening, as first her cousins, then her aunt, then the house falls asleep.

She can feel her own heart thumping loudly in anticipation.

She rises from bed, dresses silently in black jeans and a hoodie, tucks her hair up into a wool cap. Camouflage. This way she can easily be mistaken for a boy. Boys aren't safe from what is out there . . . but they are safer.

Stepping softly to cross the room, she tries the bedroom door, fully expecting to be locked in, to need to pick her way out with the pen clasp. But Aunt Joan is a trusting person. Aunt Joan thinks that wanting people to be good is the same as people being good. The door is unlocked.

Her backpack holds her new treasures: the knife from the kitchen, the flashlight, the screwdriver, wire, and clips from the tool drawer, plus money she has taken from Aunt Joan's bag, and a metal coat hanger from the closet. She moves silently down the stairs, opens the front door a millimeter at a time, as noiselessly as she can manage.

When she steps out the door, the light from the moon is so dazzling that it halts her in her tracks, and she has to stand at the doorstep to get her bearings and allow her eyes to adjust.

It has been three days since she has stopped taking the medication and the world is changing around her. She can hear the sibilant rustling of night. The murmurs are almost distinguishable. With no people, the world is so beautiful: the silhouettes of palms and olive trees in the moonlight, the whispery touch of the wind. The moon is heading for full and she can almost feel the heat of it pulsing in the velvet sky above her. It casts a trail of light down the street. The moon is showing her the way.

She starts down the driveway onto the street.

Being out in the night, on her own, is instantly freeing. She exhales a breath she seems to have been holding for two years.

But she can also feel the urgency. Once she runs, they will be looking for her. The farther she can get tonight, the safer she will be. So she hurries, slipping from shadow to shadow.

On a dark curve of the street she finds the older Honda she noticed on her walk.

She stops beside the passenger door, unfolds the coat hanger, untwists it, hooks the end, and works the wire under the soft padding between the window and the doorframe. It takes some fiddling, but she is patient. Days and weeks and years of sitting in a cell make you patient. Once she gets the hanger inside, she uses the hooked end to pull up the lock button. The lock pops open and she pulls open the door and slips in.

She slides over to the driver's seat and uses the screwdriver to pry off the lower panel of the steering column. With the flashlight she finds the bundle with the wires she needs: red for the battery, green for the ignition, yellow for the starter. She uses the knife to scrape off a tiny bit of the insulation of each wire, and clamps the clip leads onto the exposed metal. Now she clips the battery clip lead and the ignition clip lead together.

The dashboard lights come on, and her heart beats faster. She has not forgotten how to do this.

She puts the car in neutral, then touches the starter clip lead to the other attached leads. There is a spark . . . the starter motor cranks and the engine fires up.

She exhales, feels the rush of adrenaline and pleasure.

She has not been behind the wheel of a car for two years. But she can drive. She remembers everything about it.

Everything.

There was a foster home she'd lived in, some months before she was sent up to YA. Six other kids stayed in the home; their hosts were professional parents, in it for the state subsidy, as so many foster parents were.

She'd felt it before she heard it, the sneaking out. She would lie in bed, feeling the live, awake presence in the house. Then the miniscule sounds: the breath, the step . . . the sound of a lock turned and a door eased open and softly closed. And then always, a minute or two later, the faint sound of a car engine starting up, the sound of the foster parents' old Chevy. She was sure she knew who it was, who made the nighttime journeys. There was a boy, not quite sixteen, rail-thin, with the high cheekbones and sleek black hair of Native American blood. And the mornings after she heard the engine in the night, the black-haired boy always seemed at peace.

So one night she was ready. And she followed, tracing his footsteps.

Easing her bedroom door open. Gliding down the hall in bare feet, her tennis shoes clutched in one hand. Eyes fixed on the front door—

Where she was grabbed by strong, desperate hands, pulled inside the kitchen doorway. And for the second time in her life she felt a knife at her neck.

She was very still, containing her terror at the feeling of the metal on her skin.

"What do you want?" he growled. Black eyes fierce in the darkness.

"I want to go," she said, keeping her voice low and steady.

"Go where?"

"With you."

"I'm not going anywhere." The knife pressed tighter against her flesh.

"I want you to take me. I want you to teach me."

He didn't ask her what she meant. "You're a kid."

"I can still tell."

"Fuck you."

"I'll tell right now." She didn't want to, but she meant it. If you're going to threaten someone, you have to mean it.

His eyes darted to the dark corridor behind them. "You're going to fuck me up."

"You're the one who keeps talking," she whispered.

They stood in the dark, with only the sound of their breathing.

And so it began.

He would put the Chevy in neutral and they'd push the car away from the house before starting it up.

He had a key. He'd managed to steal it from the foster father and make a copy. But he would also teach her that you didn't need a key. As long as you knew the right colors of wires, sometimes all you needed were scissors or a screwdriver, and the right make of car.

She was a fast learner.

She had been watching this for years, every time she had been in a car, every time there was driving on the screen of a television. How the driver shifts the gear and works the pedals with her feet. The right one to go, the left one to stop. Turn the wheel right to go right, left to go left.

She had to sit on his coat, folded up, to see over the steering wheel. But from the moment she grasped the wheel, she knew she was home.

She kept her hands tight on the wheel, her body tense in the seat, and she watched the road and she listened as the boy gave terse orders.

And she pressed the gas pedal down and the car shot forward and she felt a rush of savage exhilaration. She felt alive.

The night. The road stretching out in front of her, a satin ribbon, lit by the moon. The power of the machine under her hands, enclosing her body. The speed of it.

A car is freedom. A car is power. A car is escape.

It is the best memory she has of the time since *The Night*. Open desert roads, pushing the pedal down to the floor. Screeching around corners.

The first time she was on guard the whole time, as she always was with older boys. But he never looked at her that way, never reached to grope her or worse. They would drive half the night, sometimes, fast as the wind, under the stars. Lowering all the windows so the wind rushed through the car, the roar filling up their ears.

Not talking, practically ever. Talking would spoil it.

Once, with the windows down, he screamed, and kept screaming for what seemed like an hour, until his voice was so ragged he could only cough. He didn't say why and she didn't ask. Whatever was in his mind, whatever had happened to him, whatever he was wrestling with—he drove it out, night after night.

It was only a matter of time before they'd be caught, they both knew it, but they couldn't stop.

One morning she woke up and he was gone.

He had not given her the signal the night before. Had shaken his head, a barely perceptible movement when she looked at him across the long, crowded dinner table.

But he had gone, himself.

The next day, the foster father stomped around looking betrayed. The mother looked martyred.

He'd been caught near the Arizona border. Sent away. Grand theft auto. Houston, they'd called him. Or maybe it was Huston. She never knew for sure. Someone called him Eric, once. She never asked where he was sent. There was nothing to be done. The system had swallowed him.

It has been two years since Eric and their midnight rides, but the feel of the car around her, the wheel in her hands, is instant relief. It takes coordination but there is no one on the road, no one for miles. She drives slowly at first, practicing slowing and speeding up. She remembers everything; her body knows what to do.

The temptation is strong to push the pedal down, to go fast, far, as far and fast as she can. Out into the desert, past the desert, out of the state, just to drive and never stop.

But there will be police out on the road and she must not attract attention.

She knows what happens to girls and also to boys who run away. She is fourteen. No one will hire her except to make her do the thing she will die before doing. She will steal what she has to and she will avoid people as much as she can. There will be no more prison. That she has decided long ago. She will not go back. She will not be taken again. They will have to kill her or she will do it herself.

She can do that. If she needs to do it, she will.

ROARKE

Chapter Thirty

Roarke stood beside his Rover, parked on the highway outside the mobile home park, feeling no real desire to get into it.

Drive back to Las Piedras? Find a hotel here? Neither option appealed.

You could go back to the bar and get shit-faced drunk.

Tempting. But probably not the best plan, either.

So he walked.

He had his parka, he had his Maglite, though the moon was bright enough he didn't actually need it.

The highway was deserted, and up ahead was a sign for a trailhead that read: *Revelation Point.* So he took it.

The breeze was cool and dry on his skin and he could still feel the trapped heat of the day rising from the sand as he walked, a pleasingly sensual mix of sensations. He breathed in the silence of the desert, and looked up at the ocean of stars.

As always, his eyes were drawn to the constellation of Cassiopeia. For some reason, it reminded him of her.

You can disappear out there, Cara. You can be free. Let it go. It's time for you to rest.

The dome of sky was vast, the landscape like an alien planet, the towering shadows of the mountains silent giants. He seemed so alone that at first he thought the music was in his mind, a faint memory.

He dropped his head and stared out through the cactus and dunes. Now he could make out the shimmering flames of a bonfire, and the dark shapes of people against it. The music was coming from there.

As he walked out toward the lights, the music became clearer, rippling through the night with a slow, stoned reverb. It was one of those gatherings this area was famous for, a generator party. A desert rock band was playing to a small crowd of people. Some had built nests of blankets and pillows in the sand beside the fire, and gasoline-powered generators provided the electricity for the instruments.

Roarke stopped on a dune, looking down at the show. It seemed out of another time, a gypsy caravan, a troupe of medieval players.

Stoned hipsters, glassy-eyed and swaying. Long-haired young women in flowing multicolored batik wear and fringe. People drinking, dancing, smoking, passing large bottles of water. Beyond the crowd, one reveler was on his knees, throwing up beside a Joshua tree, sure sign of psychedelics kicking in. But there was nothing threatening or violent about the scene, it was instead almost dreamlike.

The music had a hypnotic intensity, and the guitarist was on fire, with a commanding stage presence, enhanced by his look: a muscular build on a slim body, high cheekbones and sleek black hair that hinted at Native American blood.

Roarke stood at the edge of the crowd, listening, relaxing into the music. It was capturing something about the wind, the road, the vastness of open, uncivilized space. The kind of freedom he felt when he was driving.

He began to notice details of the crowd, the symbols and mandalas the young people wore in their clothing, their jewelry, their complicated body art. Native American images, and Mexican ones. The mysticism of the desert, so like the Haight Ashbury mysticism that seemed to draw Cara.

A pretty young woman smiled at him and he smiled back.

Another few songs later, he was sitting on a dune, feeling the music pulsing through the sand beneath him. Someone nearby offered him a Navajo blanket and he started to shake his head, but when the young man held it out again, Roarke took it and settled in.

The night got later and the music got spacier and the crowd started passing around a bottle of tea. Roarke had no illusions about what might be in it, and when his neighbor offered it, he raised a hand to decline. The Bureau had strict rules about drugs.

But you're not in the Bureau anymore, are you? Do you want out for good? Here's your chance, right here. No going back . . .

But after a moment, he passed it on without drinking.

He sat back, and he looked up at the stars, and let the music take him.

CARA

Chapter Thirty-One

The speed is exhilarating. She jams her foot down on the gas pedal, lowers all the car windows. The cold rush of air takes her breath away, makes her gasp, sends her pulse spinning.

She does not know where she will end up. But that itself is freedom. So many roads all over the country. So many places to disappear. Traveling makes you invisible. The roads have names and numbers, and you follow the signs. Highway 371 will take her through the Anza corridor, through the Indian reservations, Cahuilla, Santa Rosa . . . over the Mount San Jacinto mountain range and over to the 10, then far out into the desert.

The moon is so bright she can see as if it is daylight. Dry arroyos and luminous vistas. Boulders as big as houses. Snakelike ocotillo. Paloverde trees, psychedelically bright acid-green in the moonlight amongst the duller green of sage. Bright white trumpet vine.

The scenery is constantly shifting and the remoteness is exhilarating. *It* cannot possibly find her here.

Perhaps she does not need to die.

Even through the rush of driving, she is careful to watch the gas gauge. The indicator was low when she began, but she has driven almost an hour with no gas station in sight. Then around a mountain curve there is salvation: a wood-framed general store with a couple of pumps outside it. She pulls the car to a jerky stop at the concrete island, stares out the windshield into the dark, assessing.

The station store is closed, deserted. Prayer flags flutter on the roof of the shack behind it. A carved, standing wooden bear guards the door and a rusted metal dinosaur snarls from the top of the roof. In a fenced-off patio there are battered picnic tables under the oaks, a barbeque grill and unlit neon beer signs. She can see no one.

She unclips the battery lead from the ignition lead to kill the engine.

The wind is strong, rocking the car; she has to push back against it to wrest the driver's door open. She leans into the gusts as she walks around the car to open the gas hatch.

The old-fashioned pump is locked, but she can pick the padlock—she has done it with Eric, and on a hundred locks since. She does it quickly with her pen-clasp pick, feels the hasp pop open in her hand. She sticks the nozzle into the hole to fill the tank. The smell of gas is familiar. She inhales deeply and the memory is a rush in her ears and in her stomach. Excitement. She could drink it.

She looks up into the vast blackness of the sky. The wind swirls the stars.

The gas nozzle jerks in her hand, clicking off the flow. She replaces it in its cradle and re-locks the padlock. Then she takes a ten from the cash she stole from Aunt Joan's bag and walks to the front of the store, stoops to slide the bill underneath the door.

Something stirs in the darkness and she freezes, heart suddenly racing, eyes searching the shadows.

The wind rustles through dry grass . . . Then she sees him.

A man, slumped on the sidewalk at the side of the station store, wrapped in a dirty blanket, a bottle in a paper bag at his side. His stringy hair is long, gray and black, tied in a ponytail, and he stinks of vomit and piss and alcohol. Asleep or dead, it's hard to tell.

She starts to back up, carefully, silently. The man on the sidewalk lifts his head. A cratered face; eyes like agate, like black flint. The dry wind blows around them.

He says an Indian word: "*Naayéé' neizghání.*"

The voice is crusty, but nothing compared to the crustiness of the man who speaks. He looks thousands of years old. Proud and sad and desiccated. The road map of a lost continent is on his face.

She backs away from him, runs for the car, wrestles the door open, drops inside and locks the door. She fumbles for the starter clip and touches it to the other clips, holding her breath as she does it, willing the connection. The engine sparks to life; she feels the power.

In the rearview mirror, she sees the man still watching her as she guns the car, accelerating into the night.

Behind her, the dinosaur on the roof of the store leaps off and hits the ground with a heavy thud, then clomps off into the desert darkness.

She slams her foot down on the gas pedal, racing the car up the mountain road.

ROARKE

Chapter Thirty-Two

All around Roarke people are dancing, a whole crowd writhing to the sinuous music.

He sees a girl in a vest with an image of a wolf howling at the moon. Another wears a skull mask.

Santa Muerte. Of course she's here.

The music swirls around Roarke, taking on layers: layers of sound, layers of feeling, layers of color. His vision seems suddenly sharper, twenty-twenty dialed up to twenty-ten.

He'd passed on the tea, but he still feels high. The music is like a speeding car . . . blasting down the desert roads, taking him far, far away. Freedom.

The sand seems to be breathing and flowing, as if the whole earth is alive.

He looks up, and sees shooting stars raining down through the constellations. Cassiopeia and Orion, dancing together, melding into one.

The music pulses and pounds, an earthquake of sound, the ground shaking underneath him. In the center pit, the fire leaps up, higher and higher . . .

Fire.

He stares into it, feeling the heat on his face. And suddenly he sees a girl writhing in the flames. Her body blackened, convulsing in agony.

Burning.

No . . .

He staggers to his feet, staring into the bonfire.

The girl is gone. Only logs burn in the flames.

He breathes shallowly against the nausea roiling in his stomach. Then his gaze fixes on the sand beyond the campfire and the horror rises again.

There are girls standing in the sand. Rows and rows of burned girls. Dozens of them. Blackened bodies, arms reaching out, begging.

So many of them.

Help them. Have to help them.

He stumbles forward . . . but is stopped, as someone gently grasps his shoulders from behind.

"Easy, man. It's cool."

I'm not high, he wants to say. *Just seeing visions. Dreaming awake.*

He looks out toward the burned girls, and sees only Joshua trees.

Slowly he sits back down on the blanket on the sand. He looks up at the stars, the jeweled stars hanging above him, shooting in wild arcs.

His heart races, and the music pulses on.

CARA

Chapter Thirty-Three

Her heart is pounding and her body is flooded with sensations. As she speeds around the curves of the foothills, she seems to be driving through the creases and folds of the earth, a million years in the past. The night is alive with sound. The cries of warring native tribes. The snarling and trumpeting of dinosaurs. Time layered over time.

A stagecoach speeds past her on the road, horses kicking up clouds of dust.

She stares at it in wonder, and on some level she is aware that her brain is too overloaded to drive.

She turns her face back forward to the road, and the moon is blinding in her eyes.

The moon . . .

The moon is making her high.

She slows, pulls the car over on the shoulder, and sits still, clutching the wheel, gasping for breath.

Beside her, beyond the road, is a stretch of pure desert: huge clusters of boulders, the size of small houses. An ocean of Joshua trees, with their pitchfork silhouettes, the spiky branches.

She gets out of the car, shakily. The moon is enormous, pulsing and trembling. Standing makes her dizzy.

But the wind is wild, blowing at her, blowing through her, making her clean. She takes great gulps of it, lifts her arms and spins in it, swirling in an ocean of shadows of Joshua Trees. She is free . . .

She stops dead, midspin, as a long shadow steps from behind a boulder. All her blood turns to ice.

It is here. *It* has come for her. Here, in the middle of nowhere, under the moon, *It* will eat her as it ate her sister, her brothers, her mother and father . . .

A scream rises in her throat . . .

The shadow moves out of the dark, and in the light of the moon she sees the Indian from the service station. Not drunk now, but tall and regal.

"Girl," he says, but she doesn't know if it is him speaking or the moon. "You cannot run."

In the moment, it is literally true. She is frozen with terror. She cannot move.

He looks at her with obsidian-black eyes, says a phrase she does not understand: *"Naayéé' neizghání."* But it is his next sentence that rivets her. It is in the same alien language, but she understands every word.

"You have been scratched by evil."

Scratched. The word gives her a full-body chill, and her hand goes to her throat. How can he know precisely what happened to her?

The old man's gaze is relentless. "You must go into the darkness. You must become the darkness."

She has no idea if this is really happening. But she knows it is true. "How?" she asks, not knowing if she has spoken aloud, or in what language she speaks.

"The moon will show you. It is time for you to choose." He raises his arm, pointing to her. *"Fear the wolf . . . or be the wolf."*

She stares at him, and the night pulses around them. Then slowly he fades away.

There is nothing there but a road sign under the moon.

ROARKE

Chapter Thirty-Four

He woke to golden daylight pouring over the sand, as thick and sweet as honey, and the trace memory of trance music, of shooting stars and the exhilarating feeling of motion, of speed and freedom.

He still had the Navajo blanket wrapped around him, and his parka underneath. He was stiff from the cold, and his ears still throbbed from the music; he could feel a headache coming on. But for the moment, he felt more at peace than he had for a long, long time.

Other partyers lay still sleeping around him, cocooned in sleeping bags, huddled together.

He threw off the blanket, got gingerly to his feet. A wave of dizziness came over him at the change in position . . . and in the blinding whiteness of the sunlight, he saw the rows of burned girls from the night before, standing black and still and entreating on the pale sand.

Then his eyes adjusted to the light and he saw the truth: rows and rows of Joshua trees, their branches outstretched like limbs.

And yet the image felt as real to him now as it had in the night.

He breathed in shakily, tried to calm his racing pulse.

A voice spoke from behind him. "You okay?"

Roarke turned to see the slim black-haired guitarist from the band. The other band members were walking away across the sand, carrying their instruments, headed back toward what the world called civilization.

Roarke answered, "Yeah. I'm fine."

The guitarist stood his case in the sand and nodded out toward the radiant rising sun, the pristine calm of the desert. "Whatever else there is, there's this, right?"

Roarke looked at him, struck by the thought. "Yes," he said, and added, "Thanks for the music." The words were formal, and made him feel old, but the guitarist nodded solemn thanks.

One of the other musicians turned and called back. "Hey, Eric, you comin' or what?"

The guitarist looked at Roarke. "Need a ride somewhere?"

"I'm good."

The guitarist gave Roarke a small salute, and trudged through the sand toward his bandmates.

Roarke turned and looked back out toward the Joshua trees.

And he knew.

Instead of following the band back out toward the road, he moved away from the other sleepers, and climbed a sand dune to sit at the top.

He stayed there for some time, lifting handfuls of sand and letting the grains slip through his fingers, breathing the desert air and listening to the sounds around him: the scrabble of lizards on rocks, the call of birds, the rustle of jackrabbits in the brush. Time seemed to stop and everything seemed hyper-clear.

His phone buzzed in the pocket of his parka.

It was a moment before he reached for it. Because he knew it was Singh. And he knew what she was going to say.

He clicked on to hear the distinctive voice.

"I am sorry to call so early."

He was short of breath answering. "It's fine. I'm up. I've been up."
He was already feeling the buzz of anticipation.

She didn't waste words. "I could find no report with any evidence
that Laura Huell was raped. There was never a rape kit taken. The coroner ruled suicide: she cut her wrists and bled out. The official cause of
death was exsanguination."

That wasn't what Roarke had expected. "Where did she do it?"

"She was found in the bathroom of her parents' home."

Roarke had a sudden, unwelcome vision of the scene: that innocent
girl, slumped on a tile floor in a pool of crimson blood . . .

"There is no mention by the coroner of scarring or bruising that
could have indicated previous sexual assault. However, there is no mention that the coroner was specifically looking for such signs, either."

Maddeningly ambiguous. Some departments didn't see rape even
when they were looking for it. So in a situation where rape wasn't even
mentioned as a possibility . . .

On the other end of the connection, Singh continued. "A rape kit
was collected for Ivy Barnes. There was never a match to any other DNA
in the CODIS database. But as you know . . ."

She didn't have to finish. Even when a rape was reported, and
reported in time for DNA evidence to be collected, it was fairly rare
for the DNA to actually be tested, even more rare for it to be entered
into CODIS.

"As for the matches to previous or subsequent crimes: there were
no close matches to the attacker's MO in California, so I broadened the
search to the entire US. I found two cases in which young high school
girls were abducted and attacked in the same manner, and threatened
with burning, though no actual burning occurred."

Roarke felt a jolt of adrenaline. Singh continued.

"Those attacks took place in 1997, in Miami, and in 1999, in
Phoenix. Both these girls were abducted into a panel van by a single
assailant while walking to school early in the morning, and taken to

some unknown location several miles away, where the assaults occurred. The age of the victims corresponds to Ivy's and Laura's. There were never any viable suspects in either case."

Roarke was electrified. *That's a hit. Definitely a hit. But those were both before Ivy. Nothing after?*

Singh wasn't finished. "Then I submitted the details from each of those cases into ViCAP." She paused slightly, and Roarke had a sudden, chilled feeling. Singh continued softly. "Starting in the year 1996 I came up with seven more instances of rapes with a similar MO and victim pool: high school girls of thirteen to fifteen years of age who were abducted into a panel van by a single assailant while walking to school early in the morning, and all of them hooded or blindfolded in some way. Each of these vans was described as clean, well-maintained, with uncovered metal flooring inside, and empty. There were several different colors described, including white, dark blue, beige, and black."

Roarke looked out over the rows of Joshua trees, and for a moment, saw his vision of the night before: rows and rows of burned girls, stretching out into the desert.

"Where?" he asked, his mouth dry as dust.

"All over. Baltimore, Chicago, Dallas, Atlanta, Orlando. There is no pattern that I can see to the states in which these attacks took place except that they are almost as far removed from each other as is possible to be. It is also notable that these are quite large cities, although of course there would be more reported rapes per capita in large cities than in smaller towns. I found other incidents, including three in which girls were abducted into vans while walking to school, whose faces were also covered during the attacks. But in those cases there were multiple assailants, likely gang members. They do not appear linked."

Roarke's mind was racing. *Nine more, then, plus Ivy. Ten attacks. And that's just what Singh was able to find.* Only a tiny fraction of reported rapes were indexed in the CODIS system, and the vast majority of rapes were never reported at all.

It wasn't the counselor, he thought. And then that realization was eclipsed by a much more urgent question.

"When was the last one?"

Singh's voice was soft. "Last year."

"He's still out there," Roarke said, not realizing he'd spoken aloud until Singh answered—

"Yes. And there is another, perhaps more interesting linking factor." Singh paused, and Roarke stopped breathing for just a moment, waiting for what she would say. "All of these nine attacks occurred in the month of January."

Roarke stared out over the desert, jolted.

That sure as hell ties the rapes together. Except . . .

"The attack on Ivy was in June," he said aloud.

"Yes," Singh said. "And there are other differences. The assault on Ivy was the most severe, the only one that involved actual burning. It took place in a much smaller town, compared to all the others. And yet . . ."

"You found the others with the search criteria from Ivy's witness statement," he finished for her.

"Exactly so," she agreed.

They were both silent for a moment.

"The DNA," Roarke began.

"It is not possible to compare DNA in any of these cases, or to the DNA evidence taken from Ivy Barnes, because none of the rape kits for the other victims were ever processed."

Roarke had to sit for a moment with that.

None *of the other rape kits had been processed?*

Comparing DNA evidence from the rape kits should have been the easiest thing in the world to do. The evidence had been collected. The technology was there. A national database existed to enter the data into, and results should have been almost instantaneous.

Should have been.

In reality, hundreds of thousands of rape kits sat untested in police and crime lab storage facilities across the country. An unconscionable backlog. All of that evidence that could be used to put serial rapists away, as well as exonerate innocent men—sitting on shelves, year after year, while 98 percent of rapists go free.

He had to hold down his fury to focus on what Singh was saying.

"At the beginning of business hours I will submit requests for the rape kits that were collected from the nine attacks I have identified in my search and inform the local police departments that we are re-opening these cases on the basis that there are juveniles in potential danger. I will have our own lab process and do the comparisons to see if these attacks are linked."

There's only one problem with that, Roarke thought, with a surge of unease. *It's going to take time, and it's late January* now.

Singh added, "We must hope that the evidence has not degraded and is still testable. However, Ivy's rapist was a secretor, of blood type B positive." She meant a person whose blood type antigens could be found in their body fluids. "So if the body fluid samples in the kits can be typed, we may be able to immediately eliminate or focus on suspects by blood type comparisons, without having to wait for DNA testing."

It was a small positive, something at least.

"Meanwhile I have collected all the police reports for these assaults and have scanned and sent them through."

"Hold on . . ." Roarke clicked over to check his inbox but found he had not received emails since last night. "I'm out of range. I'll look at them ASAP."

"As for the record checks on Melvin Franzen and Principal Lethbridge, both have been married only once; Lethbridge for eighteen years, Franzen for thirty-five. Franzen's wife died four years ago, and Lethbridge is still married. Neither man has a criminal record. Both were questioned in the early stages of the investigation into the attack on Ivy, and alibied out. But it is interesting that you asked about both of them. They have the same alibi. Each other."

Roarke heard alarm bells in his head.

"Both men were at the high school, attending the Palmers Club meeting that Ivy never made it to. But I do not see how either of them could have been part of the attack. At the time Ivy Barnes was abducted, they were running the club meeting. According to the police interview, there were seven students also present at the meeting. And then Lethbridge and Franzen were at their respective jobs during the day, over at least part of the time that attack took place."

Maybe so, Roarke thought grimly. *But it seems pretty damn convenient to me.*

"In any case, Ivy reported only one assailant," Singh said, and Roarke realized she was right.

He searched his mind for a moment, and remembered. "I'm going to need another of those background checks, on a detective in the Riverside Sheriff's Department: Gilbert Ortiz. Anything you can find. Criminal charges brought and dismissed, marital difficulties . . ."

"Gilbert Ortiz," Singh repeated, and Roarke heard the clicking of her fingernails against a keyboard. Then she spoke again, more slowly. "In reading through the reports of these attacks it struck me . . . of course with your background you would know better than I—"

Roarke was instantly alert. "What are you thinking, Singh?"

"These rapes do not all seem like the same assailant to me."

"Why?"

She hesitated. "I believe when you read the reports you will see what I mean."

He nodded, as if she could see him. "All right. Thank you."

"I will update you as things progress."

And she was gone.

Roarke lowered the phone, and looked out over the Joshua trees, black silhouettes against the white glare of the sun.

Twenty years of rapes. All over the US. Undetected. Unprosecuted. *All in January. This month.*

The thought shot him to standing.

No time to lose.

He turned and started off across the sand, toward the road.

Singh clicked off the phone and put it down thoughtfully. She left the partition that served as her office, and walked into the living area of her loft space.

Epps was already in the kitchen, already making coffee in his beloved Nespresso machine. He stood at the counter dressed in pajama bottoms, barefoot and bare-torsoed, as lithe as a cat. She was as ever moved by the sight of his body, the physical expression of human form that he represented. Beauty, power, life.

He looked at her inquiringly. "Was that—"

"Yes."

Epps shook his head. "What the hell is he up to?"

It was a good question, a mystery.

"I believe it is something he must do," she told him. "Something that must be done."

He handed her a cup of tea and kissed her.

She smiled at him, then went to her meditation room and closed the door. Inside, she knelt at the altar, struck a long match . . . and lit candles for the dead girls, the violated girls, and for all the girls still in danger.

CARA

Chapter Thirty-Five

S he wakes with an image of a wolf in her head.

She is in the bed in her aunt's house . . .

. . . and is instantly aware that there is another presence in the bed. She stiffens, jerks up . . .

Then she realizes Erin has crawled into bed with her.

She lies there with her young cousin beside her: small, dark, breathing steadily in sleep. Outside, the sky is just beginning to lighten to dawn. Her limbs are strangely sore. But she feels calm, calmer than she has felt in a long, long time.

She is not sure if she has been dreaming, or if any of the night's events have even happened at all. But a voice lingers in her head:

"Fear the wolf, or be the wolf."

She rolls over onto her side, and is instantly asleep.

◆　◆　◆

When she wakes again, it is because the fine hairs on her arms are prickling . . . the feeling of danger.

She is alone in bed, and it is long past noon. She can tell by the light filtering in through the blinds.

She focuses on what woke her: the sound of a car running its motor in the driveway. There is the sound of the engine shutting off, and then there are heavy footsteps on the concrete drive, two sets of them. Men. The doorbell chimes below.

She rises from the bed, crosses to the window, and looks through a crack in the blinds, down to the driveway. Outside in the drive there is a black-and-white SUV, a police vehicle. *Riverside County Sheriff's Department* is stenciled on the side.

Downstairs in the front hall she hears the sound of the front door opening, and then voices. Her aunt, and a male voice.

She moves noiselessly to the bedroom door to listen.

"Joan Trent?" the voice asks, implacable.

"Yes, what—"

"I'm Detective Miller, Riverside County Sheriff's Department. This is Detective Ortiz. Is your niece here?"

"My niece?" Her aunt's voice is faltering.

"Your niece, Cara Lindstrom. We were informed that she's staying with you."

"Yes. Yes, she's here. What is—"

"Would you check for me, please." It is not a request.

There is a pause, and then her aunt calls, "Cara!"

She opens the guest room door and comes out of the room, wearing the high-collared shirt and leggings that she has been sleeping in, her hair unbrushed. She goes to the end of the hall and looks down the stairwell.

Two men stand behind her aunt. The older one is stocky, wearing wire-rimmed glasses. He has bushy eyebrows, a bristly gray beard. The younger one is muscular, darker, and unsmiling. She knows he is trouble the minute she sees him. He seems to be just skin stretched tight over a boiler about to explode.

He looks up the stairwell—and is obviously startled to see her. She gives him nothing.

The older one, Miller, is first to speak. "Cara Lindstrom, we're with the Riverside County Sheriff's Department. We'd like to talk to you for a moment."

She walks slowly down the stairs and stops some distance from them. She keeps herself very still as she looks from the detectives to her aunt and then asks, plaintively, "Is this about the Reaper?"

Her aunt gasps. Cara sees the older detective flinch, and is glad. She wants them thinking of the child she was, the poor little girl who survived the slaughter of her family. She wants every advantage pity can buy her. She has the strong feeling she's going to need that.

Aunt Joan looks to the detectives. "Is it?" she asks, faintly.

"No, it's not," the younger one says. Ortiz. His voice sounds too loud in the hall.

"There's no news," Cara says with no inflection. Letting the words do the accusing.

"I'm afraid not." The older one sounds defensive. *Good.*

Ortiz wants to glare at her, but is too conscious of her aunt there. Still, his anger radiates from him.

"He's still out there," Cara says, and draws into herself. Not quite a shudder, but the feeling of one.

"We . . ." the older detective starts, and then she can see him decide to take control of the conversation. "We're here to talk to you about Mr. Pierson."

She forces herself to stay quiet, not to let anything show on her face.

"Your group home counselor from Palm Desert. Have you seen him since you've been out of YA?"

She crosses her arms on her chest, defensively. It is not entirely an act. "No."

"Are you sure?" Ortiz demands. Miller shoots him a look, as if he has spoken out of turn.

Cara replies faintly, "I'm sure. Why would I want to see him?"

"You haven't been out to Palm Desert?"

She lets herself look confused. "I'm not allowed to do anything on my own."

Miller smiles. "Those are the rules. But there are ways around the rules . . ."

She looks him straight in the face. "I'm not going to do anything that gets me sent back."

Miller nods. "Fair enough. We just need to know where you were last night."

She glances toward Aunt Joan, makes her voice bewildered. "I was here."

Miller turns to her aunt. "Was she?"

Now Aunt Joan looks confused, and apprehensive. "Where else would she be?"

Ortiz speaks again, abruptly. "Has your car been driven?"

"What?"

Cara sees Miller is about to speak, but Ortiz steamrolls over him. "Is your car here?"

"The car is in the garage," Aunt Joan says. "Why?"

The word is barely out of her mouth when Ortiz demands, "We'd like to see it."

Aunt Joan answers faintly. "This is very strange . . ."

A small voice comes from behind. "She was here."

Aunt Joan and the detectives turn to look. Erin stands in the doorway of the kitchen in a T-shirt and jeans, small and dark and steady. "I had a bad dream. I went and slept with Cara." She looks at the detectives. "She was here."

Aunt Joan nods, looking relieved. "It's true, I found Erin in Cara's bed this morning."

"She was here all night?" Ortiz demands of Erin.

Aunt Joan bristles protectively. "Now look, you can't talk to my—"

"All night," Erin says.

Aunt Joan turns to the detectives. "There you are. Is there something else?"

Cara can see Ortiz is about to explode, but Miller gives him a cold look and Ortiz shuts his mouth, holding himself back.

The older detective turns back to Aunt Joan. "No, that's all we needed to know. Thanks for your time."

Ortiz stares straight at Cara. *Later,* his eyes promise. She looks back blankly. He pushes back through the front door, following Miller out.

Her aunt closes the door behind them slowly, before she turns to Cara. "What was that about?" She sounds more nervous than angry.

Cara shakes her head and gives her aunt a helpless look. "I guess something to do with the thing at school? Maybe Ms. Sharonda will know."

"Maybe," her aunt says, worriedly. She glances toward the window at the sound of the SUV starting up outside. "It's past two. You should get dressed."

Cara goes upstairs to the guest room and closes the door behind her.

So it *was* real, last night. Not a dream. Real. The moon. The car. The old Indian.

All of it.

She lies back on the bed and lets herself remember.

In the end, it had been easy. The sign said **PALM DESERT** and it led her straight to him. The moon showed her the way. The light was a path.

There was the drive over the mountain, and down the winding rattlesnake of a road toward the valley. There was the trailer home park at the base of the mountains, right off the highway, and another sign that said **GOLDEN SHADOWS PARK**.

Everything is aligned in her favor.

The mobile homes, all dark; no one at the windows, on the porches, on the paths. So easy to move silently through the night. The moon lights up the trailer park like a stage set, so she can find the unit she seeks.

There is the cheesy lock on the fiberglass front door that a baby could pop open with a plastic card. It takes ten seconds to manipulate it, and then she is easing open the door.

Inside, she becomes the dark.

The sour smell surrounds her. Unwashed dishes. Spilled beer.

The kitchen is the first room, and there are knives in a butcher block stand right on the counter so she doesn't even have to use the one she has brought from Aunt Joan's.

She moves down the short hall toward the bedroom.

The smell there is as she remembered, the stale bleach stench of sex. *It* is sprawled on the bed, sedated, semi-paralyzed by the counselor's drinking, possibly drugs, too.

Still, *It* wakes when *It* feels her coming. *It* knows her.

It glares up at her, pig eyes full of hate. The same look *It* had when *It* came through the door of her bedroom two years ago. When *It* held her down and tore at her clothes, and she kicked out in such rage and connected with soft flesh.

She had the rage, then. But now she has the knife.

She knows exactly where to put it, because she has felt a blade in her own neck. She knows, has felt, how effortlessly sharp steel cuts through skin and tissue and veins. Even now she can feel it, how close the blade came to the pulsing tube of her carotid.

Close.

But not close enough.

She does not miss.

It screams and screams and writhes and hisses. But mainly, *It* bleeds. Blood gushing from the counselor's neck, spraying the walls in pumping arcs, until the spurting becomes a gurgling, and then a trickle, and then stops. And the counselor is dead and finally *It* slips away too.

She stands shaking in the dark, breathing through the copper stink, barely able to stay upright. But it is not fear she feels.

This man, this thing, that she has been afraid of for so long, was after all nothing but soft flesh, a fragile layer of skin containing not even a bathtub's worth of blood. Six quarts. Twelve pints.

The monster may have used him as a shell, but it is a very weak vessel. People think she is just a girl, a little girl, but she is alive and he is dead. As dead as he can be.

Fear the wolf or be the wolf.

There is a humming in her head: the lightness of exhilaration.

I am the wolf.

She sits up on the bed in her aunt's guest room, then stands.

There isn't much to pack, now less than yesterday. The clothes she wore last night were discarded in a Dumpster miles away. Into a different Dumpster went the things she took from the house: the knife and the wallet on his dresser, less the money in it.

Long before dawn, the car she used was back on the street she had taken it from, the panel back in place on the steering column, concealing the peeled wires. The owner will find the car locked and the engine will start. Without any obvious signs of a break-in, it may be days, weeks, before anyone realizes the car has been tampered with, if ever.

She does pack the screwdriver and the flashlight, though. And the clip leads. She will have to hide them away for safekeeping, but having them is almost as good as having a car.

She strips the bed in the guest room and neatly re-makes it with fresh sheets from the closet.

Now she goes out to the garage to put the used sheets in the washer. She turns on the machine to the longest, hottest cycle and adds bleach to the water as well as laundry soap, to ensure that any traces of her night journey go down the drain.

Perhaps she should feel something: remorse, fear, guilt, shame. She feels none of those things, only a lightness, and a sense of . . . she does not even know what to call it. Peace, maybe. Accomplishment. Purpose.

The monster that was the counselor is no more. There is no shame in that. And she will be able to tell them now. Laura. The skeleton girl.

The monster is dead.

Upstairs again, she replaces the money she took from her aunt's hand-bag, supplementing the ten she spent for gas with a bill from the counselor's wallet. She gets her backpack from the guest bedroom and goes downstairs to the living room, where her aunt is vacuuming. Joan turns off the machine and looks at Cara, standing with her backpack in hand. "I want to go back to school," she says.

She pretends not to see the relief that lights her aunt's face. But that expression is replaced with a conflicted concern.

"Now, Cara," her aunt says gently. "Those boys could've really hurt you. I want to make sure you're safe—"

"They're bullies. They're nothing. I'm not afraid of them."

"Are you sure?" Aunt Joan asks cautiously.

"I'm not going to miss school because of them."

Her aunt is looking at her with . . . respect is not the word. It looks more like fear. "That's very grown up of you," she says faintly.

I am the wolf, Cara thinks.

"I can go any time you're ready," she says.

As Cara walks out to the car with her aunt, Erin is watching her. Cara sees her standing in the front doorway.

The two girls look at each other across the distance. Then Cara opens the passenger door of the car and gets in.

Back in Las Piedras, Aunt Joan drops her off in the circular drive of the group home. Cara walks past the palm trees, the dry fountain with the angel. As she brushes past the fountain, she stoops quickly to hide a package in the dirt and dry leaves in the basin: a package containing the flashlight, the clip leads, and the knife.

When she stops into the front office, Ms. Sharonda pauses from the work she is doing at her desk and looks her over. Her face is strange. Angry first, and then resigned.

"It's not going to work out there," Cara says.

Ms. Sharonda nods. Nothing to say about it. Kids are returned to group homes all the time.

"I'm going back to school tomorrow," Cara adds.

That provokes a flicker of surprise from the director. "Well, Eden, your bed is empty. So go on ahead." Ms. Sharonda returns to her paperwork, but Cara remains standing in the doorway until she looks up again.

"It's Cara," she says. "You can call me Cara, now."

Ms. Sharonda frowns. She takes another, deeper look at Cara. After a moment she nods once, warily, "All right. Cara."

Cara turns away and goes to her room.

At night she stands in the med line and takes her medication. In the bathroom she gags it up.

She won't be taking it, ever again. She is just beginning to see.

ROARKE

Chapter Thirty-Six

After a brief stop at a copy center to make hard copies of the reports Singh had sent and buy supplies, Roarke drove straight back to the Mission. No shower, just a quick wash and change of clothes in a gas station restroom. He knew he looked the worse for wear, but he couldn't wait to talk to the nun.

In her office, Mother Doctor poured him coffee, eyeing him with a knowing look. "Rough night?"

Not as rough as all of this is going to get, he thought. He put the cardboard box of police reports he'd printed out on her desk.

She looked startled. "You came up with all of that overnight?"

"I have a brilliant analyst on—" He'd almost said my team. He settled for, "On the case. She's the one who turned all this up."

He quickly filled her in about the other rapes Singh had uncovered.

Mother Doctor listened, getting more and more still. "Dear God. *Nine* more . . ."

Roarke knew the real truth. "Those are just the ones that she found. That were reported to begin with. It's impossible to say how many we're talking about."

"Dear God," she said again. And then after a moment, "Are you sure that they're connected, though? Abduction into a van isn't . . . well, it's not that unusual, is it?"

She was too right. Vans were the preferred vehicle of sexual predators everywhere. Portable torture chambers.

He nodded at her in acknowledgment. "It's not unusual on the surface, no. But there are too many other points in common. And it's the January date that makes it almost certain. Someone is traveling in January, renting a van, and hunting for lone girls on their way to school early in the morning."

He looked at her. "Can you think of any reason these attacks would take place in January?"

The nun frowned. "Something to do with the school calendar? Or were they three-day weekends, perhaps? Martin Luther King, Junior Day?"

"That was the first thing Singh checked." It had been in the written summary she'd sent. "It wasn't, and it couldn't have been. All the victims were abducted on their way to school. It was part of our search criteria."

"When was the last attack?" she asked. The same thing he'd asked Singh.

"Last year."

"In January," she said, and glanced at the calendar on her desk. He couldn't see it, but he knew the date. January 24.

"Exactly. January. I don't like it." It felt like they were racing a ticking clock. "This is an active, sadistic serial rapist. They don't stop. They never stop."

"But, Roarke . . . if these rapes happened all over the country . . . you have no idea where to start, do you? Every one of these attacks took place in a different city. He may not live anywhere near here."

Roarke realized why he had come straight to the Mission. He needed a sounding board, and she had a mind like a steel trap, this woman. They were thinking along parallel tracks.

"Except I keep thinking he does," he told her. "Or at least, he did."

"Why?" she asked.

"Because Ivy is the epicenter."

She tilted her head inquiringly. He stood, unable to sit still.

"Every single one of the other corresponding rapes has taken place in a big city. Not just a big town or a small city: a *big* city. Which makes me think it's possible—possible—that Ivy is the anomaly. The rapist had a schedule and a very clever, calculated plan to give him the maximum cover. But in this instance, for whatever reason, he couldn't wait, snapped, and did something closer to home. And much more out of control."

"And then there's Laura Huell," Mother Doctor said.

He looked at her, surprised . . . but not really. "Yes, exactly, Laura Huell. She was visiting Ivy, and she killed herself. So she may have been attacked. Or she may have seen something. The confluence of those two things . . . just speaks of something closer to here."

And then there's Cara. The fact that Cara was here seals the deal.

"What can I do?" the nun said simply.

"What I need to do is a timeline."

"I can give you a space to work here, if that would be helpful."

The nun seemed to have read his mind. The truth was, he was sick of his expensive but impersonal and claustrophobic hotel room. To go back there after the wild beauty of the desert seemed unbearably confining. Add to that the fact that he was slightly suspicious of Devlin. And he had a feeling he would need to talk to Mother Doctor again before the day was out.

"It would, actually," he admitted.

"Come."

He followed her out the back door again and into the garden, past the mission bell in its stone arch.

They passed through the plaza area and through another wooden door in the high wall. Outside the wall there was a grove of old oak, willow, and olive trees. In the midst of the trees was a stone-and-mortar cottage.

It looked ancient, but solid enough on the outside. When the nun opened the door and they stepped inside, Roarke was pleasantly surprised to find a minimalist but spotlessly clean interior: a room dominated by a long wood plank table, some shelving, and bare walls with a few cutout windows. There was a small kitchen area and smaller cubicle of a bedroom, painted the same white, with a cut-out window in the thick wall. The whitewashed surfaces gleamed and gave the place a sense of calm and light.

"There should be coffee in the cupboard, there. And Wi-Fi, naturally." Mother Doctor wrote out a password. "Have a shower if you like. No implication that you need one, of course."

Roarke gave her a rueful look. "No, of course not. Thank you."

"I have consultations until noon, but I'll be here for anything you need." She turned to go, then turned back, frowning.

"The police here never found anything on the man who attacked Ivy. But the information was right there, in your ViCAP system: the three assaults previous to Ivy, and the six since. How is it that you were able to turn up nine more rapes, and no one else was?"

Roarke shook his head, felt the anger again. It was a long, and heartbreaking story.

Out of eighteen thousand police agencies in the United States, only about fourteen hundred participated in the ViCAP system. Far less than one percent of violent crimes were ever reported to the database. ViCAP was supposed to revolutionize law enforcement, especially in regard to sexual assault cases. It still hadn't happened.

He gave her a partial answer. "If you really want to know, I can tell you. Many reasons, including that the system doesn't automatically compare new cases to old ones. It's a huge deficiency. Singh knows how to manipulate the database. She filters information and re-enters it. She works with it."

If only everyone else did.

The nun glanced at the watch hung around her neck. "I want to know more. I need to go. We'll talk."

When the nun had left, Roarke helped himself to the shower, standing under blissfully hot water, washing away the desert grit.

Then he fetched the rest of his files and the office supplies he'd bought from the car, brought them into the gate house, and got to work.

First he used the blank expanse of the wall to create a calendar of Post-its.

He laid out one complete January calendar for the month that Cara had been in Las Piedras: five rows of weeks, thirty-one days—and used blue Post-its to mark the dates of the significant events of the month: Cara/Eden's arrival in Las Piedras, Laura Huell's suicide, the murder of the counselor, and Ivy Barnes' death.

He stood for a moment looking at the Post-it labeled COUNSELOR MURDERED IN PALM DESERT, and spoke to Cara in his head.

So you killed the counselor that night. But it didn't work, did it? It didn't end things. Good riddance to a bad man, but he wasn't the one. He wasn't this *one.*

Another significant date occurred to him: the burning of the Wayfarers Club.

It had burned to the ground the night before Ivy had died.

"Tell me those things aren't related," he said aloud.

He made another Post-it for the burning of the club. And now that he had the blue Post-its up in place on his calendar, he could see clearly: all five events had taken place within the span of two weeks.

And there had been no corresponding rape reported in that month, not in any state in the US that Singh had found. That didn't mean there hadn't been one, somewhere. But it was interesting.

Next, he focused on the information Singh had sent him from the police reports. First, he simply listed the dates of the attacks.

On a second wall he made a second timeline, using twelve Post-its across in a straight line, and then repeating that line twenty times, twenty lines of twelve squares, to represent twenty years. He wrote a Post-it for each year, starting with 1996, to label each line.

Next he wrote the victim names and dates of the rapes that Singh had compiled on orange Post-its and put them up in the corresponding years: January 1996, 1997, 1998, 1999, 2004, 2008, 2011, 2014, 2015. For June 1999 he wrote on a red Post-it to mark the attack on Ivy.

Now, finally, he took up the reports to read them.

After reading through all nine, he was so agitated that he had to get out of the cottage.

He stepped outside and took a walk along the hillside, through the olive grove, looking down on the valley. The desert hills rolled gently down to the town, dotted with their huge boulders. He could smell the pungent scent of sage. Some bird suddenly took flight from the brush, a wild flurry of wings . . . and then there was silence again.

His thoughts stilled, and focused.

He had spotted what Singh had, about the reports. She was right: it didn't sound like a single attacker at all.

There were two of them.

CARA

Chapter Thirty-Seven

The next morning, after her first dreamless sleep in years, she is back on the group home minibus, rumbling past the horse ranches toward Las Piedras High. The day is cloaked in chilly fog; white mist swathes the hills. Winter seems to have arrived at last.

She pays no attention to the weather. She is electric with anticipation.

She has no idea what she will be walking into. Whether Martell and his jock friends will be there, and gunning for her. She almost hopes they will be. Because she knows something they don't. The voice is in her head, now.

"Fear the wolf or be the wolf."

She is expecting to have to fight. She knows that she will fight.

What she finds is far, far worse.

From the moment she walks onto the quad, she knows something is horribly wrong.

Through the fog drifting in the quad, she sees huddled clusters of students. Not the usual, casual cliques. People are talking in whispers. There is crying and shaking.

A pile of flowers and stuffed animals has grown around the center planter. Cards and ribbons laid down . . . as if on a tombstone.

It can't be.

"No," she says.

People look up, turn to her. She has spoken aloud. "*No*," she says to the watching faces, and sees people flinch back.

She twists around to face the closest group, a cluster of girls. "What happened?" she says aloud.

There are murmurs. The words, "Killed herself."

Cold fear in her stomach now. "*Who?*" she says, so loud now that everyone around her turns to look.

But she does not wait to hear the answer. She doesn't need to. She knows.

But I killed It. It's *dead.*

"Dead," she says aloud. A passing group of girls looks at her nervously. She turns away from them . . .

Across the quad, she sees the vice-principal, standing at his post outside the administration building.

He catches her gaze, looks back at her, unsmiling.

She forces herself to move away from the planter, out of the quad, first walking, then running, her face hot, buzzing.

She finds Devlin before first bell, in an upstairs hall outside the boys' bathroom. She advances on him, backing him into a side corridor. She sees guilt in his eyes. They both know why. He was there, when his road dog Martell and the wolves attacked her. He stood by and did nothing. They both know he is a coward. She has no time for his shame. She has no time for any of these things.

"What happened to her?" she demands.

"Who?" he says stupidly. She nearly loses it then, and he must see her fury, because he flinches, with actual fear.

Good, says the voice in her head. *Let him be afraid. Let them all be afraid.*

She gestures blindly toward the wall, in the direction of the quad, that hideous pile of offerings.

"Laura Huell?" he asks. "They say she killed herself."

"Why?" she says, and hears the tremor in her voice.

"I don't know. Fuck. How should I know?"

She walks in a circle, unable to hold still. "When?"

"We heard about it yesterday."

The same night. The same night.

He is staring at her, bewildered . . . and nervous. "What same night?" He takes a step back, watching her with something like alarm. She realizes she has been pacing and possibly talking to herself. She does not know how much she has said.

"How did it happen?" She makes her voice harsh, to keep it from breaking.

"I don't know. No one ever tells us anything. Look, I'm sorry—" He reaches, touches her arm.

She wrenches away from him. "*You're* sorry. Why?"

"Because it's sad. She seemed . . . like a good kid. Why wouldn't I be sorry? What else can I do?"

She stares at him. "Nothing. You can do nothing."

But I can.

She turns from Devlin, walking away blindly.

Bile rises in her. There's a bathroom close by and she veers into it.

Inside, another girl is there, at the mirror. For a moment Cara sees Laura. But then her eyes focus in the dim light and she recognizes the girl, an older one from gym class, a popular one, applying eye makeup at a sink. The girl freezes, staring into the mirror, fixed on Cara's face. Then she grabs her purse and hurries out the door, staying as far away from Cara as she can.

The door hisses shut on its pneumatic hinge and Cara is left alone in the dim, tiled room. The sound of her own harsh breathing surrounds her. Suddenly she lashes out, slams the stall doors, hitting and kicking them, one after another. Hitting to feel the pain, hitting so she doesn't scream.

She catches sight of herself in the cloudy mirror—then rushes at it and slams her hands so hard into the glass that it cracks.

She backs up, staring down at the blood dripping from her fingers. Blackness closes in.

She is standing in the dark bedroom of the mobile home, above the bleeding body of the counselor, his blood dripping from her hands . . .

She raises her head. From inside the broken mirror, a skull stares back at her. She looks into her own, black, depthless eyes . . .

Then there is nothing but her own pale face in the cracked glass.

She turns, reaches for the paper towel dispenser. She wraps a paper towel around her bleeding hand, then smooths her hair back and makes her breathing slow, slower . . .

Normal.

She manages to walk herself out, to find her English class, where she sits in a daze, choking down her feelings.

This isn't how it was supposed to be.

It's not fair.

She had done what she was told to do by the old Indian and by the moon. She went after *It.* She killed the man whose mask *It* wore. She had done battle and washed the blood off her hands and face, had thrown away her bloody clothes.

But somewhere inside she knows the truth. She has always known the truth.

She has not killed *It.* She only put away one of *Its* masks, *Its* shells. Playthings that *It* uses to taunt her. *It* doesn't die. *It* only moves on to the next willing body.

And *It* has struck here while she has been away. *It* has taken Laura, to show her *It* is not dead, that *It* never dies. *It* is playing a game. Horrible. Sick. Deadly. Taunting her. Showing her *Its* power.

She sits at her desk and digs her nails into her thighs to keep from screaming.

But some time during class something happens that wrests her at least momentarily from her savage thoughts.

It is an announcement from the front office about funeral services for Laura Huell.

Tomorrow.

She stays very still, thinking.

So It *wants to play?*

She can play.

There will be no more running.

ROARKE

Chapter Thirty-Eight

When he returned to the guardhouse, Roarke took down the orange Post-its for the 1997 and 1999 attacks and replaced them with red Post-its, like the one he'd made for Ivy.

There was a knock on the door. Roarke moved to answer it, and Mother Doctor stepped through the doorway, carrying a pot of coffee and a baking tin. Her eyes went to the improvised calendars on the walls.

"You've been busy."

In the kitchenette, she poured coffee and set the tin on the table, removed the lid. Roarke saw it contained crumbly cakes. He'd had a drive-through breakfast on the road, but now he realized he was ravenous. He reached for one.

"Homemade?"

She snorted. "Not by me." She indicated the tin lid she'd pulled open. "You've just seen the extent of my domestic skills." She took a cake for herself and stepped in front of the wall to look at Roarke's timeline.

He brushed crumbs off his hands. "Do you mind if I go through it with you? It would help me get it straight in my own mind."

"I'd be honored."

He crossed to the wall with the timeline, the rows of years, and gestured to the colored Post-its. "Two things stick out to me, here. Each attack ticks several of our boxes: the age of the victims—between thirteen and fifteen; the fact that there was a single attacker; the fact that a nondescript, unmarked panel van was used to abduct the girls; and that the attacker covered the victims' faces with a hood that he brought with him."

"Survivors," Mother Doctor said, gently. "We call them survivors."

He turned and looked at her. "Of course." He turned back to the wall. "So. We have age of survivors. Time of day. Vehicle used. Style of abduction: lying in wait, and a stealth attack. The hooding—covering the girls' faces, both to conceal his identity but also to depersonalize. The use of threats and force for control. The language: degrading, with terms like slut, bitch, whore. And the dates . . ."

That weird correlation of dates . . .

He continued, now indicating the red Post-its. "But. There were two other rapes in which the rapist actually used the threat of burning. This one in January of 1997, and this one in January of 1999. In the 1997 attack, the rapist told the girl to 'stop screaming or he'd torch her.' In this 1999 attack, the survivor reported that the rapist actually held a container of gasoline in front of her face and told her he was going to 'light her on fire and watch her cook'—but didn't go through with the threat because he was interrupted.

"Five months later he abducted Ivy and brought this fantasy to its full conclusion. And then apparently, he never used fire or the threat of burning again." He indicated the orange Post-its. "There have been all these rapes with the same MO since, that not only match the victim pool, the time of day, and the vehicle used—but that have the even more distinctive corresponding detail that the attacks took place during late January."

He stepped back from the wall and looked at Mother Doctor.

"And what's significant about all that to you?" she asked.

He pointed to the red Post-its for the 1997 and 1999 attacks. "Here the rapist seems to be escalating. Threatening to burn this survivor, then with this one actually having the gasoline with him, incorporating it into his threats. And then with Ivy . . ." He did not finish the sentence, knowing he didn't have to.

"The gasoline and burning has become part of his fantasy." He reached into his memory and quoted from a classic profiling text. "'The presence of an object or behavior during sex can quite easily lead to its eroticization and inclusion in fantasy and subsequently fantasy behavior.'" He indicated the red Post-its on the wall. "The rapist was clearly starting to get off on the idea of burning a victim. He acted out the fantasy with Ivy. But apparently none of the subsequent attacks used gasoline, or burning, either as a threat or in reality."

Roarke looked at the nun. "So what, he just dialed it back?"

Her face was intent. "I see. But could he not have felt that he'd lost control, that he *had* to 'dial it back'?" She stepped to the calendar herself, and pointed to the orange Post-its for 1996 and 1998, alternating with the red ones. "If I'm understanding your color scheme, then here and here were apparently rapes with no threat of gasoline or burning."

Roarke had noticed and wondered. But maybe the fantasy hadn't yet taken full hold.

The nun indicated a gap, the blank years from 2000 to 2004, before the orange Post-its started up again. "And here there seems to be a period of five years in which there were no attacks. Maybe he *did* scare himself after Ivy . . ."

"And then started again," Roarke said. "Only more controlled." He walked the room. "It occurred to me. He may have been more careful. Or he may have been arrested and jailed for several years. But I've never seen it work backwards in these cases. The pattern of a sadistic rapist is that his fantasy escalates. Instead what we see here is a de-escalation."

"Unless as you said, there are other attacks that aren't in the database," Mother Doctor suggested.

"Exactly." He knew it was a distinct and troubling possibility. "There could be a dozen reasons. They weren't reported to begin with. He didn't use a van, so that detail didn't ring the bells for Singh's search."

Or the survivors weren't survivors at all, he thought, uneasily.

"He also broke his January pattern with Ivy, as if he lost control, and was unable to wait. And—it's almost certain he meant to kill Ivy. It's only by a supreme act of personal will that she was able to survive."

The nun murmured something that might have been, *"Or God's . . ."*

Roarke didn't bother to argue. "There's a pattern we see in serial rapists and serial killers, a syndrome called decompensation. The fantasy tends to build, becoming more ritualized and violent, and the cooling-off period between attacks grows shorter. And at a certain point, if they're not arrested or killed, a percentage of these attackers start to unravel. They may go on a killing binge." He looked at the January calendar on the wall. "The attack on Ivy looks like decompensation to me. And I've never seen or heard of a rapist or killer pulling back from that."

Mother Doctor frowned. "So . . . you think the other attacks, these two early orange ones—and all the ones after Ivy, are not his?"

She'd read his mind.

Two different rapists.

He hadn't wanted to say it aloud. He didn't even want to think it. Not only did it muddy the investigation, it meant double the danger.

He stared at the timeline. "I don't know. They're similar on so many points. But the ones in red also differ in the level of injury to the survivors, and . . ." he paused and then said it anyway: "And the order of the specific violations. The orange ones never vary in order: anal, vaginal, oral. The red ones have no set pattern to the violation."

"Can't you compare the DNA from the rape kits?" she asked. There was a distinct note of anxiety in her voice.

That's the rub, isn't it?

He spoke reluctantly. "None of those rape kits have been tested."

She stared at him. "*What?* How can that be?"

He could feel the outrage in her voice, and he understood. There was no remotely acceptable excuse. The backlog was a national disgrace, just starting to be investigated as the human rights violation it was. Hundreds of thousands of evidence kits sitting untested in crime labs across the country. And because of that, tens of thousands of rapists that could be behind bars were roaming free.

He tried to answer, even knowing that there was no sane answer. "Money is the usual excuse. It costs a thousand to twenty-five hundred dollars to test the evidence in a rape kit. Sometimes the failure to test is plain ignorance." Law enforcement agencies often failed to send rape kits for testing because "no suspect had been identified"—these agencies apparently being completely ignorant of the fact that DNA testing was meant to *find* a suspect, and to ensure that the DNA was kept on file as evidence against further offenses.

"What a load of horseshit," the nun said suddenly.

Roarke glanced at her, startled—not because of the language, but because of the vehemence behind it.

Mother Doctor's face was hard. "That is one of the grossest miscarriages of justice I've ever heard." She shook her head. "I don't know why these things even surprise me anymore. Just when you think you've heard it all . . ." She walked the room, agitated, and Roarke sensed an anger that went far beyond the discussion. "Do you want to know what I think? They're not testing because too many people still think rape isn't a crime."

The thought was so unexpected that Roarke could only stare at her. She spoke grimly. "Oh—so you've never noticed anything missing in the Ten Commandments?"

He ran through the list in his head, but he already sensed where she was going with it.

She nodded. "There's no commandment against rape. Or against slavery, or torture, or child abuse, or spousal abuse. There are commandments against theft and swearing, but none against atrocity."

Roarke looked at her, mystified. "Then why—how can you . . ."

How on earth does she justify being a nun?

She looked back at him stonily, as if she'd heard his unspoken question. "I need structure."

Her face was expressionless and for a moment he wondered if she might be as unhinged as he felt himself unhinging.

Then she sighed. "You think it's only the Church that has failed in this regard? Look at this place. Here we are, trying to repair damage that should *never* have happened. Not in a civilized society. Not in an even halfway moral society. Keeping children well and safe, raising them without pain and fear, should be the priority of any human being. That's nowhere near anyone's priority. It doesn't make our politicians' top-ten lists. There's no political will to prevent children from being sexually abused?"

Roarke thought of *Bitch.* "I have a group for you," he said wryly, and then wished he hadn't. It was too easy to picture.

But if that's what it takes . . .

They stood at opposite ends of the room and looked at each other.

"You *are* thinking that these are two different rapists, aren't you," she said, finally.

He thought of Franzen and Lethbridge and Ortiz.

Franzen and Lethbridge, hunting together, taking alternate years, alibiing each other? Or one of them copycatting the other? Or was Pierson responsible for the three red rapes, until Cara stopped him dead?

"Maybe. Yes," he said, and then thought, *We have to get custody of those rape kits.*

CARA

Chapter Thirty-Nine

From the time she wakes up in the morning, the day of Laura Huell's funeral, she can feel it. The medication is completely gone from her body now, and there is something else there instead. Her blood is singing. She can feel it rushing in her veins. Her clothes feel too tight and too hot. The whispers buzz in the air around her, sometimes a sibilance, sometimes a guttural growling.

She goes through the morning routine of showering, dressing, eating, packing away her homework, as if the air isn't alive with sound.

Ms. Sharonda watches from the doorway of her office as she walks out with the other girls. Cara keeps her back straight, her face blank.

Normal.

There is a chill over the day, a strong wind moving darkly ominous clouds. It whips at her hair and coat, stings her face.

In front of the school, a bus is parked at the curb to take students to the funeral. A teacher stands guard beside the bus door, checking permission slips. Cara does not have a permission slip.

Wait, the wind whispers.

So she stays back on the sidewalk, watching the bus . . .

Voices simmer around the line of students waiting to board: a hoarse gasping, a reverberating low moan.

Suddenly one of the boys in line snatches at another's Walkman.

"Hey!" The other boy protests. The thief holds the device aloft, barely out of reach. The other shoves him.

"Give it *now* or I beat your ass—"

The two students face off, the teacher shoves her way through the instantly gathering crowd . . .

Cara darts forward and slips up the stairs, onto the bus, and walks quickly down the aisle to a seat far in the back, where the teacher will not be able to see her.

The cemetery is in the hills, not far from the Mission, where the skeleton girl sits sightless in her room.

Students file out of the bus in the parking lot. Cara stands close behind a taller boy as she passes the supervising teacher, but no one stops her.

Off the bus, she looks up at the yawning dark entrance of the church.

And she follows the other students up the stairs and inside.

At the front of the dim, wood-beamed chapel, there is a coffin on a stand, and a big blown-up school picture of Laura beside it, as if someone has severed her head from her body. She smiles flatly out at the crowd, the rows of people on hard benches: cheerleaders dressed in designer black, dripping with crocodile tears. Devlin and the jocks sitting in the back rows, silent, red-eyed—but not from crying. They are stoned. Martell is there, too, suspended from school but inexplicably present at the service of a girl he'd probably never had a thing to do with unless it was to tease, harass, or bully her.

And in the front, the pews are filled with clumps of men in dark suits, sitting together.

Organ music plays, the sound too loud, reverberating through Cara's body, jarring her bones. Then people get up and talk and talk. A minister. Vice-Principal Lethbridge. Their voices are like the voices in her head. Guttural grunts. Snakelike hissing. One man after another speaking, while Laura smiles mutely out of the blown-up poster, and a mile away, the skeleton girl sits in the Mission, silent.

And knowing.

Cara is sure. If anyone should be speaking over Laura's body, it is the skeleton girl. She could stand up and tell everyone what had happened. She could stare out into the rows of people with sightless eyes and point to the murderer.

Because however it happened, it was murder.

Cara looks over the crowded pews.

He's here. Of course he's going to be here.

The thought is a shiver of fear . . . and a call to action.

So who is he?

ROARKE

Chapter Forty

Mother Doctor walked the room, looking shattered, helpless. "It's January *now*. There must be something we can do."

She stopped in front of Roarke's calendar, suddenly focused on the photos of the relics he had taped to the wall. "Were the things I gave you, Ivy's things, any help?"

"I've sent the palm frond and the pyrite sample to the San Francisco lab for analysis." He was still skeptical that there was a forensic meaning to those clues. "But I think it's more likely that the palm is a direct reference to the Palmers Club, which Ivy and Laura both belonged to. The Wayfarer ring is also most likely a direct reference. Because those guys . . ."

"What?" Mother Doctor prodded.

He was silent for a moment. *Where to start? Do I want to?*

He finally said it. "I used to work as a psychological profiler."

"Huh. What a surprise." She sat in a chair, facing him. "So tell me something as a profiler."

He reluctantly reached back into his training. "Profilers have identified four main classifications of serial rapists, though the lines often blur. The typology is flawed, but it's a place to start . . ."

She spread her hands, waiting for him to continue. So he did.

"The Power Reassurance rapist is the least violent, the type who convinces himself that he's in love with his target or had some relationship with her. Definitely not the type we're looking for."

She nodded, so he continued. "The Anger Retaliatory type has anger against women in general and is out for revenge. He's generally triggered by some event and lashes out with uncontrolled violence, severely beating and wounding his victims. He will tend toward short, blitz attacks and is usually armed."

"So again, not the type we're looking for," Mother Doctor said.

"Why do you say that?" She was right, but he wanted to hear it.

"The man who commits these crimes waits a year between attacks. And the attacks are extremely well planned. Which means no external trigger. Also, you haven't mentioned him being armed. He uses brute force to subdue and terrorize these girls."

"Exactly," he said, and realized to his chagrin that he was acting exactly like a team leader.

Fuck it. Whatever works.

"Now, type three, the Power Assertive, is the opposite of the passive Power Reassurance rapist. The goal is to dominate and humiliate. He has an extreme sense of superiority and entitlement. He thinks of himself as a 'man's man,' and rape is a way for him to validate his masculinity. This type tends to be arrogant, athletic, loud—a flashy dresser who drives a flashy car, and generally projects a macho image. He'll work in a male-dominated field like construction or law enforcement—"

Roarke paused, his mind going uneasily to Ortiz. Then he continued.

"His background will usually include multiple divorces and/or domestic violence. He generally rapes away from where he lives or works. He will force the victim into repeated sex acts, generally in a specific pattern, and he uses beating and threats of violence to force compliance. But this type doesn't tend to kill; that's not the goal." Roarke glanced at Mother Doctor to see how she was taking this. She sat poised in her chair, completely focused.

"That one is sounding more like it," she said.

"I agree. I should add that it's very likely that whatever type he is, the rapist is Caucasian. The survivors Singh identified have all been white, with just one Latina. Sexual predators hunt within their own ethnic group."

She nodded intently with him.

"The fourth type, the most dangerous of all, is the Anger Excitation, or Sadistic rapist. If uncaught, this one will almost inevitably escalate to killing. In fact, the majority of serial killers start as sadistic serial rapists. This man derives sexual excitation from suffering. He degrades and tortures his victims before he kills. There is profound planning, and the fantasizing leading up to the attack is as important to him as the actual attack. He's most often within the thirty- to thirty-nine-year-old age range, married with a family, and lives in a middle class, low crime area. He's intelligent, educated, and usually has no arrest record. He's very, very good at not getting caught."

The nun stood, seeming unable to stay still, herself. "So being very general . . . the Power Assertive type would appear flashier, more macho and aggressive; and the Sadistic type would present as more of an upstanding citizen, not quite such a standout."

"Correct. So we have a mixed type, or there are two different men—or both those things." He indicated the red Post-its. "These red attacks are indicative of a sadist." Then he made a gesture encompassing the orange Post-its. "But there are many elements here of a sadist, as well. His attacks are very planned out. He stalks his victims by van, and drives the victim to a remote area where he can have complete control. He tells his victim what he plans to do with her before he does it, because it's the fear that arouses him. He's very ritualistic, performing according to a script, even adhering to a specific month. But against type, he hasn't progressed to killing."

"Unless there are others we don't know about."

Roarke looked at his Post-it calendar. "That's almost certain."

The light in the cottage was dimmer, as afternoon shadows crept across the valley.

The nun turned and faced him. "So who are you looking at for this? I know that you have someone in mind."

"Several someones." He paused. "This is by no means official . . ."

"Of course. Understood."

"Principal Lethbridge, the principal of Las Piedras High, and Mel Franzen, the Wayfarers Club president, are both Wayfarers and were both sponsors of the Palmers group which Ivy and Laura belonged to. And, unofficially, Franzen is a perfect fit for a Power Assertive type. Both were questioned at the time of Ivy's attack because Ivy was on her way to Palmers at the time of her abduction. And both used each other as an alibi."

Mother Doctor was very still. "I see . . ."

"That alibi seems to hold up," Roarke admitted. "But I'm not convinced. There's also a group home counselor by the name of Pierson who may have been responsible for a rape attempt on Cara Lindstrom." He paused, then finally said it. "I believe Cara killed him while she was here in Las Piedras."

"My God, Roarke . . ." The nun looked stunned. But not entirely.

"He may have been responsible for these three red rapes."

Her eyes were clouded. "But the orange one is still out there." She visibly pulled herself together. "What will you do next?"

"Singh is requesting the rape kits of the nine other survivors to do DNA testing. The analysis of the palm frond and the pyrite sample might give us some clue to the location that Ivy was attacked. "

"All of which takes time," the nun suggested. Her tone was raw, worried.

"Exactly. I'm also waiting for information about whether or not two other potential suspects have any affiliation with the Wayfarers."

"You have names?" the nun asked.

"I do."

"I can make a few calls."

Roarke turned to her. "I would very much appreciate that."

"It's absolutely the least I can do," the nun said. She looked about to speak, stopped, and then apparently made up her mind. "Forgive my bluntness, but you're doing this all on your own dime, aren't you?"

He hesitated, nodded acknowledgment.

"And you're paying for a hotel yourself? Why don't you stay here instead?" She spread her arms, indicating the room.

Roarke was about to decline, automatically, but the fact was, she was right. He was paying for everything himself, as well as rent on the cottage in Pismo, and it was draining his savings. He couldn't keep on like this much longer.

It was a little odd, no doubt . . . and he had to wonder if the nun wanted him close by for her own reasons. But there was no question it would be a huge help.

And there was another reason that he didn't even want to admit to himself: it just felt right. Necessary, even.

Because I'll feel closer to Ivy? To the time? Or to Cara?

Whatever it was, he was willing to go with it.

"That's very kind of you," he said aloud.

"Nonsense," she said. And then her face trembled, and he realized that she was shaking with anger. "How can anyone do anything else? We have to stop this suffering. People have to stop sending me these children."

Her voice cracked, and her anger shimmered in the darkening room. She took a breath, visibly pulled herself together. "Now, those names?"

He wrote Ortiz's name and Pierson's on a Post-it, but as he extended the slip of paper, he felt a prickle of unease. "Maybe you should leave this to me."

The nun took the slip from him, glanced at it, pocketed it. "Pierson is dead, didn't you say? And I'm hardly this attacker's type."

But Ortiz isn't dead. Roarke thought. *And he's a type. A dangerous type.*

She met his eyes. "No one will know why I'm asking, I assure you. I have my ways. Now go get your things. We have work to do."

Chapter Forty-One

Roarke went back to the hotel. In his room he picked up his very few belongings, then used the video system to check out. As he looked around the room, he felt a disproportionate sense of relief to be leaving it, for no reason he could articulate.

As he moved out through the expansive lobby with his roller bag, he heard a familiar voice behind him.

"You're leaving us?"

Roarke turned to see Chris Devlin walking toward him with a slightly uneasy smile. And Roarke had the distinct impression that this was not a chance encounter, that Devlin had been alerted to his leaving.

"I'm afraid so." Roarke stepped forward with a hand extended. "Thanks for your help."

Devlin shook hands automatically, but looked momentarily panicked. "Are you done, then?"

"With what?" Roarke asked pleasantly, determined to make Devlin spell out what he was asking, and why.

"Your . . ." Devlin looked lost for the word. "Investigation."

"Oh no. Finally got a break, in fact." Roarke took a deliberate glance at his phone, as if it had just buzzed. "I need to get moving. Thanks again."

He started off. Devlin's desperate voice followed him.

"So where are you off to?"

Roarke didn't turn, just responded with a lifted hand, as if he hadn't heard or understood.

But you've been noted, pal, he thought to himself.

Just as he returned to his car in the parking lot, his phone buzzed for real and he checked it to find a text message from Mother Doctor:

Made contact with Palm Desert Wayfarers Club. Pierson and Ortiz never members.

Roarke stared down at the text. "Damn it," he muttered.

He had to sit and close his eyes for a moment. He was aware that he was operating on no more than fumes. The exhaustion from his desert pilgrimage was reverberating in his head, buzzing in his veins. He knew he needed sleep desperately.

"Start again tomorrow," he said aloud. Maybe the rape kits would start coming through . . .

As he started the engine and left the lot, he had every intention of driving straight to the Mission. But at the intersection that would take him up the hill, he stayed stopped at the stop sign, not turning, not moving.

Because for the first time, he noticed the sign for the opposite road: a small marker for the Las Piedras Cemetery.

He checked the clock on the dash. It felt like midnight, but it was not yet nine. He needed to think, and he was also compelled.

He made the turn toward the cemetery.

The small guard house/office was a stone building like a chapel, with an antique brass bell in the tower. More mission influence.

He parked his car in the lot and stopped in at the office to ask the manager what he wanted to know.

What he found was not a surprise, but it gave him a shiver all the same. Both girls, Laura and Ivy, had been interred in the cemetery.

The manager handed him a map with two graves marked with *X*s and informed him the gates would be closing in twenty minutes.

Roarke walked under the diffuse light of old-fashioned iron street lamps, along the smooth packed-dirt paths, past curved stone benches under clusters of gnarled oaks.

The more modern part of the cemetery was well tended, the grass clipped and smooth. Most of the graves were modest; many of the headstones were simple marble rectangles set flat into the ground.

His footsteps crunched on the gravel of the paths. The cold of the night was giving him a second wind, but there was something else waking him, too: the numbing finality of the graveyard, the subliminal awareness of hundreds of the dead beneath his feet. A city of sleeping skeletons.

The older part of the cemetery was hillier, with a less-tended maze of taller stones. A wind had come up, the Santa Anas, whispering dryly in the dark through the trees.

Underneath was another crackling that set Roarke's nerves on edge.

He stopped, very aware of the familiar weight of his weapon, back on his hip. He scanned the shadows around him, under the trees, beside the standing headstones . . .

He could see no one.

Birds. Squirrels. The wind. Could be anything.

After a moment, he turned and kept walking.

He found Laura's headstone first, in a grove circled by oak trees, and stood at the base of the grave, looking at the inscription on the stone:

With her Father in Heaven

He stifled his distaste for the platitude. "Why?" he asked aloud, gently. "What happened to you?"

The night was silent. No answer from the dead girl.

It was something.

Something Laura knew. Something she feared. Something so terrible she couldn't live with it.

He turned away, to go in search of the other girl, who rested just a stone's throw from her classmate.

Dead within a week of each other, carrying their shared secret to their graves.

He walked the circular paths of the apparently deserted cemetery, looking for Ivy's headstone. His suspects, speculations and suspicions swirled in his brain, and he felt increasingly uneasy, not entirely alone.

As he approached the spot the manager had marked on the map, he found his steps slowing, his mind already reluctant to turn to thoughts of Ivy and what she had suffered. There was a sick feeling in the pit of his stomach . . . An image flashed in his head: the vision he'd had in the desert of the girl writhing in the bonfire.

He stopped at the foot of the grave, as his own terror of burning rose up, threatened to overwhelm him. He closed his eyes, felt the cool of the night air on his face, breathed in to center himself.

"I'm sorry," he whispered to Ivy. And then, before he could stop himself: "I'll find him."

He opened his eyes, focused on the headstone, the inscription under Ivy's name on the simple marble marker.

A single candle can both defy and define the darkness

The thought was intriguing, provocative, even. It occurred to him that Mother Doctor may have chosen the text.

What do I want on my tombstone?

The question came out of nowhere, startling and ominous. An image of his own name on a marble stone loomed in his head . . .

The sick feeling was roiling in his stomach, but it was no longer about Ivy. Now the feeling was unmistakable.

He was not alone.

CARA

Chapter Forty-Two

After the service, people walk out of the church, out into the cemetery, through the gravestones.

The day is bleak; a bruised sky that smells like rain, and chilly fog drifting through the old oaks at the cemetery. But Cara can feel the subdued excitement in the students beside her, the thrill of real-life horror.

She finds a thick old tree to stand beside, half-hidden, and watches the crowd, the other students, standing nervously among the graves.

Chris Devlin hangs back near a clump of trees with his jock friends. Even from a distance she can smell the pot smoke on their clothes, oozing from their pores.

Chris is looking at her. She turns away from him to survey the cluster of men in suits. Vice-Principal Lethbridge stands with them, and beside him is the big man with the pale crew-cut hair who was in the early morning Palmers meeting. Franzen.

Martell and Devlin and the jocks seem like a junior version of them. Packs.

Laura's parents, an ordinary couple, are surrounded by the men in suits, staring with blank faces down into the open wound of the grave.

Everyone casts long shadows, even though there is no sun.

The minister says more words over the coffin, then men in dark suits lower the box with Laura inside it into the ground, and people step forward to throw dirt into the hole.

Cara hears the thud of dirt raining down on the wooden lid of the casket, feels the earth pressing down on her own chest.

Her family is deep in the ground, too, in a desert cemetery in Blythe. Everyone but her. She was not allowed to go to the funeral. This is her first. Now, being here, she doesn't know why she was kept away. It's everything that comes before that is frightening.

She stays while all the others move away through the gravestones. Stays behind a tree and watches as a small earth-digger rolls over the hill it has been hiding behind. It stops beside the grave and shovels scoops of earth into the gaping hole of the grave.

In an amazingly short time, the hole is filled, and the earth digger rolls away.

The sound of the motor fades away, and the grove is quiet again, just the dull whisper of wind. Cara moves out from behind her tree, approaches slowly, stares down at the grave, the jagged edges of turf awkwardly covering it, the insipid inscription on the headstone.

The grave is as silent as Laura was in life.

Cara pictures the girl, lying mute and still, her head on a satin pillow. Six feet beneath Cara, in the ground.

"You could've talked," Cara says. "You could have told me."

Her legs feel shaky. She sits on the grave, leans her back against the headstone, closes her eyes, trying to feel the other girl, any remnant of her.

You left me. You left me.

Is it better for you now? Is it peaceful?

No. It's just dead.

Why should It *be alive and you dead?*

"You lost," she says aloud. "You let *It* win."

She has not cried in years, except in her sleep. Sometimes she wakes with her face wet, her chest and throat aching. She feels the same way now, only her eyes are dry.

Then there is another feeling. Shock. Dread.

As a shadow looms up in front of her, towering above the grave, looking down at her, featureless against the gray of the sky.

ROARKE

Chapter Forty-Three

R oarke put his hand to his holster, turned in the middle of the graves, called out harshly. "Who's there?"

Presence hovered in the silence. He unsnapped the Glock's holster, hand hovering beside the weapon. "I'm law enforcement and I'm armed. Show yourself."

A figure eased out of the shadows of the tree, hands half-raised. Roarke strained to see through the night . . . and recognized Chris Devlin.

What the hell?

Roarke moved closer, lowering his weapon, but he felt the rush of anger as the adrenaline hit his veins. "Want to explain why you're following me?"

Devlin looked flustered. "I was leaving work and I saw your car turn right in front of me . . ."

Right. Sure.

Devlin finished quickly. "And okay, I wanted to know. You're obviously . . ."

He stopped. Roarke waited, pointedly. *Obviously what?*

"You're looking into all this. Laura. Ivy Barnes."

"And what's your interest?"

Devlin looked around at the graves. "I lived it. Yeah, I was a kid. But come on. You think there's not a lot of us who wanted to know what happened?" His face was drawn. "You don't know what it was like. Living with this shit going down, all at once—and so much of it no one ever talked about. Those girls. It was like a bad dream. I feel like I spent my whole life under some kind of cloud."

That rang true. It was a whole lot of hell for one school.

Devlin opened his hands. "Ever since . . . all this stuff about Cara coming out. I can't stop thinking about it."

Roarke got that, too. The pull of the mystery. "So you followed me," he said implacably.

"I wanted to know more, that's all." Devlin paused, then met Roarke's eyes. "Maybe like you do."

Roarke felt a rush of anger at his words, but he knew that it was true. "Maybe we can exchange information, then." He glanced down at the grave. "So you know about Ivy Barnes."

The look Devlin gave him was haunted. "I didn't know her. But that's not the kind of thing you forget."

"Did you go to her funeral?"

Devlin frowned. "No. I don't think I knew about it."

In a small town, he hadn't heard about it? That meant it was kept quiet.

"Did you go to Laura Huell's funeral?"

Devlin glanced back toward the grove encircling Laura's grave. "Yeah."

"You said before you didn't know her, either."

"A bunch of us went. A lot of the school."

"Just another excuse to get out of class?"

Devlin looked angry, defensive. "There was some of that. But it wasn't all that. And my dad knew her. She played the piano—"

"At the Wayfarers Club," Roarke finished, and felt a prickling. *Wayfarers.* "Did you know Mel Franzen?"

"Sure. He was the Palmers liaison at the school."

"The junior Wayfarers Club."

"Right."

"Was he at Laura Huell's funeral?"

Devlin raised his hands. "I don't know, man. It was sixteen years ago."

"Was Cara there?"

"Yeah. Yeah, she was there."

He was sure of that, at least. And there was that same tone of voice again. The way he'd spoken about Cara before. Loss. Longing. And anger, too.

Roarke came to a sudden decision. "You want to know what happened? So do I. Are you willing to help me?"

Devlin looked startled. "Of course."

"Come on, then."

He started back through the headstones, toward Laura's grave. After a moment, Devlin followed. Above them, the old iron streetlamps showered hazy yellow light through the mist.

And Roarke could tell the moment Devlin understood where they were going; he felt the younger man tense beside him.

Roarke led Devlin through a row of trees . . . slowed and stopped in the clearing beside Laura's grave. Devlin glanced around the oak grove, the old, twisted shadowy trees, then looked at Roarke, waiting.

"I want you to close your eyes and picture yourself there, at the funeral."

Devlin stared back at him. "What is this? You going to hypnotize me?"

"Nothing like that. It's called cognitive interviewing. It's a technique for getting more detailed reports from witnesses. You can remember more about this than you think."

As he spoke, Roarke was watching Devlin closely. Even if Devlin didn't agree, if he resisted too hard, it would say something. Devlin seemed to understand that, too, because he shrugged defensively. "Go on, then."

"Eyes closed," Roarke said, and after a moment, Devlin did it. Roarke shifted on his feet to get a clearer look at Devlin's face in the lamplight. "You're going to imagine yourself back on the day of the funeral." Wind stirred the oak leaves above them as he gave the younger man a beat to think about it. Then he asked, "What time of day was it?"

It was a moment before Devlin answered. "Morning. Pretty early morning."

"How do you know?"

Devlin frowned, then his face cleared. "I was barely awake."

"Did you drive over here?"

"Martell picked me up."

"Who's Martell?"

"My buddy. Kyle Martell. We went way back. Kindergarten. Sports. You know."

"Good," Roarke said. "That's good." Devlin was cooperative, seemingly not resisting him at all, and he felt the thrill of the hunt . . . the feeling of stalking elusive prey, drawing the information out.

"What's the weather like?"

"It's cold. Wind. Fog. Lots of clouds." Devlin's shoulders jerked in an involuntary shiver. *Good. Accessing sense memory, now.*

"Do you go to church first, or the cemetery?"

"Church. Her parents were into church."

"So you're outside the church. Who else is there?"

"Lots of people. Church people. Lots of kids from school." Roarke waited, and then Devlin said, "Bunch of guys from Wayfarers."

Roarke's pulse spiked, but he let it go for the moment. He'd circle back to it, when Devlin was deeper into the memory. He kept his voice calm. "You go straight in, or smoke a little something before?"

A conflicted look crossed Devlin's face and he hesitated, then admitted it. "A joint in the car."

"So you get stoned in the car. Then you go in to the chapel. Where are you sitting?"

"In the back."

"What are you seeing?"

Devlin's face was intent in concentration. "Coffin on a stand. Big blown-up school picture of Laura in front. A lot of people crying. Preacher talking, pretending like he knew her. But that's not right, is it? I don't think anyone knew her, really."

He was doing well, much better than Roarke had expected. But Roarke was impatient to get to the cemetery. The funeral service was one thing. Setting the stage, taking the subject step-by-step through the memory was crucial setup, but what he really wanted to know were the faces at the graveside. Who was there at the interment, the actual lowering of the body into the ground. If the rapist—or rapists—had been anywhere, it would likely have been there.

"Do other people speak? Her parents?"

Devlin shook his head. "Not her parents. Fucking Lethbridge, though."

Principal Lethbridge. Who would have been the vice-principal at the time.

"Course he had to get up there and drone on."

There was a petulant tone in Devlin's voice. He sounded like a teenager, regressing slightly. Another good sign he was going deeper into the memory.

"What is he saying?"

Devlin shrugged. The gesture looked young, childish. "Who cares, right? The guy's a total tool."

"Do other family members speak? Aunts, uncles, grandparents?"

"No one like that. Some kids do."

"Who?"

"I dunno. Choir geeks, I think."

"Not you or your friend Martell, though."

"That would be stupid. We didn't know her." He raised his voice. "Nobody knew her."

He was fully into the memory now, accessing emotion, and Roarke knew he could move on.

"So it's after the funeral now. You walk out there to the gravesite?"

"Yeah."

"Maybe another joint in the car, first?"

Another hesitation. "Yeah."

"What's the weather like now?"

"Rain. It's about to rain." Around them the breeze picked up, murmuring through the trees above them.

"What do you smell?"

"That wet in the wind. And perfume. Lots of flowery shit." Devlin made a face, and Roarke could almost smell it himself, the damp and the too-sweet perfume.

"Where are you standing?"

"Under this clump of trees. A ways back."

"Who else is with you?"

"Martell. Guys from the team."

"Who else do you see?"

"The cheerleaders all in a bunch, crying. Other kids from school."

"How about adults? Look at the people at the grave. Who do you see?"

"The minister. Her parents. My mom and dad. A bunch of guys from Wayfarers."

"Do you see Franzen?"

Devlin's brow furrowed in the misty dark. "Yeah. Yeah, he's there."

Roarke felt a jolt of adrenaline. *I knew it.*

"Where is Cara?"

"She's off by herself, sort of behind a tree. Jeans and turtleneck." His face tightened in concentration. "Always a turtleneck."

It was that very thing that had set Roarke off on Cara's trail, three months ago. She wore it to cover the scar on her neck, where the Reaper had slashed her.

"Is she looking at the grave, or someone else?"

Devlin frowned. His face was focused and still, and Roarke found himself holding his breath.

Cara. Tell me something. What were you looking at? Who were you looking at?

"The Wayfarer guys. She's looking at the Wayfarer guys."

Wayfarers again. It's back to them.

Roarke kept his voice level. "Any one of them in particular?"

Devlin shook his head. "I don't know."

"Why were so many Wayfarers at the funeral, do you think?" Roarke asked.

Devlin grimaced. "They were into everything. Community fathers. That kind of shit."

"Did you also see a Latino man in a suit, early thirties, well built? Most likely on his own?"

Devlin frowned, eyes still closed. "No. No, I don't remember anyone like that."

So Ortiz wasn't there? Or Devlin just didn't notice him?

Roarke was just trying to process that, when they were hit by the strong beam of a Maglite. "Hey. You there."

Devlin's body jerked and his eyes flew open. Roarke stiffened. A man in uniform stepped forward, shining strong light in their eyes. Roarke and Devlin lifted their hands automatically.

"Cemetery's closed. You're not supposed to be here."

Roarke felt a wave of anger at the interruption, but knew the guard was just doing his job. "Sorry. We lost track of time. We're leaving now."

The guard stood watching them as they walked away, winding their way back through the dark graves, headed for the gates.

Devlin was quiet beside Roarke as they walked in the drifting mist; he seemed drained, even agitated. An intense cognitive interviewing session often had that effect. And the subject matter had been deep— maybe not exactly traumatic, but definitely not light, either.

Inside, Roarke was tired, but focused. *It's Wayfarers. Maybe Franzen. But whatever it is, it has something to do with that club. The ring, the palm frond, the presence at the funeral. It has to be.*

Through the gates ahead he could see there were only their two cars in the dark cemetery parking lot, parked some distance away from each other. As they passed through the gates, Devlin stopped abruptly.

"So you think Laura was murdered?"

Roarke tensed, but it wasn't that much of a leap, and Devlin wasn't stupid.

"I don't know that. As far as I know it was a suicide."

"Do you even have the authority to be looking into any of this?"

Then Roarke realized that he *wanted* it out that he was investigating. The best thing for him would be the rapist/killer getting wind of it and coming after him in some way, for information or for worse—but to show himself.

Bring it on, he thought, and spoke aloud.

"Two girls dead in one week. No one ever caught for what happened to Ivy. What authority do you think I need? Someone needs to do right by them."

The younger man stared at him. "Okay. Yeah."

Something occurred to Roarke. "Were you in Palmers, yourself?"

"Sort of."

"What does that mean, 'sort of'?"

Devlin shrugged. "My dad made me go to enough meetings to be counted. It was the best college scholarship in school, basically free money if you played your cards right."

Self-serving, but it made sense.

"One more thing. Your buddy Martell. I'd like to talk to him. You know where I can find him?"

A strange look crossed Devlin's face. "Sure. He's in Lompoc."

It was a Central California penitentiary.

In an instant, a whole other scenario spun out in Roarke's head. *Could it have been a student? Have I been chasing the wrong trail all along?*

"What's he in for?" he asked tensely.

Devlin looked away, into the dark. "He got sent up for securities fraud."

"How long has he been incarcerated?"

"Six years now."

Roarke sat behind the wheel of his Rover, watching Devlin drive away. For a moment there, he'd been rocked by the idea that the rapist could be someone entirely other than the men he'd been considering. But he'd just used his iPad to check, and the California Inmate Locator confirmed Kyle Martell was currently serving in Lompoc. If he'd been in jail for the last six years, he couldn't possibly have committed the latest rapes.

No, Devlin's memories had brought Roarke's focus right back to Franzen. He'd been there at the funeral. A Wayfarer. A sponsor of Palmers Club. A controlling, aggressively macho type.

Bottom line: Roarke didn't trust his alibi. And he knew a short cut to finding out what he needed to know. It wasn't the safest one. But Roarke wasn't the one in real danger.

Singh had said it: The man who raped Ivy was a secretor, blood type B positive.

What I need is your blood, asshole.

CARA

Chapter Forty-Four

S he gasps and scrambles off Laura's grave, up to her feet, to face a man in a suit. Familiar, and ominous. The policeman—detective—who came to her aunt's door. The younger, angry one.

"Cara Lindstrom," he says, and smiles at her. Not a nice smile. "Detective Ortiz, Riverside County Sheriff's Department. Remember me?"

I'm not a moron, she thinks, and says nothing.

He glances around the quiet grove, at the graves, the twisted trees. "What are you doing here?"

What are you *doing here?* she thinks back at him.

The cold wind blows through the oaks, making the leaves click together. She can see no one else on the paths between the headstones, and she is nervous that there are no other people about. Nothing around them but death.

She inches back from Ortiz, keeping distance between them, while in her mind she maps out which way to run through the tombstones. They are just minutes away from the chapel, but the trees of the grove shield the building from view. Which means no one can see them, either.

"You know why I'm here," Ortiz says.

She is acutely aware of the gun on his hip. He holds up a warning hand. "Don't try to run. We're going to have a little chat, now, just you and me. You can't run forever."

Through her apprehension, she realizes this is what the old Indian said. She can't run.

A thought flickers in her mind, the faintest hope.

What if she were to tell him? If he is a real cop, isn't it his job to stop these things? No matter what she has done, the man in the van is out there, somewhere. Maybe even right now.

"It's the same person," she says, so low that Ortiz frowns, steps forward. "What? Who is?"

"Who killed her." She looks down toward Laura's grave.

He glares at her. "She killed herself."

"*He* killed her. And the other one, too."

"The other one?"

"Ivy. He burned her."

The detective's face twists, but she can't read the expression there. Anger? Confusion? Or something else? Her heart thumps faster.

"I don't know what you're talking about. But I know what *you* did." His voice is rough, but low, as if he doesn't want even the dead to overhear. "You think you can get away with it?" She sees rage, and something else she recognizes.

That's when she knows. This is all unofficial. If he were just doing his duty, he would arrest her. That's what cops do. And he is here without his partner, who was clearly in charge.

He has nothing on her.

She knows something else, as well.

"You're afraid," she says softly.

His face doesn't turn black. It only seems as if it does.

"You little bitch," he says. "Who do you think you are? I know what you are, you dirty little whore."

He has said none of that aloud. But she hears it as clearly as if he had. She stares into his face, whispers, "*I see you. I know what you are.*"

His lips twist back in a snarl, revealing the jagged teeth of *It*—

She doesn't think, doesn't pause. She just runs.

She knows he can catch her, but she has the advantage of surprise. He has been startled by what she has said to him, and it takes him a few precious seconds to regroup.

She runs on the grass, dodging like a rabbit through the gravestones, veering around trees, sprinting for the chapel, thinking only that there is a chance there will be people there, that he will not want to be seen chasing her.

The running makes her dizzy. The clouds roil blackly above in the wind, and the heavy running steps behind her shake the ground underneath her, shooting tremors through her legs so she stumbles. Harsh panting reverberates through the air, as if all the graves around her are breathing.

She bursts through a row of trees, and the chapel is there.

And there is another service. People gathered on the steps of the church, dressed in black. Behind her, the heavy running footsteps slow to a walk. The hoarse panting and the dark whispering recedes, fading behind her.

She runs, feet pounding, doesn't slow at all, not until she is past the church, out of the cemetery, onto the street

Only then does she stop, hidden between cars. She puts her hands on the hood of one of them, doubles over to catch her breath. Her heart is pounding wildly.

Safe. But not for long.

He'll be back, wanting what he wants. And *It* is out there, too.

She waits until she can breathe again. Then she heads for the place, for the only one who understands.

ROARKE

Chapter Forty-Five

Roarke was not surprised to find that Franzen lived in an upscale house, on a street near the country club. Singh's report had mentioned that Franzen owned several hardware supply stores, in Las Piedras, Indio and—Palm Desert. A good, salt-of-the-earth kind of business that had obviously made him a more-than-comfortable living.

He stood in the dark on Franzen's porch, rang the doorbell, and hoped that his quarry was home.

Franzen answered his door himself. The look on his face when he saw Roarke was confused recognition . . . then an unconcealed anger once realization dawned.

"Mr. Roarke, was it? I have to wonder what you could be thinking, turning up at my home like this, at this hour of the night."

Roarke went for the serious, earnest approach. "I've come up with some interesting information regarding the attacks. I thought you'd want to know right away."

"The attacks?" Franzen asked. His voice was more cautious.

Roarke frowned, looked into the man's face, and lied. "The police haven't been to see you yet? That's odd. I was under the impression that they were going straight over here yesterday."

The mention of police did the trick. Franzen held the door open. "Why don't you come in?"

Roarke stepped inside, and as Franzen shut the door behind them, he turned in the hallway, slowly, so he could get a look through the various open doors into other rooms: the wide living room, an open archway into the kitchen and breakfast area.

The whole house was neat and orderly. Not entirely clean; Roarke could see dust on the mantel and bookshelves. But rigidly orderly.

He stepped to the wall, to look over a few prominently displayed framed photos: Franzen and a woman of his generation, solid, respectable.

"Your wife?" he asked the older man.

"Late wife."

Roarke knew, of course. She'd died four, nearly five years ago. Franzen had not remarried. There was no sign of another woman.

Beyond those photos there was a series of framed certificates hung on the wall. Before Roarke could get a good look, Franzen moved past him and opened a side door, ushering him in to a den that was part office, part TV room.

Franzen closed the door behind them, an odd gesture that set Roarke on alert, since they were apparently alone in the house. "Now what's all this about?"

"The police haven't talked to you about the rapes?" Roarke's eyes were glued to Franzen's face, checking for any reaction to the word *rape*.

Franzen raised his eyebrows, as if mystified.

Roarke held his gaze and lied. "Riverside County talked to me yesterday about a string of attacks on high school girls in cities all over the country, from 1996 on up to the present. They're working with local police in Atlanta. A task force was formed after the latest attack, which took place there last January." He paused, then threw a curve ball. "They said they were coming to you because of the connection between the rapes and the burning of the Wayfarers Club."

Franzen frowned, the perfect study of bewilderment. "I don't think I'm following you. The arson at the club? How do the police think those two things are connected?"

"Are you aware that the Wayfarers Club burned down the day before Ivy Barnes died?"

"Ivy Barnes," Franzen said blankly.

"Ivy Barnes," Roarke repeated, knowing Franzen knew exactly who he was talking about. "The Las Piedras High student who was abducted, raped, and set on fire."

Franzen spread his hands. "Again, I don't see the connection."

"Fire for fire? Seems pretty obvious to me."

"Let me see if I'm understanding this. The police are trying to connect all that with some attack that happened in Savannah—"

"Atlanta."

"In Atlanta last year?"

"And the year before that, and the year before that," Roarke said inexorably. "Possibly every year since Ivy was attacked here. Back then, someone was very clever. The police didn't know where to look. But now they do."

"That is some bizarre story," Franzen said slowly. "And you're working with the police on this? Or is it some *personal* interest?"

Roarke felt a flicker of menace, nothing overt, just something in the way Franzen had spoken. He answered evenly.

"I thought that with your close connection to the Palmers Club, those two girls from your own town—that you would want to assist the investigation in every way you could."

Franzen looked at him, not giving an inch. "I'll be happy to help the task force with any information it requires. Is that the extent of your 'interesting information'?"

Roarke knew Franzen was about to throw him out.

Wild thoughts were passing through his head. *I could get hair from his coat collar on the way out, from one of those coats hanging on the coat tree inside the door. Ask to use the bathroom and steal a razor . . . or there may be Kleenex in the wastebasket that would have traces of blood. I could ask for a drink, break the glass, make sure he cuts himself on it . . .*

It would never be admissible in court as evidence, but at least he would know.

But he also knew all of that was desperately crazy. And Franzen was watching him, as if he could read his thoughts.

"Why are you really here, Mr. Roarke?" he asked softly.

Roarke was startled by the sudden buzzing of the phone in his suit coat pocket. He checked the screen, saw a text from Singh.

He decided to use it. He deliberately tensed up, glanced at Franzen. "Sorry, I need to . . ." He didn't finish the sentence, but punched in his security code as if he couldn't wait to read the text, took a quick look, and then swiveled, as if jolted into action.

"Thanks for your time. I have to go." He started for the door. Franzen made a subtle move to block him.

"You said you had information."

Roarke reached past him for the doorknob. "I'll have to call you later. Excuse me." He brushed by Franzen and opened the door.

The big man bristled and Roarke thought, *Go ahead. Come at me. See what that gets you.*

But Franzen didn't follow him. He stood at the end of the hall, while Roarke walked to the front door and out.

He was sure Franzen was watching him, so he lifted the phone and pretended to make a call as he strode back through the dark to his car, parked down the block. He even took a glance back toward the house, speaking nonsense into the phone. He wanted Franzen to know he was being watched. If he was the rapist, it might give him enough pause that Roarke would have time to nail him for good—before he had the chance to devastate another life.

But he waited to phone Singh back until he was in the car, with the doors locked.

Singh's voice was always calm, always welcome. "I have some information I thought you should have right away." She hesitated. "It seemed clear that you need to expedite the elimination of suspects. So I requested the medical records for Mel Franzen and Robert Lethbridge."

Roarke felt a rush of surprise. "What? How?"

"They are material witnesses to an ongoing serial rape investigation, are they not?"

He realized what she had done. It was a little known fact that law enforcement could get medical records without a warrant—by affirming that the records were needed to identify a suspect, witness, fugitive, or missing person.

He was suddenly short of breath. "You have their blood types?"

"I do. Ivy Barnes was a Type A secretor, and the vaginal swab revealed Type A and B antigens. But Franzen and Lethbridge have blood type O: Franzen is O positive, and Lethbridge is O negative. Therefore, neither of them could have been Ivy's assailant."

Roarke sat behind the wheel, processing it.

So either I've been chasing the wrong dogs . . . or we really are looking at two different guys.

And we won't know until we get at least blood types from the evidence in the later rapes.

He looked out at Franzen's house and felt a quick gratitude that he'd showed some restraint and hadn't stolen any body fluids.

Maybe I've just gone off the rails. Maybe it's time to stop this.

"Chief? Are you there?" Singh's voice was anxious.

"It's great work. But not the greatest news," he admitted.

"I understand."

He felt a wave of frustration. *So what the hell now?*

But in the next moment, he answered his own question. "I need to get more details from these women. The survivors. I need to *talk* to them. Do you have current addresses and contact information on any of them?"

There was a pause on the line. "Is there a particular one you are thinking of?"

"Whoever you can get me. But I think . . . I need to talk to one of the ones who were threatened with burning."

"I will see what I can do," Singh said.

As he disconnected and reached to start his engine, he saw a silhouette move in the front window.

It was Franzen. Standing in the dark of his house, watching him.

CARA

Chapter Forty-Six

She stands in the garden of the Mission, looking up at the skeleton girl's window.

Going over the wall again had been easy. The tranquil gardens and the plaza seem familiar, almost welcoming, as she slips through the shady patches under the trees. But this time the heavy wooden back door is locked.

So she finds a hiding spot, behind a collection of shrubs, and waits.

Afternoon shadows lengthen in the garden; the water shimmers in the softly rushing fountain. The place seems ancient, a world out of time. Sometimes she sees the outlines of hazy figures: robed priests strolling the gravel paths, Indians working in the gardens. She knows they're not there; they're not even ghosts. It's her new, unmedicated mind playing games, like dreaming awake.

The bell in the clock tower rings out, tolling four times. And then the wooden door opens and a nun steps out. It is the older nun she had seen in the corridor, who had called out to her.

The nun walks onto the garden path, reaches into the deep pocket of her cardigan, and draws out a pack of cigarettes.

Cara waits in the shrubs until the nun has lit up, watches her stroll down the path until she is out of sight, beyond trees. Then she crosses quickly to the back door, tries it.

It opens under her hand.

Inside, she walks silently down the corridor with its gleaming adobe tiles. The sheen of them is so bright she must avert her eyes.

She looks at the wall instead, following it to the end of the passage, then hovers, stealing a glimpse around the corner . . .

There are people in the corridor. A doctor and a nurse, standing in front of the open door of the skeleton girl's room. Their voices are soft and urgent. Something is going on inside the room.

Cara tenses, worried, wondering . . .

The nurse breaks away, hurrying down the corridor, and the doctor steps back through the door.

Cara backs up noiselessly, and bolts down the hall for the back door.

She leaves the garden, but she can't bring herself to leave the Mission. Instead she sits outside, on a bench beside the wall, as the valley below turns blue with twilight.

There is a stone cottage in the grove of oak trees, but it is dark and silent, no sign of anyone in it. She is alone.

She has not eaten all day and without the medication her senses are roiling inside her. The whole night is glistening now. The moon begins to rise through the bare branches of trees. The clouds around it are golden, gossamer, silver. The light pours down from the sky and shimmers like water on the sandy ground . . .

Thoughts are rising inside her, too, overflowing like the light from the moon.

Is she dying, the skeleton girl? Is that one connection going to be taken from her, too?

She pushes the fear deep down inside her, but it rises again, threatening to overwhelm her.

It is not done.

There is not just the horror of what happened to the skeleton girl, the thing that will surely happen again. Even if Laura killed herself, that was only because of *It*. It is *It* that should be killed, and no one sees. No one sees, only her.

And there are so many of *It*.

The counselor is dead. One down. But there are all the others.

She thinks of the clump of men in suits at the funeral. The vice-principal, maybe. Ortiz definitely. And the man in the van, whoever he is, who savaged the skeleton girl, and who is waiting out there in the dark.

One of them, some of them, maybe all of them—are *It*. *It* is out there, in all *Its* many forms. Out there, making *Itself* known to amuse itself. Playing with her before *It* strikes.

So what do I do?

The moon bends closer, so close she can feel its icy heat.

You know, it whispers.

The command is so clear, she freezes where she sits.

But she does know.

It is remorseless, relentless, terrifying. But *It* can only do *Its* work within these weak vessels. They are as vulnerable as any human is; the neck the most vulnerable of all.

And she has camouflage herself. *They* see her as weak. But she is not weak. She is the wolf.

She holds her hands out and looks down at her palms. In the moonlight, she sees the red, feels the warmth of the counselor's blood spilling over her hands as his heart pumped the last of it from his body.

You know, says the moon.

She knows. She was not wrong about him. She feels no remorse. The world is a better place without him in it.

Can she do it again? Of course.

She knows *what*. But she doesn't know *who*.

She looks back toward the Mission, in the direction of the skeleton girl's room. Then she stoops to the ground, picks up a sharp-edged stone, and carves into the stone wall.

She drops the stone, steps back, looks up at the moon.

"Which?" she whispers. The night trembles around her . . .

Then the darkness in front of her moves, and she gasps out.

Standing in front of her is a huge bird, or an angel . . . a shadowy winged apparition. Her heart starts to pound. She swallows and concentrates through the roiling inside her, focuses through the shimmering . . . to see a robed figure. The older nun, the smoker.

"Hello," the nun says.

Cara moves to bolt. The nun says quickly, "It's all right. You're not in trouble. You've come to visit Ivy, haven't you? I'm glad."

Cara stays still, ready to flee, but curious, compelled.

Ivy, she thinks. *Her name is Ivy.*

"Are you a friend of hers?" the nun asks.

After a moment, Cara nods, warily.

"Well, today wasn't a good day. She's resting now. But I want you to know, you can come any time you like." She pauses, then asks, "You're from Social Services, aren't you?"

Cara tenses. The nun sees.

"I'm sorry. That's a personal question, and we don't know each other. I only wondered if that's how you know Ivy."

Cara thinks on this. So the skeleton girl is in the system, too. But she is not surprised. The men in vans, they find the homes.

She nods, and the nun sighs. She sits on the bench, but at the far end, carefully, as if asking permission. "All this . . . It must be hard for you to understand."

"I understand," Cara says flatly.

The nun looks at her, intrigued. "Do you? I'd like to hear."

She thinks the nun really does want to hear. But what is there to say? *There are monsters. It's everyone else who doesn't understand.* And how can she tell her anything, this nun, after what she has done?

They sit for some time in the silence of twilight. Finally, the nun speaks. "Maybe next time, then. You can come any time you like. Just— use the front door." She hesitates, and then says, "You know . . . I don't believe in accidents."

Cara glances at her, a quick, startled look.

The nun holds her gaze, compels her not to look away. "Maybe you found this place because you were meant to find it."

She hears herself saying, "I know I did."

For one second, she feels utter longing, to confide in this kind authority, to give this burden to someone else, to be nurtured . . .

"You are not alone," the nun says suddenly, fiercely. "And you are loved."

Cara looks down at her hands. The blood is there again, red even in the darkness, dripping. She shakes her head, and backs up, turns and heads down the hill, into the dark.

ROARKE

Chapter Forty-Seven

Roarke woke in the Mission gatehouse and lay in the narrow single bed, feeling the dark around him.

He'd returned from Franzen's house, and as soon as his head hit the pillow, he'd fallen into a black and dreamless sleep.

But now his skin was crawling, his senses on alert. He'd felt something, heard something . . .

He stood and reached for his jeans, stepped into them, and moved out of the bedroom. He glanced at his calendar on the wall, with the three names clear on the sheet of paper he'd tacked up before he'd slept: *Franzen. Lethbridge. Ortiz.*

He moved to the front door, and opened it to look out.

The moon was high about the olive grove.

Three pale figures stood in the midst of the trees: three slim, feminine shapes. One with a bloody gash in her throat. One whose wrists dripped blood. And one a living skeleton.

Roarke opened his eyes, awake for real this time. His heart was racing; his arms covered in gooseflesh, his fists gripping the bedsheets.

He pulled on clothes, went to the front door, opened it to the cold night air, and looked into the dark toward the trees. There were no ghost girls. Of course not.

He closed the door, locked it. And then it occurred to him what had awakened him. He stepped to the table and checked his phone, finding a text message from Singh, time-stamped just ten minutes ago.

He sat at the table and called her back. She picked up immediately.

"I was just about to call again. I was not sure you would want to wait for morning."

He could hear the urgency in her voice. "Go ahead, Singh."

"I have been unable to trace the first of the survivors threatened with burning, Tricia Andress, who was attacked in 1997. She was in the Social Services system, a group home girl. Since the assault she has been in and out of shelters, and frequently homeless. Her whereabouts are currently unknown."

Another group home girl, Roarke thought, uneasily. *This guy knows how to find vulnerable targets. Those girls would have no advocates pushing for investigation and prosecution, either.*

"But I have a current address and phone for Marlena Sanchez, who was attacked in Phoenix in January of 1999, five months before Ivy. She now lives in Flagstaff."

Roarke remembered the name, and the details. Sanchez had been fifteen, walking to school in the morning. The abductor pulled her into a windowless white van, bound her, and drove her somewhere undisclosed to assault her. She reported that he had a can of gasoline with him, that he held it in front of her face and threatened to "cook her." But the attack was interrupted in some way that wasn't clear in the witness statement. The assailant drove off with her, and turned her out of the van in a different location. There were several other points in common with Ivy's report of her attack, too. The rapist cuffed her to a pipe in the van. She was hooded the whole time.

He felt his skin prickling.

"Do you think she'll talk to me?"

"I believe there is a possibility. DNA evidence was collected at the time of the attack but the rape kit was never tested. However, Sanchez recently submitted a request for a test. Which has still not yet been conducted." She paused, and said dryly, "The City of Phoenix Police Department has 1,783 untested rape kits as of this year."

Roarke saw the way Singh was thinking. If Sanchez was pressing for a test, then she was looking for justice. Meaning she might very well talk to him.

"Do you wish me to place that call for you?" Singh asked.

"Yes. Please. Thank you, Singh."

"Also, I have been doing some checking into Detective Ortiz. As far as I have been able to determine, he has never been associated with the Wayfarers Club."

Roarke already knew that, but again felt that surge of frustration that he'd been wrong.

"However . . ." Singh said. "I have been monitoring his internet habits. It has been enlightening."

"You hacked him?"

"Hack is a strong word," she said. "I followed him. Not on Bureau time or systems," she added, unnecessarily. Roarke was sure that whatever she'd done, she had been more than discreet.

"He spends quite a lot of time on Reddit, in the men's rights forums. I will send through some of the comments he has posted. I believe it is information you need to have. I . . ." There was a pause on the line, and then she finished. "It is not pleasant reading."

He'd always thought of Singh as fearless, but the tone of her voice chilled him.

"I'll look at it right now," he told her.

"I will try to reach Sanchez, first thing in the morning," she said.

Roarke lowered the phone, frowning.

His phone pinged and he looked down to see an email from Singh, with a file attached.

The email said: *Ortiz has been posting under several aliases. All of the posts I have highlighted are his.*

Roarke opened the file to find a Reddit sub-forum page. He didn't have to click through into individual threads to get the picture; the opening comments under each link were the same kind of misogynistic ranting that he'd heard on the radio.

Singh had highlighted several forums. Roarke's stomach lurched as he saw the titles:

Gang Rape Cara Lindstrom
Tracking Cara Lindstrom
Kill that Lindstrom Bitch

Chapter Forty-Eight

S ingh stood in her office cubbyhole, looking down at the document that she had just sent to Roarke. She felt something welling up inside her she could not name, something that caught in her throat and made her chest tight.

She went to the doorway of the living room and stood, looking in at Epps, who sat at the table with his laptop, a glass of wine in front of him.

He looked up at her, saw her face. And instantly, he was on his feet. "What is it?"

She brought the tablet to him, open to the Reddit site. He looked down, took it. His face turned very still.

Singh sat on the sofa as he read. After a moment she curled her legs up under her, and tried to let the feelings come. "I feel . . . violated," she said. "I feel . . ." She was struggling, unable to contain the pressure of her grief.

Epps put the iPad aside, a motion like hurling it away. "I hate this." There was outrage in his voice, and loathing.

"I know," she said.

He crossed to the sofa, crouched in front of her, urgently. "Those are not men. That's not what it is."

She took his face between her hands. "I know."

"They're predators. They're not human."

"I know. I know."

He put his arms around her, and they held each other.

Chapter Forty-Nine

I t was a moment before Roarke could make himself click into the first forum. Again, Singh had highlighted posts by several commenters, apparently Ortiz's aliases. But there were hundreds of similar comments, not just those from Ortiz.

FUCKING CUNT WHORE

Stupid ass bitch needs a good raping

Imona bust dem sugar walls an leave an AIDS load in there

Hope That Slut Cunt Gets Raped By 10 Men With 9 Inch Cocks

The only question left is will Lindstrom be raped first or killed first or both?

If she ever comes near Fresno I will rape her into oblivion

Need to fuck that bitch in the ass so hard we break the Richter scale

DEATH TO FEMCUNTS

I'm gonna cut her throat and fuck the slit until she chokes on cum

The threads and comments went on and on, a maelstrom of hate. In between the vitriolic comments, there were Photoshopped photos and videos: Cara's face superimposed onto naked, bound women. Homemade torture porn.

And possibly the most chilling of all, by another of Ortiz's aliases: *Will pay $ for any verified Lindstrom sightings.*

Roarke put his iPad down, and had to force himself to breathe. He paced the small floor of the cottage, sickened. Then he grabbed his coat and walked out through the back door of the cottage.

The moon was high above the oak trees.

He sat on the bench beside the wall, and leaned his head back against the cold stone, fear and rage roiling inside him.

What is this world we live in?

It was his worst fears, confirmed. The backlash against Cara manifesting in the worst kind of depravity.

And for Ortiz, this obsession had started when she was fourteen years old.

He's a predator. Dangerous. Monstrosity masquerading as law.

And obsessed with rape.

Can you write things like that and not be a rapist?

But is he this *rapist? Or one of the two?*

Ortiz? Franzen? Lethbridge?

Who?

He turned and saw a column of writing, three words scratched into the wall beside him. Faded scratches, barely legible. And then he froze, and looked closer. They were names. Names he knew.

Lethbridge

Franzen

Ortiz

Roarke stared at the list and thought, *I'm losing my mind.*

He touched Lethbridge's name, felt the roughness of the scratches in the cold of the stone. Real.

Did I do this? Did I sleepwalk out here and do it?

He had no recollection of sitting here, no recollection of carving the names into the wall.

He knew it was not his handwriting, if handwriting was the word for lines in stone. But it was still more plausible than the other explanation.

That Cara had sat here, on this same bench, and carved these same names into the wall, sixteen years in the past.

He stood from the bench, circled around the wall to the front of the building, moving under the ghostly shadows of olive and pepper trees. It was a feeling like sleepwalking.

There was a light on in the long wing of the Mission, shining through the last window, the room at the very end of the building. Mother Doctor's office.

Of course. The coffee, the cigarettes . . . the revving engine of that mind. Of course she's an insomniac, too.

He searched the ground at his feet for pebbles, tossed them at her window as if he were a teenager, courting her.

Her face appeared at the window and she looked down, spotted him. Her eyebrows arched, and she lifted a hand to point, indicating the back door.

He met her there, and brought her around the building, through the misty dark to the bench beside the wall, where he pointed to the names in the stone. She stared, much as he had, in bewilderment, and then wonder.

"It's my list. But this was Cara," he said. "It must have been Cara. You said she visited Ivy here."

"Yes, and I found her out here, late one afternoon." Her eyes widened slightly. "Sitting here."

It was a lot to hope for, but he had to ask. "Do you remember anything about what she said?"

The nun stared off into the dark, where mist curled through the olive trees. "She had come to see Ivy, and I tried to get her to talk—"

"Did she mention any of these men?" He gestured to the list.

"No. She didn't say much, really. I didn't press her. I felt that she would come back, and I didn't want to scare her away . . ."

"What day was that, that you saw her? Was it before Laura Huell died, or after?"

The nun sat on the bench, her eyes sharpening as she remembered. "It was the day of the funeral. I'd seen the notice in the paper that morning."

So . . . it was just after she killed Pierson. She wouldn't have been likely to talk to any authority figure honestly after that.

He looked at the scratched list of men on the wall, and realized he had needed the nun there just to corroborate that the writing was actually there, that he was not dreaming or hallucinating. It was surreal, but Cara had been here, had been thinking the same thoughts . . . and planning the same thing.

He turned to Mother Doctor. "Those things you gave me, from Ivy's room . . . I'm pretty sure what they mean, and what this means—" he gestured to the list on the wall "—is that Cara went after Ivy's attacker."

"Went after him?"

"To kill him."

The nun's eyes went still in the dark. After a moment she half-laughed, uneasily. "Roarke. She was fourteen years old. You can't mean . . . you think that child went after a serial rapist? Maybe a killer?"

"She's been doing it for a long time. It had to start somewhere. I'm fairly sure she'd already killed Pierson by then. And if anything could make someone kill . . ." He stopped, and heard himself saying what Epps had said to him, not that long ago. "It's who she is. It's what she does. Her mission."

She was watching him. "Because she sees evil." There was no skepticism in her voice, only interest.

"Do you think that's possible?" he asked, and realized he was desperate to know.

She looked off over the darkness of the valley. "I see the effects of evil every day. Is it possible to see it, actually *see* it in a perpetrator?" She lifted her shoulders slightly. "I often meet parents who make something in me recoil. In other cultures, people have no trouble believing that a shaman can see human energy. That they can read the quality of a human being. I don't see anything so farfetched about that." She met his eyes. "Don't *you* know, sometimes?"

Roarke and Epps had talked about it. Briefly, carefully. But they had both agreed: there was such a thing as Blue Sense. The intuition, or just heightened perception, that made cops sense danger, that whispered, *Something's behind that door,* or *Watch that guy at the corner table . . .*

"Yes," he said aloud to the nun.

"Then that's the answer. If you can sense it, and I can sense it, then I have no problem whatsoever believing that a child can see it. If there's anything I know, it's that children are more highly attuned to the world than we ever remember to be."

Roarke nodded slowly.

Mother Doctor lifted her hands. "And I can't help but think . . . Joan of Arc was just thirteen when her visions told her to drive the English out of France."

Roarke looked at her, startled.

She nodded. "So in the past, we have a fourteen-year-old girl on a mission. Who was willing to risk her life to go after someone she considered evil. And in the present we have—you. Also on a mission, obviously."

He didn't know what to say to that. It seemed that he'd lost any mission he ever had.

She seemed to read his thoughts. "Don't kid yourself. I deal with law enforcement regularly. I know the type. But it's more than a mission, for you." She looked at him directly. "I need to ask you something. Are you trying to find her? And I don't mean in a law enforcement sense. Your interest in Cara goes far beyond any law enforcement duty."

He felt a hot rush of shame.

She shook her head. "I'm not blind. And I did meet her. She was compelling then. Now . . . I can only imagine."

He closed his eyes for a moment. "I don't want to find her."

Suddenly all he could think of were the toxic words from the Reddit forums, and again the fear for her rose up, choking him, so that he could barely speak. He would rather she were dead than ever have to face that mob. "I hope . . . I never hear from her or about her, ever again. I should never have come at all—"

"But you did," she said sharply. "So you have a choice to make. What outcome do you want, here?"

Her words were a command, a welcome slap in the face, and he remembered the girls. The rows and rows of burned girls. Laura. Ivy.

He looked at the stone wall, at the scratched names. "I want to finish this," he said. "Make sure that whoever it is, is never able to hurt anyone ever again."

"And what is the next right step?"

"There's a survivor I can talk to. If she's willing to talk to me."

"Then that's what you do."

Back in the cottage, he realized Mother Doctor was right. Singh wouldn't be able to talk to Marlena Sanchez until the morning, but he could be there, on site, to meet her as soon as she said yes. Or to try to see her anyway if she said no.

He used his iPad and called up MapQuest to be sure, but Flagstaff was an eight-hour drive, and he was feeling too much urgency to lose the time a sixteen-hour round trip would take. This time of year the roads up into the mountains could easily be shut down due to snow.

The closest airport was Ontario International, less than an hour away on the 15, and Southwest had a flight to Flagstaff at 6:00 a.m. He booked it online, and grabbed his roller bag to pack, again.

He started up the Rover in the parking lot of the Mission, and looked out through the windshield at the garden wall, the skull and crossbones above the wooden gate.

He had the haunted feeling that he was leaving young Cara alone, helpless. He knew it made no sense. The danger was sixteen years in the past.

Be safe, he told her in his head.

Then he shook off the feeling, and drove.

CARA

Chapter Fifty

It is long past dinner when she returns from the Mission to the group home. The moment she walks through the door, Ms. Sharonda steps out of her office, drawn up to her full height like an avenging angel. She looks toward the massive clock on the wall, and her face is ominous. "You see the time there. You know the rules—"

Cara stands facing her. "I'm sorry I'm late. I went to a funeral."

Ms. Sharonda's eyes narrow. "You knew that Huell girl?"

"She was in my Social Studies class. We talked sometimes."

It is true enough.

The director is silent for a moment. At last she says, "That's hard. I'm sorry to hear it." She studies Cara. "How are you feeling?"

Are you sad? Do you have thoughts of harming yourself? Do you have thoughts of harming others?

Is there any kind of *Normal* answer she can give?

"I don't know," she says. Suddenly she feels lightheaded. She swallows. At the end of the hall behind Ms. Sharonda, Laura stands in the corner, with a pool of blood at her feet.

"Did she say anything to you? About what she was thinking?"

Cara turns her eyes away from the vision of the bleeding girl, shakes her head quickly.

Ms. Sharonda makes a sound that is not quite a sigh. "Suicide is what happens when a person is overwhelmed by feelings. They feel unable to cope." She looks at Cara fiercely. "That kind of moment will always pass. But in the moment it feels like things will never get better. You got to ride out those feelings."

"Because it gets better," Cara says flatly, and looks Ms. Sharonda in the face.

Ms. Sharonda doesn't answer right away. "Sometimes it gets better. I can't tell you it always does, because you know that's bullshit. But you got a choice to make here."

Cara thinks of moonlight and Joshua trees and blood.

"I've made it," she says.

Ms. Sharonda raises her eyebrows, waiting.

"She gave up. But you can't give up. You can't let them win."

Ms. Sharonda looks at her for a long time, and Cara wonders what she sees. "Okay then." She straightens. "But next time you need to go somewhere you go through channels. You talk to me first. Are we clear?"

"We're clear."

Cara turns and goes down the hall to her room, thinking of the list she scratched into the stone wall of the Mission.

She is clear. She has never been more clear in her life.

The next day she starts, with the first name on her list.

She walks past the snarling wolf mural, into the administration building, and into Lethbridge's office, telling the secretary, "He said I should come in and talk to him."

The vice-principal looks up from his desk as she steps in through the door. He registers her, leans back in his big chair in surprise. And there is something else on his face, but she doesn't know what. Lethbridge is a harder read than Detective Ortiz.

"Well, hello, Eden. What can I do for you?"

She doesn't bother to correct him about the name. "I've been thinking about what you said about college prep. I want to sign up for some clubs. I want to sign up for Palmers."

He spreads his hands. "I'm so pleased, C—Eden. Palmers is a very worthwhile program."

"You're the sponsor."

"I'm one of them, yes. Palmers is a youth service club, a branch of the Wayfarers Club—"

"I know," she interrupts him. "Laura played piano there, for dinners and meetings and things." She had been listening at the funeral, to the pretty, useless things that people said in the church. Now she looks straight at him. "She told me all about it." She emphasizes the word *all*, just slightly, but enough for him to notice.

Lethbridge's smile fades. "Laura is . . . It was a tragic loss. You knew her, then?"

"She was really nice to me," Cara lies.

"Yes, she was that kind of person," he says, also lying.

Cara holds his gaze. "She really liked Palmers, though. She liked talking about it."

The VP gives her another smile. This one looks weak, worried. "She talked about Palmers?"

Cara nods. "A whole lot. And Wayfarers, too."

"What did she tell you?"

She looks across the desk. "You know." She waits a good long beat so that he can imagine all kinds of responses, before she finishes, "Stuff."

He clears his throat uncomfortably. "I'm glad to know we made a difference in her life. But Eden, if Laura said anything . . . if there's anything that might bring her parents some understanding . . . I really do need to know that."

She looks back at him blankly. "What kinds of things?"

"Just . . . anything that you might remember her saying."

"I'll try," she says, and turns to leave. Then she turns quickly back. "Oh wait, I remember now."

It is almost comic, the look of alarm on his face. Comic, and telling. She waits a beat to keep him suspended, then she says—

"You have to call Ms. Lewis to get permission for me to go to meetings."

He blinks, forces another smile. "I'll do that."

She can feel his agitation like a current in the air behind her as she walks out the door.

ROARKE

Chapter Fifty-One

Flagstaff was freezing, a good fifty degrees colder than Southern California, with snow frosting the pine trees, icy drifts banked up beside the streets. People on the sidewalks were bundled in alpaca coats, wrapped in wool scarves, hats, boots, thermal leggings.

Roarke cruised the historic downtown of the former silver mining territory in the rental car he'd picked up at the airport. He'd driven through the city before, en route to some job he'd already forgotten, but had never spent any time here. He was struck by the unique style of it: Wild West with a dash of New Age mysticism. Many of its historic buildings had been restored; some of the hotels were award-winning period recreations. But the old storefronts now housed boutiques, rock crystal shops and microbreweries.

It was an eclectic collection of people, too: skiers and New Agers and stag parties and conventioneers. Banners hung over the entrances of several of the hotels: WELCOME NATIONAL LIONS CONVENTION.

Marlena Sanchez had agreed to meet him in her shop, a clothing store on one of the touristy side streets. No girly dresses here, though.

Roarke walked in through the door to find a storefront populated by rows of female mannequins dressed in angular clothes with sharp lines, lots of combat trousers and chain link ornaments. The shop had a wide window with round armchairs placed to make a comfortable seating area.

Marlena stood looking him over. She was dark-haired and cocoa-skinned, with a coiled-spring muscularity under her severe dark jeans and gray sweater. Her eyes were wary and watchful.

The same age as Cara, Roarke couldn't help but think.

She had put the CLOSED sign in the window, but she stayed within reach of the door, as if giving herself an escape route. Roarke took his cue and sat in one of the chairs beside the broad front window, a good distance from her. She remained standing.

"I appreciate you talking to me," he began.

"I'm not doing it for you," she said stiffly.

"I appreciate that, too."

She stared out the window at the street, the people walking by. "Seventeen years, and they haven't found this guy."

"I know," he said, inadequately.

"You know they didn't even test the rape kit. I started hassling them a year ago. I'm still waiting."

"That's a crime," he said. He could not have meant anything more. "My field office has requested the kit. We'll do everything we can to expedite the testing."

"You think he's still . . ." She trailed off, shuddered. He waited, letting her take the lead. "So what do you want from me?" she finally asked, her voice flat.

"I've seen the police report," Roarke said. "I'm afraid what I need is more details about him. Anything you can remember. Voice. Smells. Speech patterns."

"You want me to relive it, you mean," she said, her voice harsh. "Christ, you're not asking much, are you?" He could see her hands were shaking.

"I can take you through it if that would be easier. Ask questions. You can take as long as you like to answer. Whatever will help you."

She didn't respond, and he knew he had to say more.

"The thing is—we've found a pattern of these attacks. They happen in January. The last one was last year—"

She turned on him savagely. "All right. *All right.*"

"Thank you."

"Just do it." She was agitated, breathing hard. He knew he had to get her to relax enough to remember.

"Are you comfortable here?"

She half shrugged. Then she glanced at the plate glass of the window. She stepped to the wall and pulled on a cord, dropping a blind across the glass.

Good, Roarke thought. *Thank you.* She wasn't happy. Who would be? But she was willing.

"Would you prefer to sit or stand?" he asked aloud. He wanted to offer her all the choices he could, to let her feel that she was in control.

After a long moment, she sat in the other armchair, across from him.

"You can close your eyes, if that will help."

She made a contemptuous sound, but after a moment, she shut her eyes.

"You were walking to school in the morning that day?"

Her posture had already stiffened. "Yes."

"What was the weather like? The temperature?"

"It was January. It was cold."

"Raining?"

"In Phoenix?" she shot back. "Dry cold. It was dark but . . . it was morning," she said plaintively, her voice for a moment just a child's. "I thought bad things only happened at night."

Then her face hardened. The cynicism was back. "If you can believe that." She made a gesture as if she were reaching for a cigarette, then faltered and clasped her hands together tightly.

"Did you always walk to school?" Roarke asked. *Could he have been watching you for days?* he meant.

"I missed the bus." Her voice was an agony of regret, and he thought he could guess what she was thinking. What if she'd been five minutes earlier? What if her parents had given her a ride to school? It only took the smallest lapse, the tiniest error, to plunge someone into a living hell . . .

But the information was useful already. It meant the abduction was opportunistic. The rapist wouldn't have been able to grab her if she'd gotten the bus. Roarke made a mental note and moved on.

"As you were walking, were there any cars driving on the street?"

"Once in a while. Not many. It was early, it was still pretty quiet."

"Were you aware of a vehicle following you?"

She stiffened again. It was a moment before she answered. "I saw a van go by but it didn't stop. It was parked when I went around the corner. I walked by it. There was no one around. Then . . . then I got grabbed from behind."

Roarke had a sense of déjà vu. *Definitely the same MO. Exactly how Ivy had described the abduction in her police statement.*

I'm so sorry, he said to Marlena in his head. He waited a moment before he continued. "Did you have a sense of how big he was?"

Her voice was savage. "I'll tell you what. *I* wasn't big. He was a lot bigger than me. A lot bigger."

"Did you ever at any point see him? Any part of him?"

"He put a hood . . . over my head, you know?" She cleared her throat. "I screamed, and he punched me in the face . . . he said he would kill me if I made another sound." Her voice was labored. Roarke could see that her jaw had tightened to the point that she was having difficulty speaking. "He broke my nose. I was bleeding the whole time, under the hood. Sometimes I was . . . choking . . . on the blood. I thought I was going to die."

Roarke, who didn't pray, found himself praying he would say the right thing. He tried to put all the feelings he had into his next words. "You didn't. I think you're incredibly brave."

She took a shuddering breath, then glanced at him and nodded.

"What kind of hood was it?" He looked around the shop, at the clothing. "Can you tell me what kind of material?"

She closed her eyes again. "Canvas. It was like a canvas bag."

"Was he wearing a watch? Or any jewelry . . . ?"

She shook her head. "I don't think so. I don't know."

No ring, then? Roarke tried to contain his disappointment. "You said in the report he was fleshy?"

"He was big. Not fat, but . . . solid."

"Did he say anything to you? Talk to you?"

Her voice was dark, bitter. "Oh yeah." She changed her tone, mimicking. 'Shut up and take it, whore. You're a dirty little bitch . . .'" She gagged slightly.

Roarke had noticed a bottle of water beside the cash register. He stood and walked to get it, brought it to the window and set the bottle gently in front of Marlena. She picked it up with shaking hands and drank. After a moment, Roarke continued.

"What was his voice like?"

"He was white." Before Roarke could say anything, she added, "You can tell by the voice." She sounded defensive. "You can. Plus, he . . . used it."

"Used what?"

"He called me a Mexican cunt."

"I'm sorry," he said again.

"It wasn't you." She drank more water, then added, "His voice was fake."

"Fake how?"

"Like, he was making it lower. Rougher. Yelling and whispering at the same time. All the time he was . . ."

She had been very detailed in the police report. He had sodomized her, beaten her with his fists and choked her, then raped her orally, holding the bag over her eyes.

"I either passed out or just checked out for a while when he was . . ." She was overcome with savage, angry sobs for some time before she could continue. "But then I smelled it. The gas.

"He was holding something in front of my face and he shook it. A metal can with liquid in it. Sloshing. The gas. He said he was going to burn me.

"I was begging him. I didn't even know what I was saying." She shuddered convulsively. "He described the whole thing, you know? That he would pour gas all over me and set me on fire. How my flesh would cook. How it would smell. He said I would feel my flesh melting and my bones charring and that I would be screaming until my throat burned and then I would be screaming inside. He was getting off on it. That was the worst part of it. It made him . . . excited."

Roarke sat with his hands on his knees and breathed through his own fury. *I am going to get you, you sick fuck.*

She was shivering uncontrollably. "I thought I was going to die," she repeated. "I was sure he was going to kill me. When he started talking about burning me, I *wanted* to die—"

Roarke leaned forward urgently, without touching her. "He didn't kill you. You are strong. You are here. You're here in Flagstaff, in your own shop."

She took another shuddering breath. He waited some minutes while she got hold of herself again, then asked very gently, "Do you know why he stopped? Did you say something, do something?"

She shook her head, kept shaking it. "Something happened. I'm still not sure what. I think I heard a car, and maybe that scared him, because he suddenly climbed back in the front seat and drove off fast. He drove . . . maybe a few minutes, then stopped and pulled me out of the back and dumped me on the ground. It was some parking lot."

So that the cops couldn't get tire tracks, Roarke thought. *At this point the guy was thinking. He wasn't taking chances. But he backed off on the burning . . .*

He wanted to touch her hand. He made himself stay still in his chair. "I'm so sorry," he said.

Her voice cracked. "He did it with someone, though. That's why you're here."

"I'm afraid so. One that I'm sure of, anyway."

She swallowed. "He burned her?"

Roarke paused. "Yes."

Marlena sat very still. Then her chest heaved and she bolted up from her chair, ran to the back of the store. Roarke could hear her retching.

He sat in the armchair, and looked out through the lowered blind at the passing people.

Two teenage girls in colorful coats walked side by side, staring down at their phones as they texted. Much the same age as Marlena would have been . . .

And Ivy, and Laura . . .

After some time, Marlena came back, her eyes red. She sat down again, but Roarke could see she was starting to space out, detach from her surroundings.

She's had enough. No one should have to go through this again.

He cleared his throat. "Before I go, can I ask why . . . what was it that made you go back to the police about the rape kit?"

"My therapist." She looked away from him. "For fifteen . . . sixteen years all I wanted to do was forget it ever happened. I went through a lot of pills and booze and other shit to make it go away."

She looked out the window.

"January's not a great time of year for me, for obvious reasons. I think maybe I wanted to live in snow so January would *look* different, you know? But last year it was just—bad. These . . . nightmares. Flashbacks. I knew I'd better get . . . something. Help.

"I started working with Lyn, she got me into a support group, and people were talking about the rape kit backlog. So I called up the cops and I found out they never ran the DNA."

They never ran the DNA. And six months later this guy set Ivy on fire, Roarke thought, beyond fury. *This madness. It has to change.*

"We're going to run it now," he said, his voice hard.

She sat for a long moment, silent, but Roarke had the feeling she was working up to something. He waited, and finally she spoke.

"I dream about it. It never goes away. I'm never not afraid. Because I know he's out there. That he could show up again, anywhere. Anyone on the street could be him." She looked at him, with dull, dark eyes. "This is a *monster.* He's out there. And I never know if I'm looking right at him."

Roarke walked around downtown Flagstaff for almost an hour to clear his head. Then he went into the lobby of a hotel, where a painstaking historic renovation created a weird time warp back to an 1850s saloon. He sat on a glass-enclosed Victorian balcony and ordered a beer instead of lunch. It came, but he didn't touch it.

He looked out over the townspeople and tourists. He had half a mind to get in his rental car, drive to Phoenix, walk into the police department and demand the kit himself.

Might not go over so well.

He stared down at the street, watching a bundled-up bachelor party pedaling a PubCrawler down the street: a bizarre combination group bicycle and functional bar.

The phrase *boys will be boys* floated through his head.

And then that thought bumped against another.

He scanned the street, focusing on the hotels, on the draped banners:

WELCOME NATIONAL LIONS CONVENTION.

Roarke suddenly felt a cold that had nothing to do with the icy weather.

He pushed the beer aside, pulled out his iPad and called up the file with the list of rapes that Singh had compiled: the dates and cities of the attacks.

Then he jumped onto to the internet and looked up the National Wayfarers Association website.

There was a tab for *Events and Conferences.* Clicking on it got him to a list of past conventions, with the cities and dates.

Roarke could barely hold the iPad, and he realized his hands were shaking. He clicked back and forth between screens, running down the lists, comparing the cities and dates of the rapes to the Wayfarer convention list.

There had been a Wayfarer national convention in January for the last twenty years, exactly corresponding to the cities and dates of each rape.

Except for Ivy.

But the thing that stopped him, chilled his blood, was the current convention page.

He stared down at the date in paralyzed disbelief.

This year's convention was this week. Starting tomorrow. In Dallas.

Roarke grabbed for his phone, punched in the numbers for the convention hotel.

"Yes, I'd like to be connected to one of your guests," he told the first live person who answered, and waited impatiently through the inevitable transfer.

"I'd like to speak to Mel Franzen, please."

"One moment, please . . ."

Roarke waited in agonized impatience. The receptionist came back on. "I'm sorry, Mr. Franzen hasn't checked in yet. Would you like me to transfer you to voice mail?"

"No. Thank you," Roarke said. "Can you connect me with Robert Lethbridge instead?"

"One moment, sir . . . I'm sorry, we have no Robert Lethbridge registered."

"Thank you," Roarke said numbly, and disconnected. He stared out at the mountains.

It's Franzen, then. This is what he does. He goes to the conventions where he's going to have plenty of alibi witnesses, he rents a van, and he cruises the schools in the early morning looking for girls walking alone.

Both meticulously planned and opportunistic. Crimes spread out so far over different jurisdictions that no one had ever connected them.

He stood up at the table, looking down at his phone.

Dallas. It was late afternoon already.

What could he do? Alert local police?

And tell them what? To put a twenty-four hour tail on Franzen because he thought he might be planning to hunt down a high school girl?

He had no evidence. No contact with the Dallas PD.

Other customers at surrounding tables were staring at him. He threw money down on the table and ran through the bar, heading for the street, for his rental car.

No time to book. He would get to the airport and take the first flight he could get.

CARA

Chapter Fifty-Two

The Wayfarers Club is an easy walk from the school. She tells Lethbridge she wants to go to a meeting to see what the club is like, and once Lethbridge has talked to Ms. Sharonda, Cara goes the next day.

It is an old, columned building, with steps up to the portico and symbols that look Greek on the arch above the doors. A big concrete compass stands on the front lawn.

She goes to the parking lot at the side of the building first and walks through the rows of cars. There are lots of expensive ones with security systems, the kind that are harder to steal, she notes idly. But that is not her mission here. She is looking for the white van.

There is no van of any color.

She goes up the steps of the building and into the hall.

There are more compasses inside, and a hallway full of pictures of men in suits, several polished wooden boards with attached wooden plaques and names carved into them.

Loud talking and laughter comes from an open set of double doors halfway down the hall.

She approaches with caution to look in.

The meeting is all men inside, standing and sitting in rows and row of folding chairs.

Some of them stop talking as she stands there in the doorway, looking around. Many of them look at her furtively. Some are not so furtive.

It is a terrible, uncomfortable feeling, the eyes on her, like being on stage, like being on display. The smell of too-strong cologne rolls from the men and surrounds her. Every instinct she has is on alert for danger. She wonders how Laura could stand it. She has to force herself to stand still, not to turn and flee.

One of the men comes up to her. He is tall, and broad, much bigger than she is. Franzen, the crew-cut man from the Palmers meeting, who was also at Laura's funeral, standing near the grave. He gives her a smile with too many teeth.

"Are you Eden?" he asks. "Vice-Principal Lethbridge said you wanted to attend our general meeting today. That's very industrious of you. I'm Mel Franzen, the Palmers coordinator."

He has an oily interest in her, but so many men do. He sticks out a hand for her to shake. The clasp of his fingers is strong and damp, unpleasant, but she keeps her face still. She feels the bite of the large ring he wears on his middle finger, and glances down to see it has that same compass symbol. The vice-principal has one, too.

"I'm looking for activities," she says automatically. "To build my resume."

"Of course you are." He does not let go of her hand. "And it's our mission to help bright young people like you." She pulls her fingers away from his grasp, and has to force herself not to wipe her palm on her jeans. As she does, she sees a flash of something in his eyes. *Anger?* But his voice is calm and friendly when he speaks.

"We're about to begin. Why don't you take a seat?"

She turns and finds a chair in a back row on the aisle, the one nearest the door so she can flee.

Some other man in a suit takes the stage and calls the meeting to order.

The meeting is a succession of speakers, men talking loudly and laughing, voting on things she doesn't understand and doesn't care about. An accountant reports on finances. Someone gets up to talk about a pancake breakfast. There are many mentions of "the community" and "the youth."

She keeps looking over the rows of men in suits. All of them seem old. All of them seem too loud. They are a pack, like Martell and the jocks. There is nothing good about packs.

There are so many of them, and she doesn't know what she is looking for.

She looks at the silent piano in the corner. Laura came here, and sat in the middle of this. Week after week, that silent, frightened girl on display for the pack.

Why? Why would you? Why would anyone?

Then her ears prick up at a familiar name, as the man called Franzen takes the podium again.

"Our deepest sympathies go out to the Huell family for the loss of their daughter. The chapter is collecting donations that will serve to establish a memorial scholarship fund. See Pete to contribute. Also, as the family is in mourning, Dave Huell will be unable to serve as delegate to the national convention this month. We will need to elect a new delegate. Can I ask for volunteers, for brothers who will be able to fly out to Houston next week . . ."

Some of the men raise their hands, and Cara loses interest again.

She is the first to leave the meeting.

In the corridor, before anyone else comes out, she ducks inside one of the other doors. It is some sort of smaller meeting room, with a large conference table in the center and bookcases against the walls. There are more of the compass symbols here, more charts and plaques, a glass case full of trophies.

She closes the door most of the way, stands against the wall by the doorway, listening to the heavy sound of shoes on the polished floor of the hall, to loud male chatter. After a time, the hall is silent.

Then she opens the door silently, just a crack, peers out. There is no one in the hall. She eases through the door and makes her feet light and silent as she walks down the hall toward the rectangular glow from the last office. She stops beside the doorway and listens, hears no one moving. She sneaks a look inside.

There is a large desk, shelves and filing cabinets.

She looks over the desk, with its desktop computer, pencil jar, a calendar blotter, an in and out box for papers. She takes a glance at the computer, at the filing cabinets . . . takes a step through the door . . .

What can she look for here? What could she find that would tell her something? Would Ivy's name be in the files? Would Laura's? Would that tell her anything, anyway? Surely the things that happened to those girls would never be written down and filed away.

Someone speaks from the doorway behind her. "We meet again."

That oily, jovial voice.

She turns to face Franzen. He is standing in the doorway, blocking it.

"I thought you'd gone," he says pleasantly, but there is an edge in his tone now.

She swallows, tries to keep her voice steady. "I came back. Vice-Principal Lethbridge said I really should sign up. So that's what I want to do."

She watches him, looking for any signs, not knowing what she's looking for. She had thought that she would be able to see, that somehow *It* would reveal itself, show *Its* teeth, make some move. But everything about Franzen is cloudy. All she sees is a man in a suit with a blustery face.

He is watching her, too. "Is that all?"

She doesn't know what he's asking, so she is silent.

"Is that the real reason you're here?"

She wants to shake him, to shock him. "I'm a friend of Ivy's," she says quickly.

It is as if he has stopped breathing. For no more than a moment, but she can feel the pause, the stillness. Then his face moves again. He raises his eyebrows.

"Ivy?"

"Yes," she says, and looks straight into his face, waiting for the lie. If he pretends he knows nothing, she will know. It will be proof.

He shakes his head. "We are all so very distressed about that whole—business. That poor girl. The club is helping with her medical bills."

And suddenly Cara knows what to say. "She said I should join the club."

It works like a charm. Franzen seems to pale under his crew cut. "She *said?*"

"She said I would learn a lot."

She keeps her face innocent, but she can feel his agitation. He cannot believe this conversation is happening. All the power has shifted to her.

"When was that, that you spoke to her?" he asks. He is trying to keep a friendly tone but she can hear the urgency in his voice.

"I visit her. At the Mission."

"And she's speaking?"

"Oh yes. More every day." She watches his face, and decides to go further. "If she wants me to come here, there must be a reason, right? And not just Ivy. Laura came, too. Someone has to do it now that they're gone."

His eyes narrow. "Do what?"

She shrugs. "That's what I'm here for. To learn."

"You want to learn. That's interesting. You want—to learn."

His voice has become soft—and ugly. Her stomach lurches. The change in him is so fast she knows that she has made a mistake. And she is here, alone with him . . .

She glances at the door. He glances at it too, then back to her, his face weirdly blank. He is solidly in front of the doorway, and he is so much bigger than she is. But she knows that on the desk behind her is a pencil jar . . . and in that jar is a pair of scissors.

She takes a step backward, feels the edge of the desk against her thighs . . . eases her hand behind her back . . .

There is a step behind Franzen. He twists around to look. Another man in a suit glances inside the office, sees Cara.

"I didn't know you had company."

She takes her chance and darts out, lunging straight ahead and pushing between the two men.

"Eden!" Franzen calls from behind her, but she runs down the hallway, toward the front door, and slams out.

Outside, she runs down the front steps and veers to the right, ducking out of sight around the side of the building. She pauses there, her back pressed against the wall, listening for any sound of someone following her . . .

There is only the dry whisper of palm fronds in the trees above.

She pushes off from the wall and circles the entire building, making her way around to the parking lot again. She stops and hides in another cluster of trees right up against the building, where she is concealed by the thick dry trunks, but can watch the lot and also the front door.

There are very few cars left in the lot, and still no van. But she remains hidden in the trees, and waits, and watches.

Franzen steps out through the front door, turns around and locks it. He walks past the columns, down the steps, past the concrete compass, into the parking lot. Then he stops beside a car in a front parking space: a big, gleaming black Lexus. He opens the door, squeezes himself inside.

The Lexus starts up with a roar, and Franzen drives out of the parking lot.

She watches it go.

It could still be him, she thinks. *He wouldn't be driving the van. He's hiding it. Of course he is. He won't drive it where people will see him. He has it in a special place, and he only uses it to go out hunting. He might change license plates, too.* It is what you do when you steal a car. Eric had taught her that, as well.

She has an unfinished feeling, but there is nothing more she can do here. She steps out of the palm trees, and walks for the sidewalk.

There is a bus stop halfway down the street, and she heads for it. She is just fishing for money in the pocket of her jeans when she sees it: the white van, waiting at the corner, at the stop sign at the end of the street, its turn signal blinking right.

For one heart-stopped moment she is unable to move. Then she bolts, runs as fast as she can toward the corner, to see who is driving. But when she rounds the corner to the next street, the van is far down the block. Too far to see a driver. Too far to see a license plate number. It accelerates, disappears into the distance.

Cara halts on the sidewalk, bent over, hands on her knees, panting. Her thoughts are reeling.

But Franzen just got into the Lexus.

So there was someone else *in the van.*

The man who interrupted them in the office?

She'd been so focused on just getting out, she hadn't looked closely at his face.

She straightens, moves back to the bus stop bench and sits down. As her breathing returns to normal, she thinks quickly back over the rows and rows of men at the meeting. There are just so many of them, and they look so much alike.

But the van was here. Outside that meeting.

It is close.

She looks back down the block at the club house.

So many, and only one of me. She feels a wave of anguished helplessness.

I can't do it.

As soon as she thinks it, another voice speaks in her head that for once, she recognizes. The nun's. A strong voice, firm and kind.

You are not alone.

And she realizes the nun is right.

ROARKE

Chapter Fifty-Three

It was early evening by the time Roarke landed in Dallas. The taxi took him to the downtown hotel, cruising past the urban green space of Klyde Warren Park and the futuristic orb of Reunion Tower. But there would be no time for sightseeing.

The Wayfarers convention had taken over the whole hotel. There was a registration room and staff rooms down one corridor; the hotel's TV monitor projected a schedule of events.

Roarke stopped in front of the screen to study it. There had been an opening banquet, which he'd already missed.

But the real action of any convention started in the bar.

And that's where Roarke found Franzen, in a crowd of well-lubricated conventioneers.

Roarke stared across the low-lit bar at the big man, laughing with the other men. He shouldered his way through the crowd.

Franzen saw Roarke coming and for an instant there was that moment of trying to place him. And then it hit him, and all geniality vanished.

Franzen closed his hand around Roarke's forearm and used the grip to steer Roarke to the side of the room. "What's the meaning of this?" he demanded, not loudly enough to attract attention.

Roarke removed Franzen's hand from his sleeve. "I think you'll want to talk somewhere more private," he said, letting his voice carry the implicit threat.

Franzen's eyes burned at him, but he turned and they moved further away from the bar, into a hallway with Art Deco lamps casting triangles of light all the way down the corridor.

Franzen turned on Roarke. "Explain yourself."

Roarke opted for open, casual menace. "I just wanted to let you know that I'm here. I'm watching you. Wherever you go this weekend, I'll be there. In case you had any extracurricular plans."

Franzen's jaw and fists were clenched, a barely contained fury. "I don't know what the hell your problem is, *Mr.* Roarke. But this is harassment and you'll be hearing from my lawyer—"

"Oh, I'm happy to stay the requisite fifty feet away. But you've heard of the buddy system, haven't you? Where you go, I go. Buddy."

For a few seething seconds, Roarke thought Franzen would haul off and punch him. *Just try it*, he lasered at the man, silently. *Give me an excuse.*

But Franzen dropped his hands and turned without a word, heading back to the bar.

And Roarke followed. Staying the requisite fifty feet away. He found a high stool against the wall in the bar and ordered himself a tonic and lime. When the glass came, he waited until the next time Franzen glanced across the room at him and raised the glass in a mocking salute. Franzen glared at him and turned away.

At this point, Roarke was sure that he'd already done what he'd set out to do. If Franzen was the rapist, he would have to be insane to try anything this weekend, in Dallas, knowing that he was under this kind of scrutiny. And the rapist's MO was the complete opposite of insane: he operated under the most meticulously crafted safety procedures.

But Roarke had been dead serious. He wasn't going anywhere. If he had to camp outside Franzen's hotel room door, he would.

There would be no fourteen-year-old girl snatched by a monster on her way to school tomorrow. Not here. Not by Franzen.

I swear it.

He downed his tonic and lime and signaled for another.

CARA

Chapter Fifty-Four

The low light on the curved walls of the Mission hall looks like torch-light, and Cara feels as if she's in another age entirely.

She taps so softly on the door that no one could hear her knocking . . . except a girl who can hear the dark.

The door opens, and there she stands, in the oval of light. The skeleton girl. Faceless. Eyeless. But somehow, she knows. She opens the door further to let Cara in.

Cara closes the door behind her.

The skeleton girl turns and lies back down on the bed.

There is nothing in the darkness but the sound of their breathing.

Cara walks slowly to the bed and lies down beside her. Then Cara puts her arms around Ivy and lies, holding her.

The night folds around them and they huddle in bed and speak together without words. They speak of a man who has long ago become something other than a man. They speak of cruelty, of soul-crushing violation. They speak of the darkest fears of children, who know that monsters are real.

And when Cara finally dreams, she dreams Ivy's nightmare, just as she has told it.

The walk to school in chilly predawn. The sense of someone, something . . . following, hovering, and then the quick grab. The chains welded into the wall of the van. The duct tape and gasoline. The brutal invasion of her body and the unspeakable pain of burning, her skin, her hair, her eyes on fire . . .

The stinking malevolence of the man.

He. It. The monster. The man with the monster inside.

When the monster has used her in every way she could be used, he drags her from her metal prison and hurls her to the ground.

He rips the canvas hood off her head, and that is when she knows that she is going to die. She has one last glimpse of the world . . . the golden glittering sand, the sky, the feathery shadows of palm trees against the brilliance of the sun . . .

And then burning, blinding pain.

Chapter Fifty-Five

S he leaves the Mission in the dark. Out through the gardens, blanketed in shrouds of mist. Out through the heavy wood door in the wall.

She is silent, drawn into herself, exhausted and sickened by the things she has seen.

But she knows where to find him now.

ROARKE

Chapter Fifty-Six

Roarke was dead on his feet when he returned to the Mission. Two days in Dallas following Franzen around the convention and around downtown.

Franzen had been a good little conventioneer, following the schedule, attending nothing but meetings and meals. But Roarke knew he'd made an enemy for life, and though he didn't regret the surveillance as a preventative measure, there was also no concrete evidence proving that Franzen was responsible for any rapes at all. That would have to wait for the DNA tests. Singh had gotten custody of two of the kits so far, and they were on the way to the San Francisco Bureau's lab. But the soonest they'd have results from the expedited tests was three days.

When he unlocked the guardhouse door, and turned on the light, there was a parcel on the table inside the cottage, a padded mailer with a return address that was as familiar as his own name.

The Bureau.

He pulled his coat off and tore the mailer open . . . to find the palm frond and the lump of pyrite, a thick folded-up map, a stapled document, and a note from Lam:

Geologic and botanical reports. I can talk you through it if that's easier. Call anytime.

Roarke quickly flipped through the materials: a topographical map of Southern California and several text reports, along with scanned photos of palm trees.

He looked at the time, decided to take Lam at his word. He reached for his phone.

The tech greeted him with his usual effusive cheerfulness. "Long time no hear. Hope things are okay down your way."

Roarke didn't know how to answer that. "I'm keeping on. I got the package, appreciate it."

"Well, we've got a mixed bag of results, here. Hopefully something will come up cherries. The geological is pretty useless. Pyrite is a very common mineral, found in a wide variety of geological formations, from sedimentary, magmatic, hydrothermal, and metamorphic deposits. There's no way to identify a specific region that this particular specimen came from."

Roarke closed his eyes. No surprise there, but his heart sank.

"The botanicals are a little more promising. The palm is *Washingtonia filifera*, also known as the desert fan palm, the California fan palm, or California palm. Here's what's interesting. Most of the palm trees we see in cities are not native to California. In fact, your *Washingtonia filifera* is the *only* native palm of Southern California."

Roarke felt a sudden flare of hope. "Go on . . ."

"You can see a typical tree in the photos I sent." Roarke reached for the photos as Lam added, "Although apparently it's not actually a tree, it's an evergreen monocot, with a tree-like growth pattern. It has a sturdy columnar trunk and waxy green fan-shaped leaves, and it's a big mother: grows fifty to sixty-six feet tall, sometimes up to eighty, and twenty to thirty feet broad, with fronds up to thirteen feet long. When the fronds die they remain attached and drop down to cloak the trunk in that skirt-like formation you see in the photos there."

Roarke flipped through the photo scans, but the palms looked like any other wild-growing palm tree. He'd seen hundreds, thousands of them in the last week.

"They're found in the Palm Springs area, the Colorado River area, and various other canyons. Unfortunately, not only are they not rare, they're quite common to the Santa Rosa/San Jacinto Mountain area, Indio, Coachella, Anza-Borrego, Joshua Tree, et cetera, et cetera."

Nothing but bad news, Roarke thought bleakly.

"But here's something that may help you. These palms need deep ground water and are typically found in spring- and stream-fed oases, and in riparian areas, meaning the interface between land and a river or stream."

Oases. Well, that's a start, I guess.

"So . . . I thought I'd mash up two different geological maps for the Las Piedras region in Riverside County: a Landsat GeoCover 2000 satellite image, and a river map, so you can take a look at water sources. You never know, right?"

"Right," Roarke agreed, trying to sound more positive than he felt. "I really appreciate it, Lam."

"No problemo," the tech assured him. "Anything else we can do, just shout."

Roarke disconnected, and felt a wave of what he realized was homesickness. For the Bureau, for his team, for the techs. For a long time, they'd been as close to family as he got. He was better with them. Not alone.

He turned to the table and unfolded the map Lam had sent. It was full color, with blue dots and veins representing lakes, creeks, streams, and other water sources. And it was as big as the table. Roarke stared down at it glumly.

What do you think you're going to do, search the whole of Riverside County for evidence of a sixteen-year-old crime?

The police and sheriff's department had searched a five-mile radius from where they found Ivy and found nothing.

"But were they searching for evergreen monocots in riparian areas?" he asked aloud.

Right. Just a little crime lab humor there.

It was absurd, not a clue at all. What was he going to do, just drive around looking for palm trees on river beds? Talk about a needle in a haystack . . .

And then he stopped, thinking.

But that's not really true, is it?

He took the map over to the one remaining bare wall and taped it up. Then he grabbed a marker and made an X at the spot on the highway where Ivy had been found.

She couldn't have walked more than a mile. It would be a miracle if she'd walked that far.

He took the marker and a ruler and drew a line representing a mile on the map, a straight line out from the X. Then he did three more lines out, and connected the quadrants to make a circle.

But even before he completed the circle, he'd seen it.

The tiny blue squiggle with the name beside it: Pyrite Creek.

CARA

Chapter Fifty-Seven

The moon is full, as bright as day. The world below it is glowing blue shadows.

She has no trouble finding a car. The world is full of cars. There will always be a ride to wherever she needs to go.

And she knows where she is going. Ivy has told her, and the map is in her head.

It is not far, by minutes, but for anyone who didn't know, it would be nearly impossible to find. A state road that turns into a half-paved road. Past the city, past the ramshackle houses spaced far apart in the unincorporated areas on the fringe, out into the desert. Up toward the mountains, almost to the Cahuilla Reservation, so close that no one would be inclined to go near it.

Side roads turn into dirt gulleys and then there is the arroyo she has been looking for. She can see the grove of old palm trees in the former riverbed. The lair will be close now.

But it is so deserted, so quiet, she knows she cannot approach by car. She turns the stolen Accord around and drives back a bit, then leaves the vehicle on an unpaved side road so she can walk in the rest of the way.

It is easy . . . she just follows the dry riverbed, looking for the sign.

Moonlight on the sand. A billion stars above. The wind breathing through the sand dunes, stirring sand in whorls.

She walks for ten minutes, fifteen, with only the dry touch of the wind and the moonlight to lead her. The smell of sage and juniper, and then the metallic smell of ground water.

Then around a bend, she sees them. The two entwined palm trees Ivy had shown her rise above the dry riverbed, marking the spot.

She scrambles up the sloping, sandy wall of the arroyo, boosts herself over the top. She stands up, to face a fence of barbed wire hung with posted warning signs. One of them is just the crude image of a gun muzzle, aimed point blank. She ignores it.

There are worse things here than a gun.

She steps to the fence, carefully pulls two strands of barbed wire open so she can climb through.

Up the rise, the two small, dark buildings are there, a cabin and a shed, just as in her dreaming.

She keeps her flashlight off. The moonlight is bright enough for her to see, strong enough that she moves quickly to the shadows beside the shed to avoid being seen herself.

The shed door is locked with a hasp and padlock that she knows she can break with her screwdriver. Instead she backs up, and circles the rickety building, scanning the wooden walls until she finds a gap between planks. She drops her flashlight, reaches into her jacket for the screwdriver, and forces the blade into the gap to break off a piece of plank so she can look inside with the flashlight.

The shed is black and empty. She maneuvers the beam of light around the walls, sees rusted shelves cluttered with cans and tools. Chains hang from a hook on the wall.

The chains welded into the wall of the van. The duct tape and gasoline. Her skin, her hair, her eyes on fire . . .

She pulls away from the hole and sits with her back against the outside wall of the shed, forcing herself to breathe through a wave of nausea.

Then she hardens herself and stands.

She approaches the cabin from the side, staring ahead, looking for any signs of inhabitation.

The cabin is dark, although when she gets up closer she realizes there is black material over the one small window. If there is light inside, if the monster is inside, she will not be able to see *It*.

She is very, very slow, her feet whispering against the sand, as she moves up to the cabin. Her breath seems to reverberate in the silence of the night.

She stops in front of the door. There is a steel plate with a hasp, and a padlock hanging from it.

The door is locked from the outside.

She hovers, thoughts coming quickly. He may be here. He may have parked the van on a side road, as she did.

There is time to back away. To run away.

Instead, she reaches for the lock, examining it. It is a heavy combination lock, a Master 17 series. Thick, intimidating, and easy to open.

She has her tools: her ballpoint pen clasp flattened into a lock pick. And of course, a knife.

She grasps the lock, slides in her homemade pick and pushes down the spring plate inside to release the shackle. The lock pops open in her hand.

Her heart is pounding out of her chest as she pulls open the hasp, and then the door. The creak of it is deafening. She freezes, every limb ready to bolt . . .

But nothing stirs inside.

The cabin is dark and stale, a revolting smell she knows too well. She uses her flashlight to scan the room: a filthy mattress, stacks of magazines against the wall, a kitchenette with a sink and hot plate and shelves with cans of food. And a set of metal shelves. Not for books, but with something very interesting to her.

She doesn't know how much time she has. But now she knows she has a chance.

ROARKE

Chapter Fifty-Eight

The riverbed called Pyrite Creek wound through an unincorporated area next to the Cahuilla Reservation.

Roarke drove out toward it on a state road which turned into a half-paved road which turned into a dirt road. With every mile there seemed to be more layers of stars in the black dome of sky. There had been no town for miles, though every few miles he caught sight of dwellings: mobile homes with built-on additions, ramshackle houses that had started as sheds but that one makeshift room at a time had become something somewhat resembling a house . . . all as far from any building or safety code as anyone could imagine and all too far away from each other for anyone to call anyone else a neighbor. It was all so close to the Cahuilla Reservation that not many people would venture near it.

And then there was nothing but the desert. Chaparral, sage scrub, oak woodland. Arroyos and rock falls from the mountains.

And Pyrite Creek: a riverbed that these days would only see water during a flash flood.

The only thing to follow was the riverbed, so Roarke followed it, grateful for his four-wheel drive. The high full moon marked his way. Wolf Moon. Bitter Moon.

And then there they were. The palm trees. An oasis of them. And in the vast empty canvas of the desert, they were as good as a billboard.

Roarke stopped the Rover, turned it off.

There was instant silence in the vast expanse of the desert.

He sat, looking out the windshield, up at the palms. Breathing out, breathing in. Centering himself.

Are you ready for this? For what might be here?

He reached for the glove compartment, took out the Maglite and plastic handcuffs stowed there. He checked his weapon, holstered it, and got out of the car.

The desert air was cold and dry, a light breeze ebbing and flowing like water, and the silence was deep, encompassing, soporific.

He breathed it all in, and headed up the wall of the arroyo, scrambling up soft sand. There would be more of a view there.

He crested the top of the ridge, and it was only then could he see there was clearly a property. The buildings were hidden from the bottom of the arroyo, but at the top of the ridge, he could see the spread.

There was a fence: cruel rows of barbed wire sagging between posts that no one had bothered to straighten in years. NO TRESPASSING signs and OWNER WITH GUN warnings: one just a threatening graphic of a gun muzzle.

And behind the fence, up a slight rise—a crude cabin, and some distance away, a large shed.

Roarke walked toward the fence, carefully lifted one of the barbed wire strands and climbed through.

He moved across the sand, under two entwined palm trees on the ᵉ of the ridge, approaching the cabin, drawing his Glock, already ᵍ he would have to kick in the door.

closer up, he saw a steel plate with a hasp on the door, and no ᵍ it.

He stepped forward. The door opened under his hand.

He pushed it open and moved inside, leading with his weapon . . .

A single room, and it was a ghost cabin now. Sand had filtered in through cracks and covered everything in drifts. Not even a footprint in the silt on the floor. Empty.

He lowered the Glock.

Looking around, he was willing to bet that that no one had been there for years and years.

He holstered his weapon, pulled out the Maglite and turned it on, playing the beam around the cabin.

There was a mattress in the corner. Underneath the layers of sand, the cloth was stained and vile.

Stacks of magazines stood against the wall. Even as he stepped toward them, he knew what they would be.

He picked a handful up, went through six or seven in quick succession, looking down at teenage girls forced into twisted parodies of adult women. Every bodily orifice filled with the genitalia of adult men. Bound. Gagged. Hooded.

He stopped opening the magazines, but continued through the stack, checking dates. The last date he could find on a magazine was 2000.

He dropped the last magazine and turned away from it, using the Maglite to explore further.

Beside a crude sink, there was a hot plate, and open shelving with rusted cans of food. Roarke checked the cans, and found no expiration dates past 2002.

No one's been here since then.

"Fourteen years at least . . ." he said aloud into the stillness.

He turned in the cabin, sweeping the flashlight around him.

And then the light found the most chilling sight of all. On a metal shelf, the rows of gasoline cans.

◆ ◆ ◆

Roarke left the cabin, and stood under the inky sky, the stars glittering in the vast dome above.

Once he'd gathered himself, he turned and walked toward the shed.

It was big, and better constructed than the shack. It was built to keep people out. There was a padlock on the door.

Roarke looked around him to find a large enough stone, and smashed the lock until it broke. He slipped the lock out of the frame and pulled opened the door. It creaked and shivered under his hands as he moved the door open enough to get through.

Flashlight in his left hand, Glock in his right, he directed the Maglite beam inside.

The white side of the van reflected his light back on him. The windshield stared like a big black eye.

Roarke approached the side door of the van cautiously, his heart beating faster. He gripped the door handle, pulled the door open with a shriek of rusty hinge.

He stepped back, shone the flashlight inside. The beam caught glimpses of hell.

The floor was plain metal, grooves. Easy to wash.

There were handcuffs welded to the floor. There were chains. Coiled rope. A can of gasoline.

Ivy's prison.

He had to swallow back bile.

But he knew he had the key now. It was sixteen years later, but there would still be trace evidence, if it wasn't too degraded. Hair. Blood. Fiber.

He found a cloth rag on the dirt floor and used it to open the driver's door. On the console between the two front seats, there was a man's vallet. Roarke used the rag to pick it up, opened it on the front seat.

Inside were a few bills, a driver's license with a familiar name, and hotograph of a family: a man, a woman, and a schoolgirl with a smile. Roarke recognized her instantly.

Huell.

CARA

CHAPTER FIFTY-NINE

After she has walked all around the property and found what she needs to find and done what she needs to do, she sits and waits outside the cabin, watching the night. Looking up at the stars outside the radiant circle of the moon.

The palm fronds rustle in the riverbed below, and the moon whispers calming things. She is not alone. She can feel Ivy with her, and Laura. And someone else, too, she thinks. Someone she doesn't recognize.

The nun's words come back to her, fierce with conviction.

"You are not alone. And you are loved."

She hears the engine, first, the bumping and straining of the van over the rough, sandy terrain.

She stays by the side of the cabin, the knife in one jacket pocket, something else she has found in the other.

The white van drives up to the shed, and a man gets out. She ca' see his face perfectly in the moonlight.

He is not the one she is expecting, but when she sees him, it all makes sense.

An ordinary-looking man, with a monster inside.

She watches as Laura's father moves up to the shed, unlocks the padlock on the door.

As he parks the van inside, she hides herself on the other side of the cabin, out of sight of the shed, and readies herself. Checks the knife. Breathes and centers herself.

She hears his footsteps crunching heavily on the sand as he approaches the cabin now. In front of the cabin door, he reaches for the lock. She hears his grunt of disbelief as he finds it already open, his lair violated.

"Who the fuck . . . ?" he snarls. He backs away from the doorway, twists around . . .

She steps out into the moonlight, lets him see her.

She doesn't know how she looks, standing there in the light, but she can tell by his startled shock there is something more to her than usual. Something not *Normal*.

She stands, hands at her side, motionless. Defenseless.

"What are you doing here?" he demands.

She doesn't answer, just looks at him. Now she sees the quickening of lust on his face, and something much darker twisting underneath. When he speaks again, it is the voice of *It*.

"You're a long way from home, little girl. Are you lost?"

She stays still, knowing he will come to her.

"Does anyone know you're here?"

"No."

No one will ever know I was here.

She waits for a moment and then finishes. "Ivy sent me."

It stops him. "Ivy sent you?" he says softly.

Laura."

Now she feels the confusion and anger in him.

"They told me about you," she says.

"Told you—"

"Everything."

She stares him in the face. She sees the burning eyes and jagged mouth of the beast. And then she turns and runs. Across the sand, away from the cabin, toward the riverbed and the ridge she discovered earlier.

He is fast behind her, but she knows where she is going and it is not far. She darts suddenly sideways, up the ridge, running straight up, then dropping to her hands and knees to crawl for the last steep bit. She can hear him panting behind her, scrabbling up the sand after her like a huge, skittering spider.

She thinks of Ivy, of fire and horror and intolerable pain, and the terror propels her upward. She clambers over the top of the ridge.

And in the split second that he cannot see her, she veers away from the second drop-off, darts sideways toward a large flat rock and throws herself down behind it.

The man reaches the top of the ridge, hauls himself up to standing and steps to the edge of the second hole to look down—

Now.

—and in that moment she is up on her feet, running at him from behind and shoving him with all her strength . . . her own strength, and Laura's, and Ivy's. Over the edge.

He stumbles forward, arms cartwheeling in vain as he falls . . .

. . . down into the hole . . .

And hits the ground with a heavy thud.

She gasps through the galloping of her heart, steps to the edge of the hole and looks down on him.

He is fifteen feet below, trapped in the dry well he has been using as a trash pit. An ant in an ant lion's den. He has fallen on the layer of full plastic garden bags at the bottom, barely covered with sand.

And the sand below him is wet and dark.

As he gets to his feet, she can see the smell hit him. He knows what is soaking the sand. The dozen gallon cans of gas that line the metal shelving in the cabin are empty now.

"Fuck . . . You fucking little cunt—" he rages.

She holds up the silver lighter she found in the cabin. It gleams in the moonlight.

And then his face changes as the panic sets in. "Wait. You can't do that. You can't . . ."

She flicks the lighter and tosses it into the pit.

It is a dozen gallons of gas. The flames are instant. A whoosh of blue fire, racing over the bottom of the pit and up the sides.

Laura's father screams as the flames engulf him.

Cara stares down, feeling the heat of the fire on her face, glowing orange.

He is screaming, his shrieks rising into the dark. He tries to run from side to side, but the entire pit is burning. His clothes are burning, and now his hair . . .

She backs away from the pit, and sits down in the sand under the moon, waiting for *It* to die.

ROARKE

Chapter Sixty

The pit wasn't far away from the cabin. Roarke found the ridge, first, and at the top, he found the gasoline, a full, rusted can behind a large flat rock. Beyond it, the drop down into the old natural well, long run dry.

There was a lump at the bottom, fifteen feet down, covered in sand—but he recognized the shape of a few pale protruding sticks.

He scrambled down the side of the pit and used a branch to uncover it. A human body, long since reduced to cracked and blackened bones. Eye sockets staring up out of the charred skull.

He had seen another body Cara had burned, more recently. He could see it, what had happened.

He knew he was looking at Ivy's killer. And Laura's, too.

Maybe he'd abused her. Or maybe he'd never touched her. But she'd discovered what he was, and couldn't live with it. She'd visited Ivy, and she knew that her father was a monster.

As he stared down he saw something silver in the sand beside the skull. He stooped to pick it up, felt the weight of it in his hand.

He stood, in the middle of a burned-out pit, the sky crusted with millions of stars above him.

And knew that justice had been done.

Inside the cabin, he sat down in the one chair and reached into his pocket for his phone, but there was no signal to be found. He disconnected, looked around at the cabin. The filthy mattress, the stacks of magazines. A time capsule of evil.

And the monster who lived in it had been snuffed out of existence by a teenage girl.

You did it, Cara. You stopped this one.

There was another one out there. But the rape kit comparisons were coming.

"We'll get him, too," he promised her, aloud. "We've got him."

He sat, not moving, and it occurred to him that Marlena was free now. He could tell her the monster was dead. Nausea roiled in his gut, after-effects of adrenaline and relief . . .

No.

Not relief—

He twisted in the chair, reaching for his holster . . . as the door opened across the room.

The doorway filled up with Mel Franzen. Big. Smiling. And pointing a Ruger.

"Don't move, Mr. Roarke."

There was relish in his voice, and Roarke froze, eyes fixed on the Ruger. He knew he was in trouble. And this time Cara was nowhere near to save him. No Cara, no Epps. He could die out here in the middle of the desert and no one would ever know where he was, what had happened . . .

"Take that weapon out and slide it over here," Franzen said. His gun was aimed dead center at Roarke's chest, and the man knew how to hold a weapon. None of it was good news.

Roarke reached slowly for his holster, unsnapped it, drew out the Glock.

Franzen's aim never faltered. "On the floor."

Roarke leaned forward and placed it on the rough wood planking, then kicked it to the side, out of Franzen's reach, still in his own peripheral vision.

Franzen chuckled. "You're a stubborn motherfucker, aren't you, Mr. Roarke? Persistent, too."

"It's *Agent* Roarke. And my team knows where I am."

Franzen shook his head. "Oh, I very much doubt that." He looked Roarke over. "No. You're a lone wolf, through and through."

Keep him talking, Roarke thought. *These guys love to talk.* "You weren't, though. Not always. Did you know your rape buddy is dead?"

Franzen nodded, almost distractedly. "Knew he had to be. Minute he disappeared, I knew he'd have to be. He burned himself out, so to speak." He glanced around the cabin. "You've done me a favor. I always thought he had a place. I never knew where. It's been on my mind, all these years, what he might have had hidden out here."

"There's some interesting stuff, all right," Roarke said. "I've been having a look around." *And if he thinks I can tell him what I've found, maybe he won't shoot me right off the bat.* "Quite the setup you had. Planning everything around the conventions, so you'd be out of town and accounted for. You gave each other the perfect cover."

He was lucky. Franzen had to preen a little. "Of course. If anyone came asking, we were having breakfast together, doing business before a meeting. Having a morning stroll about the city."

"Every January. And you alternated years." The timeline made sense to him now, the orange and red.

"That's right. Everything nice and orderly. It was a great setup until he lost the plot."

"And he went after Ivy. Right in your own backyard."

"The rule was, nothing anywhere close to home. No one from the fucking *state*." Franzen's face darkened, and Roarke saw for a moment what his victims had seen. "And then he flips out. Someone right under our roof. Someone from the *club*. Stalking her. Taking her from just blocks away. Burning her . . . and leaving her out here without taking care of it for good. Stupid. Sloppy."

"Must have scared you. The cops all over it. And a live witness." Roarke said softly.

"If you want to call it that. She was the walking dead."

Roarke felt the heat of fury. He had to swallow hard to contain it, and it was a longer moment before he could speak again. "Was Laura a witness, too? Did one of you kill her?"

"She took care of that all on her own." Franzen smiled. "And even then, the cops were too stupid to follow up. Easy as pie."

"No one ever came knocking at your door. It was just the two of you, then? No other Wayfarers involved?"

"Our little secret. And it turned out I didn't need Dave after all. It's worked out so much better without him."

His face turned hard. He motioned toward the door with the gun. "We're going to take a walk now. Stand up. Nice and slow. Any move I don't like, I shoot until this piece is empty."

Roarke stood up from the chair.

"Now walk. One step every ten seconds. Anything faster than that, you get shot where you stand. Got it?"

"I got it," Roarke said, his voice grating. His mind was racing, calculating quickly.

He'd expected Franzen to just kill him inside the cabin. Burn the cabin down around him. But to be truly safe, he'd have to burn the cabin, and the shed, and the van beyond recognition. And that size of that fire would draw attention.

Better to bury him out in the desert. Let the sand take care of him, like it had taken care of Huell.

Which meant Roarke had a chance. Not the greatest odds . . . but a chance.

So in slow motion, one step at a time, he moved across the cabin floor.

Out the cabin door now, with Franzen right behind him and the muzzle of his gun pressed into his back.

Out away from the cabin, toward the ridge, and the pit.

The moonlight brought out a stark clarity in the desert landscape, and Roarke's thoughts seemed hyper-clear as well, as he walked one excruciating step at a time over the sand, with Franzen right behind him and the Ruger in the center of his back.

Cara was here, in this place, with a monster. She survived it. You can, too.

He wasn't afraid of dying. Which was probably a good thing, because dying was a definite possibility.

In the arroyo below them, the palm fronds swayed in the slight, dry breeze, and he caught the metallic scent of ground water on the wind. Not a bad place to spend eternity, if that's how it happened.

But this man shouldn't be allowed to live.

They were almost to the well now. Franzen clearly intended to save himself the trouble of digging.

Roarke thought of Cara, standing under the moon. Fourteen years old, throwing a silver lighter into a pit of sand soaked in gasoline. The sense of her presence was almost palpable.

And when he saw the small tree backlit by moonlight, he knew what he had to do.

He twisted his head toward the tree in shock, and whispered from his soul, "Cara."

He felt Franzen swivel to look, felt him angle the gun toward the tree . . . and in that split second, Roarke shoved himself backward with all the power in him. Franzen was bigger but Roarke was younger, fitter. And he was angry.

Franzen stumbled back, firing wildly and missing. The explosion reverberated in the night, and Roarke was on him, both hands grabbing Franzen's gun arm and twisting and jerking at the same time, using his full strength to pull the arm from the shoulder socket.

Franzen howled in pain and rage. Roarke twisted the Ruger away from him and lunged with his whole weight, shoving Franzen backward into the pit.

He heard the Wayfarer hit the bottom with a sickening thud. Another shriek of pain.

Roarke stood on the ridge, breathing through the adrenaline pounding in his head. He walked to the edge of the pit and looked down.

Fifteen feet below, Franzen clutched his dislocated arm, gaping down at the bones at his feet, the charred skull.

Two monsters, one alive, one dead.

Roarke stared down.

Here is justice. No one has found this place in sixteen years. I could soak the pit, toss the lighter in, light him on fire. Send him to hell with his friend.

His flesh melting and his bones charring, screaming until his throat burns and then screaming inside.

For Ivy. For Laura. For Marlena. For Cara. For all the dead girls, and the violated girls, and all the girls still in danger.

He reached into his pocket and drew out the silver lighter he'd picked up from the pit.

Yes or no?

He flicked the lighter. And sixteen years later, it burst into flame.

He held it over the pit, and looked down at Franzen's cowering bulk.

Burn him. Let them rot together. It's justice.

Then he snapped the lighter closed.

CARA

Chapter Sixty-One

She sits at the edge of the blackened pit, under the moon, in a night landscape so drenched in light it looks like day.

The screaming has stopped. The man is dead. She has killed *It*.

But It *never dies.*

There will always be others.

The thought threatens to overwhelm her.

She could bury herself now, in the desert sand. She could rest. She would die within days. It would hurt, it would be agony, maybe, but *The Game* would be over. She would not have to fight, to be ever on her guard, to live in fear. Surely the peace of nothingness would be preferable to this life of fear and memory.

She sits for some time. Then she climbs down into the pit, stands above the stinking, smoldering corpse, reaches down and snaps off the ring finger to take the ring.

Chapter Sixty-Two

It is just dawn, the sun glimmering over the hills, when she walks up the driveway toward the group home.

The house is dark, and she must use her lock pick on the front door to get in.

She closes the door quietly behind her, takes a step toward the hall toward her bedroom—

Then she freezes at the sense of a presence behind her in the dark.

She twists around.

Ms. Sharonda stands up from the couch in the lounge. They look at each other across the unlit hall. When she speaks, the director's voice is hard.

"Detective Ortiz was by last night, wanting to talk to you."

Cara is very still, very aware of the number of steps to the door. She has no idea what's coming, but she is ready to fight or flee. She will not go back to jail. Not ever.

Finally, Ms. Sharonda speaks. "Pack your bag. You've been transferred."

It is not at all what she expected.

"It's a home out by the Arizona border," the director says flatly. "Just as well you weren't here long enough to make any friends. It's three and a half hours from here, the end of the county. Gonna be hard for anybody to visit you out there."

Cara suddenly has the feeling of another conversation going on, an underlying meaning.

Ms. Sharonda stares straight into her face. "I told you before. I don't want to see you back here. Ever. You get out now and you don't come back."

Cara meets her eyes, and understands she has been reprieved.

The minivan takes her away before anyone else wakes.

She sits in the back seat and watches the road signs. The roads all have numbers. If you know the numbers, you always know where you are. This time, though, she knows the roads without the signs. Through the Anza corridor and the Indian reservations. Up over the San Jacinto and Santa Rosa Mountains. Down the sidewinding road into the Coachella Valley. And then far, far out into the desert, to the town when she spent the only happy years of her life . . . until *It* struck for the first time and took her family, and tried to take her.

When the minivan drops her at her new "home," the driver calls her back and gives her her transfer papers. She glances down at the top page and something catches her attention, makes her look again.

When she stands in front of this group home director's desk, he takes her papers and files them without looking, without seeing what she has seen.

The transfer is dated the day before. As if the night and the man and the pit had never existed.

Ms. Sharonda has made her choice, too.

ROARKE

Chapter Sixty-Three

It was three days of police work before he could get back to the Mission. And of course he found Mother Doctor out in the gardens of the *asistencia,* walking and smoking.

They moved together out through the garden gate, beyond the wall, where the children couldn't hear, and sat on the bench that Cara had sat on so long ago, and he told her the story of his night journey.

He didn't know if Cara had ever known about Franzen. He did know that she had been transferred away from the group home. And Franzen had stopped his attacks cold, for five years after Ivy died.

He was in custody now. There were already two DNA matches from the rape kits. And Roarke was looking forward to walking into the Palm Desert station and laying the DNA evidence against Huell out in front of any detective except Ortiz.

Roarke didn't say it to Mother Doctor. But Ortiz was a whole new problem.

His posts in the men's forums meant he was after Cara, intending evil and death. Could Roarke prove it? Was there anything he could do that would be within the law? He didn't know.

He would have to think.

But not now.

He stood from the bench, reached into his coat pocket. "I thought you would want this." He handed Mother Doctor back the satin surplice with its relics.

She looked at the package, didn't take it. "You should keep them—"

He shook his head. "They belong here."

She nodded, took the packet, tucked it back in the pocket of her own coat. Then she looked him over. "So you're going back to work. Formally, I mean."

She had seen the service weapon in the holster on his hip, of course. She never missed a trick.

He spoke carefully. "Most people don't know this about the Bureau. We have a certain latitude to set our own agenda. To direct resources where we feel they're most immediately necessary. *If* we've put in the time . . . and have a certain influence. Which means my team and I . . . we can build a permanent task force to make crimes against children the priority. Wherever that's happening. On the streets. In the juvenile justice system. In their own homes. I just wanted you to know."

She reached for his hands, squeezed them hard. "Thank you."

"Thank *you*."

He stood from the bench, started to turn away. Her voice stopped him. Gentle, reproving.

"There's something else, Roarke. I know it. Are you going to tell me?"

He stood still for a long moment before he finally spoke. "It's Cara. I know where she is."

It had come to him as he stood out in the desert moonscape. He might be wrong, but he didn't think he was wrong. He'd seen where she grew up now. It made sense.

Mother Doctor's eyes widened slightly, and her voice was cautious. "What are you going to do?"

He knew he would ask himself that question a million times in the next days. About Cara. About Ortiz. But right now, he said the only thing he could say.

"I don't know."

She shook her head. "Nobody said it was easy."

In spite of himself, he smiled at her. "No. They never did."

CARA

Chapter Sixty-Four

I t is done.

The director of this new group home is nowhere near as vigilant as Ms. Sharonda. The night after her arrival Cara sneaks out in the dead of night and takes a car from the street.

There are cars everywhere. There will always be cars, and roads to take her where she needs to go.

Back in Las Piedras she sets the fire. The dry palm trees surrounding the Wayfarers Club are a hazard. They go up like massive torches and the fire spreads in seconds to the gasoline she has used to drench the foundation. The Santa Anas breathe their hot breath, fanning the blaze.

She stands for a moment with the glow on her face, then before the trucks can come, she slips through the dark to the car, and away.

One more stop. One last visit to the Mission, to give Ivy the relics of her journey into the desert: the palm frond, the glittering stone, and the silver ring from the monster's hand. Proof of the end.

It is not justice. There is no justice when such things are allowed to happen. When monsters roam free in the world, and people do nothing. There will never be justice while *It* is allowed to live.

But it is something. Ivy can rest now. In that way, she is the lucky one.

Now Cara sits on the bed of her new room, looking out the window at the desert hills. The day is sunny. The room is drenched with the light.

It is not home. But it is not jail. There are worse places.

It will be waiting for her here, undoubtedly. *It* is everywhere.

It never dies.

But she knows things now. There are voices in her head.

A fierce one that sounds like the old Indian.

"You are the wolf."

And a gentler one, the nun.

"You are not alone. And you are loved."

Author's Note

B efore I was a full-time screenwriter and author, I worked as a teacher in the Los Angeles County juvenile court system. I have not in any way exaggerated the plight of children and teens in the Social Services and justice system. Abuses and neglect are rampant in every state, not just in California. Good people in the system fight a heartbreaking battle to make a difference, but real change will never happen until we all make it our responsibility to educate ourselves about what's really going on in our own communities and find ways to help, from spreading the word through social media to volunteering, advocating, and donating to organizations that pick up the slack.

I donate every month to Children of the Night, MISSSEY, and the Covenant House, who rescue and work with homeless, trafficked and sexually exploited teens; and to Planned Parenthood, which works tirelessly to ensure that every child is planned, wanted, and cared for. If you'd like to learn more about organizations in your country, state and community, I have links to places you can start on my website, http://alexandrasokoloff.com.

> "Bad men need nothing more to compass their ends, than that good men should look on and do nothing."
>
> —*John Stuart Mill*

Acknowledgments

The verse Cara reads for Ms. Sharonda is from "Nemesis Necklace" in *The Couple Who Fell to Earth* (C&R Press), by the astonishing poet Michelle Bitting: http://www.michellebitting.com.

The quote on Ivy's tombstone is Anne Frank's, from *The Diary of a Young Girl: A single candle can both defy and define the darkness.*

The profiling text that Roarke references extensively and quotes to Mother Doctor from is *Behavior Evidence: Understanding Motives and Developing Suspects in Unsolved Serial Rapes Through Behavioral Profiling Techniques*, by Brent E. Turvey, MS. I am greatly indebted to Brent Turvey for all his textbooks and papers on criminal profiling and forensic science, and I highly recommend that any author or reader who would like to read further on these subjects consult the Forensic Solutions website: http://www.corpus-delicti.com, for books and classes.

A million thanks to:

My awesome editors, JoVon Sotak, Jacque Ben-Zekry, and Charlotte Herscher, and the rest of the team/family at Thomas & Mercer: Sarah Shaw, Grace Doyle, Alan Turkus, and Anh Schluep.

My brilliant agents, Scott Miller, Frank Wuliger, and Lee Keele.

Copyeditor Hannah Buehler, especially for her help sorting this complex timeline!

My priceless early readers: Diane Coates Peoples, Joan Tregarthen Huston, and Helena Rybak.

Pearl Ruscio-Metcalf, for helping me hear young Cara's voice.

Lee Lofland and his Writers Police Academy trainers/instructors: Dave Pauly, Katherine Ramsland, Corporal Dee Jackson, Andy Russell,

Marco Conelli, Lieutenant Randy Shepard, and Robert Skiff, for forensics, investigative, and tactical help.

R.C. Bray for his terrific narrative interpretations of the books.

P.J. Nunn, Timoney Korbar, Amanda Wilson, Adam Cruz, and the WriterSpace.com team for brilliant publicity support.

Robert Gregory Browne, for the series cover concept.

The initial inspiration for the Huntress from Val McDermid, Denise Mina, and Lee Child, at the San Francisco Bouchercon.

My writing group, the Weymouth Seven: Margaret Maron, Mary Kay Andrews, Diane Chamberlain, Sarah Shaber, Brenda Witchger and Katy Munger.

Webmistresses extraordinaire: Madeira James and Jen Forbus at Xuni.com.

The Dorland Mountain Arts Colony, for providing such a gorgeous and inspiring writing retreat. The view from that mountain helped me create the fictional but very nearby town of Las Piedras.

Tracy Fenton, Helen Boyce, and the awesome administrators and readers of THE Book Club, who've been so supportive on the other side of the pond.

Craig Robertson, for too many things to list, including that this year we had the same book and editing deadlines twice and managed not to kill each other.

I love to hear from readers! Visit my website at http://alexandra-sokoloff.com to contact me, join my mailing list, find me on social media, and win cool stuff.

About the Author

Alexandra Sokoloff has won the Thriller Award and been nominated for the Bram Stoker, Anthony, and Black Quill Awards for her supernatural thrillers *The Harrowing, The Price, The Unseen, Book of Shadows, The Shifters*, and *The Space Between*. She has also earned a second Thriller Award nomination for her Huntress/FBI Thrillers series (*Huntress Moon, Blood Moon, Cold Moon*, and *Bitter Moon*). The *New York Times Book Review* has called her a "daughter of Mary Shelley" and declared her books "some of the most original and freshly unnerving work in the genre."

As a screenwriter, she has written original screenplays and novel adaptations for numerous Hollywood studios, and is the author of three nonfiction writing workbooks: *Stealing Hollywood, Screenwriting Tricks for Authors*, and *Writing Love*. She also writes the acclaimed blog www.ScreenwritingTricks.com, based on her writing workshops and books, and has penned erotic paranormal fiction, including *The Shifters*, Book 2 of The Keepers trilogy, and *Keeper of the Shadows*, from The Keepers L.A. She lives in Los Angeles and in Scotland with crime author Craig Robertson.